KINGDOM OF LIES

By

Brittany Pyle

Edited by TJ Shiree and Kaitlyn Shiels
Cover art and design by Owen Beck
Interior map by Inkarnate

ISBN 979-8-218-55705-8

First Edition December 2024

This book is dedicated to those whose heart yearns for adventure, the unknown is out there. Don't let anything hold you back from finding yourself.

This book is also dedicated to Kait, without you, this book wouldn't be where it is today.

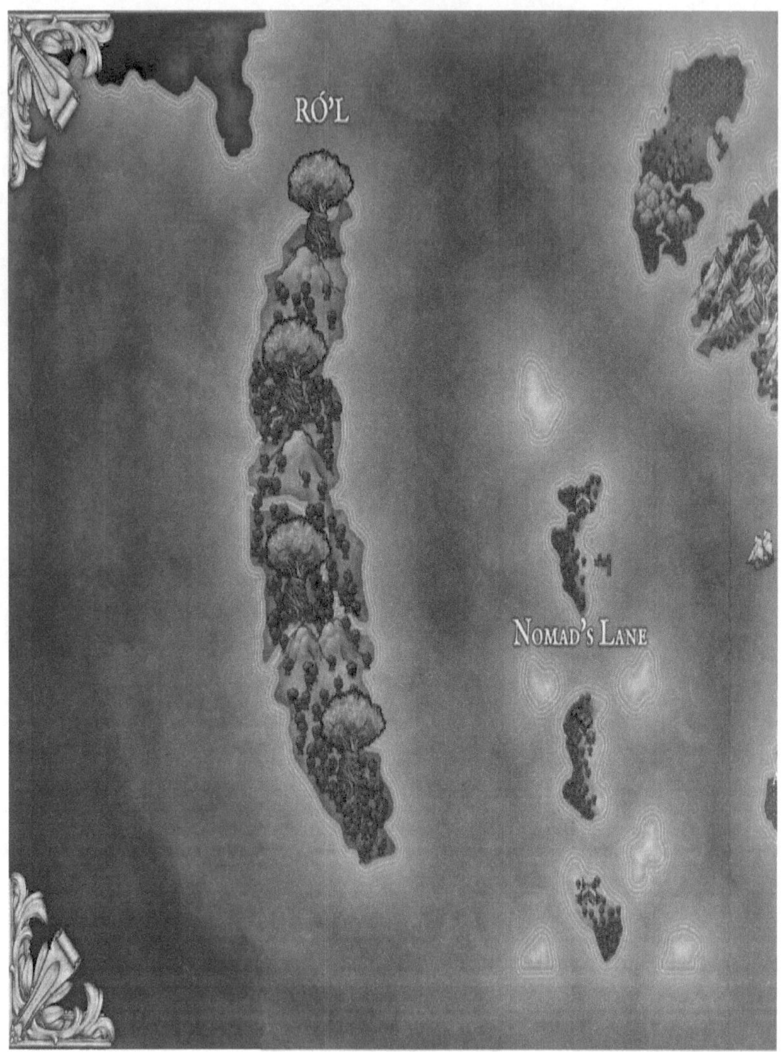

RÓ'L
NOMAD'S LANE

Esnia
Kingdom of Fel
Kingdom of M'Ralz
Kingdom of Lo'kil
Felkiern
Ashfall

Prologue

Growing up, I wasn't like the other children, especially not like my sisters. While they spent their days up in their rooms trading secrets, sewing beautiful dresses, and dreaming about kissing princes so they could someday become royalty themselves, I was outside running around with my brothers. We would run through the trees, dodging stray branches and brambles that would tear through our clothing, desperate to deceive the imaginary villains we dreamt of. We would use fallen branches to fend off the ones we couldn't outrun and slide through the mud to evade the ferocious beasts of the wild that clawed their way out of our waking dreams. The world was beautiful and unimaginably big for someone as small as me, and I had dreamt of conquering it all. There was never a thought in my mind that someone like me could ever be like my sisters. Especially when I could be the adventurer I had always dreamt of being.

By the time my brothers and I came back home, the dress that my mother had made me wear would be muddied and torn. She would always shake her head at me and mutter to herself how I was too much like her as a child. Every time it happened, I apologized with my head hung low before I went upstairs to clean the dress myself. One day, however, after a day of running through the woods, I came home and scowled at her. I was tired of being reprimanded for being myself and for wanting to have an enjoyable childhood. So I decided to say something back; my anger boiled over as it had threatened to escape my tightening chest.

"How am I just like you?" I snapped. "I've never heard anything about you growing up." My eyebrows were furrowed in anger and my mouth twisted into a sneer.

Although she gave me that kind and understanding smile she always had, a part of me knew it was a mask to hide the pain. Slowly, she placed the towel she had in her hand down, untied the apron that was hanging over her neck, and sat at the kitchen table.

She didn't show any frustration towards me as she silently waited for me to join her. With a hesitant look towards her, I felt the anger slowly fade to confusion before I finally walked the couple steps it took to join her at the table.

She cleared her throat, placed her folded hands on the table, and began. "I've never told you of my childhood because I didn't want to tell you a story without a happy ending. I wanted to wait until you were older, but it seems that you're ready."

My expression slowly faded from confusion to shock. My knitted brows and tight-lipped frown slowly faded to widened eyes and a slackened jaw. I knew I should have said something, but I whispered the few words my mind could come up with. "...What happened?"

She looked down at her hands before patting the seat next to her. She wanted me to be closer to her instead of on the other side of the table. "Come here, my love. Let me tell you a story."

When she finished the history of her life, my cheeks were stained with tears. Over the years, her tale became my favorite and my love and respect for my mother grew without end. She told it many times throughout her life, and every time, I listened to her just as intently as the last. I always memorized it throughout my childhood, and it did not take long until I knew it like it was my own story. It always began the same way. And so, with a smile, she said:

"There once was a girl who lived in the small village of Felkeirn..."

Part One

Chapter One

Verona was always a heavy sleeper. She could sleep through a disaster, or a war if it happened right on her very bed. It was one of the many things that drove her parents insane, taking every ounce of their strength to wake her, especially this morning.

"Wake up, Verona!" her mother whispered harshly, frustration heavy in her voice as she shook her daughter awake. "Don't make me get your father in here, or worse, don't make me get Novaak. You know how he'll wake you up if he gets in here. That boy will have all of his muddy paws all over you."

Verona groaned, rolled over, and placed a pillow right over her head. Waves of curly rust-colored hair tumbled over her eyes. "Oh no! Not Novaak!" she grumbled sarcastically, her voice still rough from sleep.

Her mother sighed in desperation as she walked over to Verona's window. She opened the curtains up to let some of the morning light into the room. "I don't know what to do with you anymore! Get up! It's time to run errands. Your chore today is to travel to Ashfall, so that is why you need to get up now!"

Verona slowly pushed herself up into a sitting position on her bed. She was groggy from waking up. Slowly, she brought a hand up to rub her eyes. That's when it finally clicked. The words her mother said made her feel wide awake. "...I do?!" she said excitedly but wearily, as she thought it was another tactic to make her get up. Though her eyes were wide with hope.

Going into town was her favorite errand. She was intimately familiar with her small village of Felkeirn, full of endless hills of farmland that stretched as far as her eyes could see. In her village, there were several houses that a few families occupied, and she could name every person with ease. It was a small and simple village with only a few buildings in the heart of it. To Verona, it was barren and would never hold a candle to any other town or kingdom.

The town of Ashfall, where she ran errands, was nothing like her tiny wasteland of a village. It was extensive and exciting in every way imaginable. In Ashfall, there were stands of food she had never seen before, shops selling jewelry, a place where children learned during the day, and so many more people, too. There were so many other places in there that Verona still had yet to explore but that was because she loved to spend time with her friend, Mariam, who would always take so much of her time.

When Verona was younger, her parents would send her on errand runs in Ashfall. Because she was so young and new to the town, she felt so lost as she drowned in a sea of unknown people. Being in a big town, it was one of the many things that she wasn't used to. It scared the living daylights out of her. Then Mariam, who was a few years older than her and knew every inch of the town, swooped in and saved her when Verona needed someone the most. Mariam had shown her where she wanted to go, all while talking her ear off the entire day. Since that moment, they had become thick as thieves, and Verona looked forward to every chance of seeing her best friend. She loved Mariam like a sister and she could hardly remember any moments before she knew her.

Her mother let out a huge sigh as she waved a hand in front of her face, breaking her from the thoughts that clouded her mind. Verona rubbed her tired eyes, waking up a little more, and finally focused on her mother. Many people who knew her family had always told Verona that she was a spitting image of her mother when she was younger. She had shaken it off, but looking at her mother now, she knew they had been right. To their matching red-orange hair with blonde streaks, their pale skin splashed with freckles, a full set of pink lips, along with wide amber eyes filled with golden specks. Their faces were both heart-shaped, though her mother's held the start of wrinkles that told many great years full of laughter and fun. Her hair had started to fade from the natural red-orange color into a dull imitation with streaks of gray.

As Verona finally emerged from her thoughts, she could see the daydreaming and loving expression that her mother normally held was now twisted with a hint of concern. "I thought you were getting up. Hurry up, get dressed, and come back as soon as possible, please. I worry when you go into town."

Verona rolled her eyes as she stood from the bed. "I know you do, Mother. Though I'll be fine, I can take care of myself. I just turned eighteen last month, don't you remember? Besides, I know everyone there. If I have a problem, I know who to go to."

"I know, I know. I still worry, I am your mother. While you get ready, I will see if Novaak is up for a journey today." With a heavy sigh and the worry still plastered on her face, she walked out and left Verona to get ready.

Verona quietly threw on a simple dress that her mother had made her and softly stepped out of the room where she and her six siblings slept every night. Even though she was the oldest and held a lot of responsibility on her shoulders, her younger siblings also helped and had their own chores on the farm. Some of them, especially the younger ones, loved to help and followed their father around every minute of every day. Though it was hard to try and get even the youngest to do some of the harder chores because they often disappeared to play in the multitude of barns they owned. Though, she had to admit, that had been her favorite part of her own childhood. Verona loved the carefree times she had, playing around on their land.

With soft and quiet steps, she went down the stairs and into the kitchen. The earthy and nutty smell of a hot cup of coffee filled the air along with the warm and sweet smell of freshly baked bread. Verona's stomach growled in protest as she walked towards the inviting smell. That's when she saw her father sitting at the table. He lifted his cup to his mouth and took a sip.

"Good morning, Father," Verona said as she placed a kiss on his wrinkled cheek. Unlike her mother, her father's hair was fully gray along with the scruff on his jaw. His once-black hair had faded years ago from the stress of keeping the family farm running. He had a rounded face, thin lips, and a sharp nose. His skin was a dark tan, weathered from years of working outside under the sun. The eyes that graced his face were deep-set and constantly full of concern, but they were a blue so vivid they could blend with the sky above them. Those same eyes looked up to meet Verona.

"Glad to see you're finally up," he said, his voice still rough with sleep. It sounded gruff and stern to anyone who did not know him, though, to Verona, she had grown to love it and knew deep down it was full of love that he reserved for only them.

"Hey, it's better than nothing. Would you rather me still be sleeping in, Father?" she asked with a sly smile that slowly painted her lips as her father shook his head and chuckled at her words. Quickly, she cleared her throat before continuing, knowing she had little time to waste. "What would you like me to get when I go into town today?" she asked eagerly.

"We're running low on food for our Roagals," he said, nodding to them in the fields, towering over everything.

Verona looked out of the window of their house and out to the field to see a herd of beasts wandering the grassy plains. She remembered when they had enough money to buy their first one. Her parents were elated because they knew it would be a turn for the better. Roagals were large, working beasts, mainly used for farming and moving objects too heavy for a human being to lift on their own. Even now, they were massive to Verona as the ten-foot-tall beasts roamed the lands and towered over everything in their path.

By the time Verona was in her teens, she grew brave enough to walk into the field with them. Looking back, it seemed silly, but she remembered what it felt like seeing them up close. The first Roagal Verona saw had a medium-sized snout, relying on its excellent sense of smell or the lead of a handler to direct them as they had no eyes. Despite having no outer ear, its sense of hearing allowed it to hear for miles. The males had short horns jutting from the chin. But the females' horns were twice the length and curved in a spiral pattern to help them protect their young. Near the back base of the skull, a flat plane jutted out a few feet.

Its body was thick with corded muscle, and its skin was rough and wrinkled. Its legs were cylindrical and beefy, rendering it to excel at its one and only purpose: pulling. The Roagals had a short, nubby tail that always made Verona laugh. To her, it was simply breathtaking being so close to such a massive beast.

She looked back towards her father as a question popped into her mind. "Will I be trading grain and food again, or will I be using money?"

"Food, but try to sell some grain too. We should have enough food to spare to make it through next winter. We made it through this one and thank the gods it is spring. At the pace we are at now, I cannot say about the year after," he told her, his eyes wandering back to his drink. As she nodded in turn to her father's request, Verona softly put a hand on his shoulder in reassurance before moving away.

As Verona started to walk toward the door, a thunderous echo sounded from the stairs. With a smile gracing her lips once more, she knew what it was from. Six bodies had come barreling down the staircase.

First was the youngest, Wymond. Everyone had called him Wy. He had just turned five over the winter and thought he knew everything. He spent his days playing more than working but thought himself to be the boss of the house as he followed their father everywhere. Father picked Wy up and placed him into his lap after he descended the stairs. After Wymond was Willow. She was eight and one of the quietest of their family. She kept to herself most of the time and often daydreamed the day away. Though Tawnie, who was eleven, always acted as Willow's voice. She was the loudest, funniest, and sassiest. Tawnie never took no as an option and always found her own way around things. Cerelia, the next sibling, was fourteen and fully showed that she was in her beginning teenage years. It was all drama for her and she thought herself better than all of her siblings. Then it was the twins, Thomas and Graham. They were both sixteen and the hardest workers next to Verona. They took up chores that the others didn't want to do and did everything without a complaint. Verona was proud of those two and she was also the closest to them. They helped Verona through tough times, and she did the same for them. They were fully devoted to each other, and she didn't know what she would do without them.

Verona chatted amongst her siblings for a few moments as she grabbed a slice of bread along with them as well. However, she felt the stress of time ticking away so she walked outside to where her mother was standing next to Novaak. "Is he coming today?"

"I'm not sure if the poor boy can make it. He's getting too old for these trips." Her mother knelt next to Novaak as she ran a brush through his fur.

Verona squatted down to pet Novaak on the muzzle. "He's still got some fight left in him, don't you, boy?"

Novaak lifted his head and growled before head-butting Verona affectionately. Novaak was a wild Rilasi, the most beautiful creature to ever roam their lands with their slim muzzle, long neck, and sleek, wiry body built for long-distance running. Long, yet soft, hair covered their body. Though the hair was short and almost down to the skin around their head, lower legs, and paws. A set of long, pointed ears sat further on the back of their skull and always stood up tall. They had thin, slitted eyes that sat on either side of their thin muzzle. Though the one thing that stood out the most to Verona was a mouth full of razor-sharp teeth. Their canines were long and prominent. Whiskers shot out below their square pink noses. Rilasi's usually never looked the same with their fur, color, and tail. Novaak had the usual Rilasi crest on the back of his long neck and a long tail to go with it. However, his once golden-brown fur was rare for his kind; it now had grayed over the years.

With a sigh, Verona stood up and faced her mother. "I should be going soon, shouldn't I?"

She nodded and pursed her lips in worry. "If you want to make it before the markets open, then yes, but like I said, please hurry back. You know I can't stop worrying about you."

Verona gave her mother a sweet smile with a hug and walked back into the house, packing some bags of food and grain into a wagon. As soon as she was leaving, her siblings walked outside to start their chores. One by one, they said their goodbyes to her, and Wymond gave her the biggest hug he could. She walked up to her parents for one last hug and told them that she loved them, and then she took her first step on her journey into town.

⁂

The flatlands stretched on for miles in the wide, expansive landscape before her. Fields of endless tilled dirt lay on either side of the stone-paved road that she was walking on. They were being prepared to plant once more in the upcoming months, though for now,

they would lay empty and muddied. A handful of trees
dotted across the landscape, though it wasn't enough
to provide any sort of wooded area. Water flooded the
ditches bordering on either side of the road and in
them were tall standing grasses that danced with the
soft breeze this morning. The smell of burning wood
and the strong earth scent of early spring hung thick in
the air. For Verona, she loved the smell because it
meant warmer months were ahead. They were finally
out of the colder, darker days. A few white puffy
clouds drifted above in the clear blue sky. It had been a
while since they had a day like today, and with a smile,
Verona closed her eyes and soaked up the sun's warm
rays. The sound of chirping and birdsong filled the air
and joined in with the melody of the breeze gliding
through the dancing grass.

Just as she was starting to feel weightless
amongst the world around her, a loud crack of leathery
wings broke the song of the morning melody. Verona's
eyes snapped open quickly as they took to the skies.
There above her, a Daekari blocked out the sun. A gasp
filled her throat, and amazement ran through her body
like tingles against her skin. They were rare to see;
Daekari were not native to Esnia and this one was far
from its home amongst the Jagged Coast. They could
often travel this far if a Daeki rider was seated on its

back, though the beast was far too high in the sky for Verona to tell. All Verona could make out was its large, leathery body, a tail that was the same length as itself, four massive wings that beat in the sky like drums, and its large head that was as big as a Roagal. Verona memorized the scene before her, hoping to never forget it.

Verona walked with a wheelbarrow full of crops and a bag full of food on her back. She hummed songs on her way into town to keep her spirits high. Usually, the road was not very busy during this time of day. She was used to long hours of walking by herself, but today, it was crowded with people going towards different villages, towns, or even one of the three kingdoms. People were walking or riding Rilasi's, while the kids were playing in the road, filling up the air with the sweet sound of laughter. Even though Verona felt timid with the new people that crowded the road, she did enjoy this. She liked the small conversations she had with those who passed. They made her feel a lot less alone in this world.

Hours passed into her journey when she spotted someone unusual. Every man she had seen on this trail was wearing the usual garments of trousers and a tunic, but this man was clad in full armor with weapons strapped to him. He stood out in the crowd with the various weapons attached to his body; however, he looked as if he was trying to blend in, with his shoulders slumped and a vacant expression on his face. The closer she got to him, the more she could see what he truly looked like. His dark skin stood in stark contrast to the silver of his armor. He looked a little older than Verona, but only by a handful of years since his face still held onto that sliver of innocence. His black hair was cropped close to his scalp, and he had a sharp jawline that she swore could have been sharper than his weapons. She felt that he could be kind by the laugh lines forming around his full lips and a sharp, angled nose. Although it was clear he had been through a handful of fights with the scars that littered his face: one diagonal on his nose, one slicing through his left brow, and one jaggedly etched on his right cheekbone.

Verona quickened her pace to close the gap between them. In that short journey, she battled with herself whether she should say something, though curiosity eventually won.

"I'm sorry, sir, can I bother you for a little while?" she asked, with her jaw hung loose and eyes widened in amazement. As soon as she said something to him, they both slowed their pace.

With a quick glance, she looked down at his armor. It seemed well-weathered and very old. Though she could tell he took great care in keeping it in excellent condition as it had a shine to it still. In the middle of the chest was a symbol of a Daekari. Verona could tell that symbol was important, though she did not know enough about the great families of Esnia to know who he could be. Her eyes traveled back towards his face, and she gave him a warm smile of reassurance.

The man looked a little shocked at first that someone would come up to him, but it did not take long for his demeanor to become relaxed. He gave himself a little chuckle, Verona thought it could have been out of shock or embarrassment, though she gave him a soft smile in reassurance. He looked towards her with those liquid gold eyes of his. "Of course you can, little one."

Verona scrunched her face at the nickname he had already given her and stood a little straighter. "You look like an adventurer... Are you one by chance?" she asked a little brazenly.

As soon as she had called him an adventurer, he rubbed the back of his head in nervousness. "Well, I guess that would be a term for what I am, in a way. Can I wonder why you would ask?" he questioned her back.

"Well," Verona started, quickening her pace to keep up with the stranger, "I ask because, well, I guess I'm a bit jealous, that's all. Seems to me you're living the dream." Her words left a bitter taste, like sand, on her tongue. Though the bitterness was quickly taken over by a strong wave of sadness. "I just wish I could be an adventurer too."

The man looked puzzled. "Of course, you can. Anyone can be an adventurer. No one can tell you what to be. As long as you put your heart into it and it's what you truly want, then it's only you that is truly holding yourself back."

Verona sighed. Her eyes wandered to the path before them. If only she could go and explore the world. If only she could just let herself be free and fight the evil that lurked in the shadows of the world. To free magic from the grasp of its chains, to demolish the god slayers, and to free the souls stuck in Azarath. Though as soon as she had that thought of running away and doing what she truly loved, all she could see was the faces of her parents filled with disappointment. In her mind, she saw that they would struggle; she feared that the farm may collapse without her there. All that fear pooled in the back of her mind. Those tiny, destructive thoughts were what truly held her back from doing what she loved, and she couldn't face being the reason her parents suffered. She would rather be stuck on the farm for the rest of her life than watch that happen.

She looked away from the man, her lips pulled in a tight line from the stress of her thoughts. "I wish I could lie and say that nothing is holding me back, but I have duties and a family tradition that I cannot ignore."

The man looked into the horizon towards the people who walked past them. "When I was your age, I thought the same thing. My family had a job that ran through the generations. A tradition, just like yours. I thought that I was destined to become just like them because I shared their blood and their last name and that it was my duty to carry it on. Though their ideals did not match with mine. When I didn't see the way they did, I broke those chains. I broke those bindings that held me down and created my own path in life. My family didn't suffer because of me, they didn't starve or hate me. They just moved on. You can do that too, break what holds you down and become who you are meant to be." The man's golden eyes glowed fiercely as his determination and might shone deep within his words.

Looking down towards her feet, Verona spared a few beats of silence before she replied. "I know it's mostly fear holding me back, and I'm just placing the blame on my parents, but I just don't know if I'm ready to take that leap yet." She gave the man a wry and playful smile. Though the sadness still broke through the cracks of her demeanor. "Maybe in a few more years, I will take that leap, and you can show me all the wonders in the world, train me to fight with swords, and dance in royal ballrooms."

He laughed. "I promise I will find you when it is time, though in the meantime, have this." He dug through a small pack tied to his waist for a brief second, then held out a teal-colored stone. It seemed almost translucent, though shiny streaks of blue and green swirled around its smooth texture. It reminded her of the jewelry her mother would wear all the time. It was her favorite stone, and Verona loved it too.

She grabbed the stone out of his hand with a smile. "It's a sea stone, isn't it? What's the meaning behind it? My mother loves these stones and wears them all the time."

He nodded in affirmation. "Correct, they are actually the stones of adventurers. It was a popular rock for people like me to grab on trips to the sea. If your mother wasn't given it as a gift, then she had to have been an adventurer herself."

The statement that was just laid out before her shocked her to her core. There was no way her own mother traveled around the country, seeing the sights and people that Verona wanted to see. She shook her head in confusion, with her brows drawn in tight as she looked back up at the man. "There's no way that she was someone like you. She married my father young and has been running the farm ever since. That's what she's told me before."

The smile he once held slowly started to fade from his features. A deep somberness blanketed over his face. "Sometimes we hide knowledge from the people we love the most so we don't hurt them in the ways we fear. She must have done so knowing what you desire most."

There was so much Verona had to talk to her mother about. There was so much that she needed to know right away. If her mother was an adventurer, then she could do that as well. Verona didn't need to keep the tradition solely on her shoulders. She could pass it to a sibling who wanted it more. She had a life she needed to live, and she had to tell her parents that. Verona looked up to say more but was caught off guard by the town that loomed closely before them. She scowled for a second, wishing for more time, but she was excited to finally be here, to finally see Mariam.

She gave the adventurer one last smile. "This is where I'm going. I need to do some trading for my farm. Are you stopping here as well?"

He shook his head. "No, unfortunately, I am not. I'm actually going with many of the people on this road. We have traveled together for days now, and we're making our way to the kingdom of M'ralz for the Magnolia festival."

Verona slowed her pace for a second, trying to dig through her memory about the festival. It confused her briefly before she remembered a tradition Mariam had told her about a year ago. "It's the festival that celebrates the coming of spring and love, right? It's in celebration of Valencia, the goddess of new beginnings, secret lovers, and bringer of spring."

He nodded his head in agreement. "Yes, though there's more to it. There's so much life in such a small festival. While the true festival starts in a couple of months time, the spring equinox is only a week away and many people celebrate until the last day of the festival. I am one of those people," He lightly chuckled. "If you can make it, do so. It is definitely a sight worth seeing."

Verona smiled at the thought of going and seeing what the festival was truly about. At that moment, she made up her mind. It was time to tell her parents how she felt when she got back home. Though before she did that, she needed to complete this last errand.

With hope in her eyes, she looked back at the man. "I will be there. I'll take the first step to become who I want to be." She paused in her step before looking a little sheepishly. "I don't think I ever got your name."

The man gave a slight chuckle. "You can call me Calder. And yourself?"

Verona reached out her hand. "It's nice to meet you, Calder. I'm Verona."

He took her hand and shook it, relaying the same sentiments. The two eventually split and moved onto their separate paths. Before entering the town, she gave one look down at the stone in her left hand. She thought about everything she had learned from her conversation with Calder. While it had been a shock to learn, it was a good step towards the future she always wanted. Verona glanced back at Calder one last time. She smiled and then took her first step past the gate and into Ashfall.

Chapter Two

Ancient stone walls loomed around the bustling town. They once served as a way for archers and other guards to protect the town. Now, in a time of peace, its only purpose was a place for the white flowering vines to thrive. In the early morning hours, the sounds of chatter and childish giggles filled the air as the people in the town went about their day. The first few buildings Verona saw as she entered the town were the community hall, which held meetings and information for passing travelers, and the local inn for them to stay in.

On the cobbled stone road beyond those first structures were several merchant shops selling everything people could want, from jewelry and weapons to baked goods and pottery. The clanging of a hammer hitting metal reverberated off of the stone buildings, the sizzle of steaming water following behind it. Chatter filled the spaces as the shopkeepers were bartering prices with their customers. The slap of wet clay came from the pottery shop as Verona walked by. She took a peek inside to see an artist at work, making bowls and plates. As soon as she passed the bakery, Verona closed her eyes and took a deep breath in. The sweet smell of confectionaries, chocolate, and freshly baked bread filled her senses and made her mouth water. While this part of town was her favorite to explore, she had to keep moving.

When she reached the center of town, the crowded street unfurled into a wide, open market. Wooden stalls scattered the grassy knolls. In that very place, Verona could find anything that she would ever want to buy. While there were the merchant's quarters that sold more quality goods, the market, which would soon open, was there for arts, trinkets, farm fresh food, and empty stalls for travelers to sell their goods.

From the market, there was a street that went to the left of town, leading to the working quarters. On that street held the smith's shop, the armory, livery, fletchers, carpenters, butchers, and a few others. The street that led to the right held smaller, nondescript shops and many of the local taverns. The rest of the town was filled with houses behind the working quarters and taverns. As you walked further toward the back, the houses became grander and larger compared to the smaller, ramshackle houses near the front.

By the time Verona made her way to the center of the town, the grassy knoll and stalls stood empty. There wasn't a single soul in sight. She quickly looked around before moving her cart towards a young woman passing by.

"I'm sorry to bother you," Verona spoke softly and sincerely. "I'm here for the market. It's been a while, so my memory is a little hazy. Do you know when it starts for the day? I think I made it here a little early."

The woman stopped in her tracks for a quick second to let Verona know that she was a little under an hour early. Verona gave her a quick 'thank you' before setting her cart off the road and leaning against it for a rest. How could she waste an hour? An idea popped into her mind, and without a second thought, she picked up her cart and headed toward a familiar house.

Verona placed her cart on the side of the stone wall, walked up the stairs, and knocked on the heavy wooden door. It didn't take long for a familiar blonde to open the door, with worried eyes and a set of eyebrows knitted in confusion. Verona couldn't help but grin widely at her friend, excitement buzzing across her skin as she reveled in the fact she was finally able to see her once more. She took in the sight of her friend; she looked exactly like the last time she had seen her. Mariam was beautiful, so beautiful, in fact, that she looked as if she was born from royalty.

She was jealous of Mariam, she couldn't lie about it. Verona was labeled tall for a female, often standing face-to-face with grown men. She was strong from the years working on her family's farm and her body was toned to the point of barely any femininity to it at all. Her skin was littered with freckles and her curly hair was on the edge of being untamable. Mariam, on the other hand, was petite, her body curved in all the right places. Her skin was tanned from days spent basking in the meadows and her shiny golden hair fell in perfect waves, with not a single strand out of place. Her teeth were perfectly white and straight, framed by a full set of dusty pink lips. Mariam also had a dusting of light brown freckles that plastered her cheeks and the bridge of her nose. They made her green eyes, flecked with golden streaks, stand out to their fullest potential. Though it also was the impossibly long lashes that framed them as well. She was perfect in every way, but Verona couldn't let that bother her. Mariam was like family to her, and she wouldn't let a sense of competition ruin that for them.

Verona softly laughed at Mariam, whose confusion slowly turned to shock. "Hello, Mariam."

Mariam's face lit up brightly as realization finally hit her. A buzz of excitement ran through her as she finally hugged her in what felt like years. "Oh, Verona! It's been too long since I've last seen you! Come inside. You have the time to, right?"

Verona nodded and walked into the house. The inside was beautiful, as it had always been. She couldn't help but be amazed every time she saw it. As she stepped past the door, she admired the wood and white stone framing the walls. The inside was dimly lit by a large fireplace that sat in the middle of the right wall. Other small wax candles littered the room on several of the tables and bookcases that decorated the large room. Over by the fireplace, a small table and a couple of chairs sat with a large fur blanket draped over one of them. Above the fireplace were several heads of beasts that Mariam's father had hunted over the years. A large standing dresser leaned against the wall to the right of the fireplace, and in the middle of the room was a large table that was placed over a fur rug.

Several books were opened and sat on the table, likely from Mariam who must have been there only moments ago. To the left of the table were several mid-sized bookcases that were overflowing with books, many of them Verona had looked at herself and read in this very room. Several potted plants were scattered amongst the room for decoration, and numerous paintings and decorative drapery were placed amongst the walls as well. Large wooden arches stretched across the ceiling, held up by decorative steel brackets. Hanging down from them were antlered chandeliers that supported large wax candlesticks. In the back of the room were a couple of doorways and also a stairway up to the second floor.

As Mariam and Verona were about to sit down at the table to talk, realization struck Mariam's features. "Oh, Verona. I forgot I would meet Ren and Beatrice at The Wilted Rose. Will you come with me? They would be elated to see you again, and we have so much to talk about."

A sense of disappointment blanketed Verona. She would have rather spent the time she had in a place that was more comfortable to her, though if she needed to go to a tavern and sit down with others to talk to Mariam, then that's what she would do. So, with a smile, she gave Mariam a nod, and the two of them walked out of the house and onto the streets.

As Mariam and Verona walked towards the tavern, an itch rose up in her to tell Mariam what she learned. She wanted to blurt it out about the stone, the festival, Calder, her plan, and everything in between. Verona stared out into the street in front of them as they continued their walk. She tried to devise a way to start the conversation, but she couldn't figure out how to, so she just said what was on her mind. "I think I'm going to tell my parents that I don't want the farm anymore. I saw an adventurer on my way here, and he made me feel like that's what I truly wanted to do. I want to explore, Mariam."

Mariam looked at her, shell-shocked by what Verona said. She placed a hand on Verona's arm and gently stopped her. "You don't know, do you?"

Verona looked at her with an expression that was nothing but fear and nervousness. "What don't I know, Mariam?"

"Your brother Thomas, last time he came here, was telling me that he wanted the farm from you. I don't know why he hasn't said anything yet. It's been ages since he came here. Though I figured that he would have said something, so that is why I did not say something last time I saw you. I told him he should say something right away to you, but it's Thomas, so of course, he didn't say a word." Mariam huffed out a breath in utter annoyance at Verona's own brother.

Verona couldn't say anything back. She felt as if her whole world was turned upside down again and again. Her brother wanted the farm! He was the second oldest, so it would work out perfectly. She could live her own life and travel all of the unknown lands around them, and her family would be okay without her there. She became so lost in her thoughts that she didn't realize they'd arrived at their destination until Mariam started to open the door to the Wilted Rose Tavern.

As they stepped into the old wooden tavern with gray stone walls, a blonde woman with a too-tight bodice walked quickly over to them and pulled Verona into an equally too-tight hug.

"Oh, Ver! It's been way too long since you have been here. I have missed you so much. Why didn't you stop by last time? I forgive you, though, because I get to see you now." The woman crooned loudly in Verona's ear.

Verona gave a light chuckle before peeling herself from the body that held onto her. She looked fully at the woman before her. Long, graying blonde hair was pulled back from her face and braided into a tail down her back. Her gray-blue eyes reminded Verona of a vengeful storm cloud on a warm summer day. At that moment, those same eyes overflowed with love as they looked at her. The bridge of her nose was twisted and broken, showing obvious signs of trying to break up one too many bar fights. Though the tip of her nose was round and almost button-like. Her lips were full with a strong cupid's bow and they were now turned up into a large smile. The face of the woman before her was sharp and angular. To Verona, it was as familiar to her as her own mother's face was. "Hello, Aunt Regina. I know I haven't stopped by in a while, I've missed you too! Could we get a table for the four of us? We have Ren and Beatrice arriving soon."

She led them through the maze of tables before bringing them to a private table in the corner. While Verona had called Regina her Aunt, it was far from the case. Regina was in fact Mariam's Aunt, though since they had been friends for so long, Verona had been a part of Mariam's family for years now. They had watched her grow up, talked when she came into town, and even called Verona one of their own. While she didn't get to see them often anymore, she still loved them like her own and missed them just the same.

As they sat down, Verona thanked Regina. It was only a matter of moments before the two other women showed up and took their places among the empty seats. She knew what the other two friends liked to talk about most, so she leaned in to start the conversation.

"Okay," Verona said while a smile started to bloom on her lips. "What gossip have I missed since I've last been here?"

The three ladies before her smiled. Ren, who had olive skin, black hair, and almond-shaped eyes, sat next to her and smiled. "Oh, you know, just the usual. The town's lord is still sleeping with the blacksmith's wife. The blacksmith is sleeping with the lord's wife, but they've been trying to hide it from each other. They haven't caught on yet, but everyone in the town knows. More people are moving in, and it's helping the town a lot. Some say that we have a neighboring town that wants to take us over, but we've been hearing that for years." She looked over towards the bar and rolled her eyes. "Also, Mav is still Mav."

Hearing the familiar name at the end, Verona glanced towards the bar, seeing the messy-haired, dirty-blonde man sitting there. Verona could see him clearly from where she was sitting. His jawbone was sharp as steel and covered in a fine layer of blonde stubble that was barely trimmed neatly. Years in the sun were responsible for the few dark freckles that dusted his cheekbones and his dark tone of olive skin. A slightly large and crooked nose sat in the middle of his face, broken from the years of starting bar fights. Large eyes were framed by dark blonde eyelashes. Even from here, Verona could see a set of hazel eyes with gray flecks that reminded her of an early spring day filled with endless fog. Verona could see a large pink scar that poked out from the collar of his gray shirt and led from the middle of his neck down towards his chest. Mav was tall, so tall that Verona felt petite in his midst, even from where she sat. Although he wore loose clothing as he sat there slouched over on his chair, Verona could tell his body was toned in every way imaginable. She couldn't help but blush at the thought but shook it out of her head. This was not the time or place to gush about a man who spent his days in a bar.

She had heard so much about him that she didn't know what to think. He was the same age as her, both eighteen and on the brink of adulthood. Gossip was often spread around about his troubled background. He didn't have any family here and no house; he lived in the inns or taverns around town and was never seen sober. Many laughed at him, made fun of him, and tossed him out when he was so drunk he could barely even walk. Verona felt nothing but pity for the poor man.

Verona sighed, looking back at her friends. "Looks like he's still the same him, being the town drunk and clown as usual." She felt a tinge of disgust at the words, but she knew her friends would look at her weirdly if she had said anything else.

She had forgotten to lower her voice, not thinking anyone would hear. When a hand landed on her shoulder, Verona jumped. Her friends' faces were pale, and she had a good feeling about who was right behind her. The man leaned in towards her ear, and she felt a puff of hot air against her face. The foul smell of a breath tinged with alcohol assaulted her senses and she knew exactly who was nearly touching her face. She shivered with a mix of anxiety and disgust with how close Mav was. Verona wanted to move, but she would never give him that satisfaction of seeing her feel small next to someone the likes of him.

"Hello, Mav," she said, her voice absent of any emotion.

He chuckled, getting amusement from her reaction. "You know, darling," he slurred into her ear, his lilting seaside accent thicker and more pronounced, his breath reeked of mead and other kinds of drinks he already had today. "When you talk about someone that's in the same room as you, it would be wise to talk a little more quietly so they don't hear you. You can offend someone by saying things like that."

Verona gritted her teeth in annoyance, she moved her chair farther away and faced him.

"Well, I'm sorry you can't handle the truth, Mav. Also, maybe you shouldn't be eavesdropping on other people's conversations, that's rude too." Verona snapped back with an eyebrow raised.

Aunt Regina came quickly over with a sheepish expression. Worry was deeply clouded in her eyes. Swiftly, she grabbed Mav's shoulders and moved him away from the girls. "I think you've had enough to drink for the day. I have a room already set up for you upstairs." She waved over another one of the barmaids who took him away and up the stairs where a room was waiting for him at the top.

The group could hear Mav grumble as he was escorted away. Verona shivered, feigning disgust to the other ladies around her. While she felt a need to help the poor boy, she knew she could not say that to anyone, so all she knew she could do was play a part. "I'm glad he's gone," she whispered.

Regina sighed, shaking her head. "He's just as bad as he's ever been. I feel bad for the kid, he needs someone to pull him out of the hole he's in. He used to be better than that. A lot of people who knew him before always said he was a great kid growing up. Though you know all about him, everyone who comes here often does. I don't know why I'm rambling to you." She laughed, though no humor was anywhere on her solemn features. "I just wish he would get the help he needed."

She couldn't wrap her head around that, for someone who was so hollow and broken to have been someone so great and liked. She couldn't imagine what pain or suffering he had gone through to bring him to such a point. She wanted to reach out to him, wanted to bring to light what she thought. Though this town was ruthless in how they thought of him, Verona knew she had to play along with them. Verona sent a quick thought to the gods to help heal him, and she prayed for herself to never go through a tragedy so horrific enough for her to end up like that.

Before Regina left their table, they had all ordered their food. After a few lighter conversations, they had food in front of them. While they ate, it didn't take long for them to completely forget about Mav as laughter filled the air around them.

• • •

For Verona, time passed too quickly in her favorite town. It was past midday, her errands were done, and she knew that it was time for her to leave and head back home. Verona and Mariam stood near the exit of the town gate with bags and a cart in tow. They both cried out in frustration as they gave each other the biggest hugs they could.

Verona slowly peeled herself away from Mariam as she tried to wipe away the tears that built up in her eyes. "I don't want to go home, Mariam. I wish I could stay here with you forever."

41

Her friend sniffled at the hard goodbye. "I know, Verona, I wish you could, too. Though you have to go home. You need to tell your parents how you feel. I'm sure they will understand. After that, you can come straight here; I'll have a room waiting just for you."

Verona loved the thought of that, to spend every day she could with Mariam, to bring her on adventures with her, and to see the world like she always wanted to. They had promised, if it came to fruition, that they would live out their dreams on the road no matter the circumstance. At this moment, it felt as if she was brushing her fingertips against that very dream. She pulled away from Mariam and gave her a wide grin. "I'll be expecting that bed to be made when I'm back in a few days."

"It will be done, Verona," Mariam responded softly.

With hopefulness and excitement running through her veins, Verona took her first step back home.

As Verona walked back, the road before her was a little more quiet. She saw only a few people, many who had their heads hung in exhaustion, carrying sleeping children, or just not willing to talk. She felt the same way, though; she couldn't wait to be home and to finally lay in her own bed. Though the weariness was violently clawing at her heels, she kept on pushing, putting one tired leg in front of the other. She didn't notice the scenery change around her for quite some time; it took a woman's loud sob of grief for her to finally look up. When she did, Verona thought she was escorted straight into a living nightmare.

The first thing Verona comprehended was a sky full of looming darkness, though it confused her. *Why was the sky black? Why wasn't it the beautiful colors of a sunset? It's not night yet.* Other thoughts raced through her mind until she was forcibly snapped back into reality. Fire roared on the horizon, stretching on for miles, burning endless fields of crops and houses in its path of destruction. Ash rained down on the world like a fresh coat of snow. Verona looked around in shock, trying to find where the screaming had come from. That's when she saw the mass of bodies. The many people who walked towards her held a blank stare, too shell-shocked to even be in the present. Their faces were covered in a layer of black soot. Some had burnt rags covering their bodies from being torched by the flame.

She gasped loudly as she finally saw the source of the scream. A few yards away, a mother was kneeling, holding her lifeless child to her chest. She couldn't tell why the child was so red until Verona came closer and saw the burnt flesh that covered the child from head to toe. Verona looked away, the slick feeling of bile rose into her throat, and her lips twisted into a sneer of revulsion. Tears pricked at her eyes. She finally realized where these people were coming from, why they were heading towards her. The fire was coming from the same direction as her home. The feeling of disgust quickly built up tenfold as anxiety clouded her thoughts and her eyes widened in fear. Her legs shook almost overwhelmingly, she couldn't breathe, couldn't get a single breath past her rapidly closing throat. Her eyes were getting blurry. Why was it so hard for her to see anything in front of her? She felt so light-headed as she was gasping for breath. Her eyes were darting around as panic and fear enveloped her, squeezing her so tight. Everything was becoming so hard to do. All she wanted to do was lie down and scream. Though deep in her mind, she knew that this panic and fear was only crippling her. With deep, even breaths, her ever-spinning world slowed down. She looked around for someone, anyone to talk to.

"Ma'am, please! Where did you come from? Did you pass Felkeirn? Are the people of Felkeirn safe?" Verona spoke loudly, her voice echoing her fear.

The woman looked towards Verona, her eyes red and full of tears. "I escaped from Felkeirn. I was hiding there when my home burned down this morning, but the flames, it-" Sobs wracked the woman's body as everything came back to her. The fear, the feeling of it all, she was reliving it all again. "It came there too. It's all gone. Everything is gone."

Verona shook her head. "No, that can't be true. Did everyone make it out? My family lives there. Did you see a woman that looks like me? She would be with her husband and six children. Have you seen them?" Her breath quickened, her lungs couldn't keep up as her vision blurred further. Verona's skin felt far too tight, her mind too clouded as the panic and fear crept up her body once more. She wanted it gone, she just wanted it all to stop.

The woman shook her head and walked past Verona. She ran her hands through her hair, feeling tears well up in her eyes once more. She was only half an hour away from home if she walked with the cart. So, with a quick, irrational decision, she dropped it and ran.

She ran past children who were walking alone, screaming for their mothers. She ran past men carrying their injured wives. She passed others too stunned to even move as they lay there crumpled on the ground. Verona couldn't stop. As much as she wanted to help them, she had to find her family. She had to know they were alive and well. She gritted her teeth and pushed her too-tired body even more. She was almost there, she was so close to home. As she drew nearer, the world around her grew hotter, the flames edged in and threatened to take her as another one of their victims. It was becoming harder for her to see as more ash clogged the air in front of her. Sweat dripped down her forehead and into her face. She lifted her arm, wiping it away. Though as she pulled it away and looked down, her arm was covered in soot, and she knew she looked like the other people she'd passed.

Verona halted to a stop as she saw what was once her house. Black charred wood laid in a large rubble with broken stones and scorched hay.

Everything was burned. She could see pieces of a bed frame sticking up from the rubble, along with other pieces of furniture that were once items they cherished, now blacked char and broken pieces amongst the carnage. They had to have seen it coming, they had to have gotten out. Though the little ones, her youngest siblings, wouldn't know what to do. Her mind went to the worst scenario... what if they didn't get out? Her breath caught in her throat. A loud, ugly sob escaped her as she dropped to her knees. She wanted them all to be alive and safe. She couldn't live without them.

"Mother! Father!" she screamed out in desperate panic as a sob wracked her body.

For a second, all Verona could hear was the roar of the fire circling her, coming closer and closer to destroy what was left of her home. She then heard a groan, and Verona gasped. Pulling herself up, she ran to the rubble. Hearing the groan again, she climbed up to where it was coming from.

"Hello? Mom? Dad? Is it you? Are you okay?" she said into the burnt ruins, hopefulness was tinged in her voice as most of the fear vanished from inside of her.

"Verona?" A familiar voice whispered back.

She knew that voice, it was her mother. Kneeling on the wood before her, she started to dig.

The broken pieces of her house were still hot to the touch, and every time she grabbed something to move it out of the way, she could feel her skin sizzle and burn. A scream was lodged in her throat, but Verona gritted her teeth as she felt the pain run up her arms. She pushed every feeling down. She had to. Someone was alive down there and they needed her to keep going. Her body was telling her to stop as she felt her skin melt, tears were running down her cheeks in protest, but she couldn't stop, not when lives depended on it. Verona lay down, getting deeper into the pile. She pushed away one last piece of wood and finally found a pocket of open space.

The space was large and dark. Verona had to take a moment for her eyes to adjust to the darkness below her, though when she did, she saw the burnt body in her view. There she was, her mother, lying underneath a large wooden beam. It was one of those exact beams that once held up their house; a beam that Verona knew just by looking at it, she would not be able to lift by herself. Her mother was badly burned. Her skin was covered in residue and charred in large patches all over her body. Rags of barely-there clothing hung to her body and were soaked in blood. Her once beautiful red-orange hair was almost burnt away. The only part of her that remained the same was her golden amber eyes, which were now full of suffering and agony. In her arms was a too-small body, curled up tightly but unmoving. Verona couldn't stop the mangled sob that escaped her as she saw Wymond, who her mother protected until his last moments. Her father lay under another beam, his eyes were closed and would never open again. Smaller hands and arms surrounded them in the small pocket, sticking out from the rubble that closed in on them. They were all gone, the fire took them all.

"Mother," Verona said softly. She pushed away her own pain and fear as she reached down to comfort her mother.

"Verona. You're alive," she said with a smile.

"Yes, Mama, I'm here for you. I'm going to get you out," Verona said softly as she looked down at her mother, desperation deep in her voice.

Her mother was silent for a few too long heartbeats. "I can't get out. I am too weak and badly burned," she whispered. Her eyes traveled down to Wymond. "I can't leave them here."

Her mother coughed loudly, even saying just a couple of words was hard. She was struggling to breathe from the smoke and debris that filled her lungs. Her voice, which was once a sweet melody, was nothing more than a rattle of death.

Tears flowed down Verona's face as the agony and fear swallowed her whole once more. "No, no, no, no. I can't leave you here. I can't lose you, too, Mama. You're all that I have left."

Her mother gave her a sorrowful grimace, tears running down her face. Even being this close to death, she was still trying to be strong for her own daughter. "Save yourself, please do it for me. I love you, Ver. Live for me."

Verona lay there in the burning ruins, reaching down towards her mother. She cried, calling out for her as she watched her mother take her last breath. Laying there in silence, time passed slowly. The sunset fell into the earth, and the stars slowly began to burn bright, unaware of what had happened during the day. The sorrow and fear slowly burned out, and nothingness took their place. Emptiness was a comfort to her. She wanted to feel numb as she gave herself to the glowing embers, hoping they would consume her too. Though when the sun had risen once more, and she was still there, lying amongst the rubble, able to see what had happened once more, rage had taken over every space in her body. Verona bared her teeth as it consumed her.

Something had broken inside her that very morning. Something that would never be able to be repaired and was now filled with revolting hatred. A feeling so dark, it was easy to take over her, though she was nothing but vulnerable, and so it was easy for her to feel it. She did the only thing she could do. She screamed. The anger ran through her tenfold as it escaped her. She wanted everyone to hear it, even the gods and death. Verona would show her vengeance to whoever did this. They would pay for every ounce of pain they had given her. That was a promise she would keep, one that would keep her alive.

Chapter Three

Verona stumbled from the ruins, her mind hazy and uncomprehending. She didn't know where she was going, just that she needed to get out of there. The flames licked at her heels; it was so uncomfortably hot. She tried to grab anything she could as she stumbled again, the tree she reached for crumbled to ash before her and burned her skin once more. She cried out in pain, pulling her hand back. Her skin was a swollen, red mass with blisters already forming on her palm. She looked up towards the sky above. It looked so dark from the ash that eradicated the sun. Her world faded in and out before her. She gritted her teeth, trying to focus on the path she was

on, though everything was still blurry to her. She shook
her head, trying to get rid of the feeling. After a
heartbeat of reprieve, she tried to move forward, but
her foot caught on a rock, and her entire world fell
down with her. She felt a blow to the head and gasped
in shock as the pain enveloped her. Reaching up, she
felt her temple. Something wet and sticky slid down
her palm.

Verona whimpered as she pulled herself to her
knees, her head bowed in frustration as tears welled in
her eyes. "I can't do this anymore! I can't do this. I'm
sorry, Mama."

The fire around her grew even closer with each
heartbeat. The flames danced around, creating figures
of those who she had loved and taunting her in
unimaginable ways. Verona screamed at the fire, telling
it to go away as she flung a branch into it, disrupting its
taunting rhythm. Although the fire once again began
its dance, showing her mother, alive and happy, telling
her again the last thing she told her. *Live for me,* it
whispered in its crackling way. The tears flowed down
her soot-smothered face. She was on the cusp of giving
up. She gave one last primal scream into the flames as
she pulled herself up. The pain that shot through her
entire body was unbearable, but she had to move. She
had to keep that promise to her mother.

Verona leaped through the small opening in the flames and landed on the road, scraping her knees as she fell on hard rocks. She slowly pushed herself up, a gasp escaped her lips as every nerve in her body felt tinged with pain. Painstakingly, she started to stumble down the road before her. Her vision faded in and out as an ache started to swell inside of her head. Her hearing was gone except for a sharp ringing that echoed throughout her body. She saw more people up ahead of her and tried to call for help, but her voice was so hoarse she couldn't utter a sound. She couldn't do anything but follow the others, forming a group of half-dead, injured beings. She didn't know where they were going or which road they were on, but she thought that it had to be towards safety. A mother was beside her carrying her lifeless child. Verona tried to reach out to comfort her, but the mother stared toward the horizon with emotionless eyes. If she could, Verona would have shed a tear for the scene she saw before her. Though with her soot-clogged eyes, she looked forward and walked towards the rising sun.

Soon, she saw the entryway of a town she knew all too well. The group she was in blended with other refugees; they all huddled together in a mass of injured bodies. People from the town were drawing in, and gasps sounded through the growing crowd. Some were running away to get healers, while others were too shocked at the sight before them to even move. A familiar head of golden blonde locks bounced towards her group. As soon as the two locked eyes, Verona fell to the ground in relief. A set of soft hands caught her fall, and the last thing Verona saw was Mariam's wide, fear-stricken eyes looking back at her as her friend was yelling at her

"Stay with me, Verona. I'm going to get you help, I just need you to stay with me. I need you to stay with me, please! Please, Verona!" Mariam was screaming as her eyes darted around in fear.

Verona opened her lips to reassure her friend that she was alright, though as soon as she tried, the darkness consumed her being and pulled her into its depths as consciousness evaded her.

Chapter Four

Verona had woken in a bed framed by familiar walls; this room was one she used time and time again when she had to stay in Ashfall. Though this time was unlike the others. This time, she did not want to be at Mariam's house, nor did she want to be anywhere near Ashfall. She wanted to be in a place where she could mourn and wanted to be close to her family. She wanted to be consumed by the flames with them. As she tore the covers off her body so she could travel back to her home, she saw the bandages that covered the burns. Something inside of her snapped as her vision blurred out of focus. They covered it all. They covered the evidence that reminded her of her family. They covered the torture she had gone through to try and save them. A tear rolled down her cheek as she drew in a shaky breath. They couldn't do this to her, they couldn't minimize her feelings and try to shield her from them. She wanted them off her. She wanted these bandages gone. The tears were rolling down her cheeks faster as her throat tightened and her body shook as she started to feel suffocated. A whimper escaped her lips as her fingers moved on their own accord, ferociously clawing at the tightly wrapped bandages.

"I want them off, I want them gone. Get them off of me, get them off, get them off," she whispered, her hoarse voice cracking with desperation and never-ending pain.

The anxiety rolled through her as her throat tightened more, her vision darkening, her limbs shaking, and her mind reeling. She couldn't do this anymore, all this pain, all this suffering she had gone through that was all for nothing. Her fingers clawed faster, tearing bandages, cracking nails, and breaking skin.

"I want them all off! I want them all off! I want them all off!" She started to scream. She didn't care who heard her because, in the end, she wanted them to feel the same pain she was feeling now.

Pain soon seared her body as the bandages were finally off with fresh claw marks that had now accompanied the burns. She looked down at her cracked and bloodied fingers. She had spent the rest of that day watching the blood under her fingernails slowly dry. No one had come and checked on her, no one came to ask if she was okay. Day had soon become night, and she drifted off to sleep. Though when she closed her eyes, fire danced in her dreams, burned bodies chased after her, and no matter what she did to try and stop it, she watched her house burn over and over again until her eyes fluttered open once more.

When the sun had finally crested the horizon, a servant entered her room. The girl's eyes widened at the scene before her as she took in the torn bandages littering the room and bloody fingerprints dotted across the sheets, accompanied by a broken girl staring out the window, trying to escape from reality. Verona knew the girl had walked into the room, knew that she would soon start to work on the scene around here, and knew that she should talk to her. Though she never moved her unyielding eyes from the window-framed horizon. She was waiting for them to walk into this town, was waiting for them to find her and to tell her that everything was okay. They had to be out there, they had to be alive.

Without turning her eyes, she grievously whispered to the girl. "Has my family come into town yet?"

The girl stepped into her view before kneeling down to look at Verona's arms. She hesitated for a heartbeat before looking fully at the broken girl before her. "M'lady told me that your family is gone, miss. She told me that she went to see for herself to see if she could help them. I am truly sorry for your loss."

Verona's eyes twitched before they went wild, vision snapping towards the girl in front of her. "No, they're not gone. They'll be here any day now." Her breath quickened as the sobs started to wrack her body. "They're still alive out there. They are. They just don't know where to find me. I need to go and find them."

When Verona started to rise to escape the house, the girl gently pushed her back towards the bed. "I am sorry, but what m'lady says is true. I am truly sorry."

The girl quickly took care of Verona, rewrapping her wounds, redressing the bed, and cleaning the room as quickly as she could. Before she fully left Verona alone, a plate of food was dropped off on the dresser before her. Though, as hours passed, the food lay there untouched and unbothered.

Days passed before her. Other servants walked into the room, dropping off food, checking her bandages, and trying to take care of her. However, the only things she said to them were about her parents and whether they had arrived in town yet. Every time someone said 'no' or 'I'm sorry' or 'm'lady said', it was kindling to an ever-growing fire. She hated when they told her those words; they were not the truth. Her parents were still out there suffering, and no one wanted to help them.

When the end of the week came, the last 'no' she received about her parents that day made her snap. The plate of food she had received that morning ended up splattered against the window; shards of ceramic lay broken on the floor as the food slowly smeared down the glass. She slowly bruised her fists as she banged against the locked door for hours on end. She wanted out. She wanted to yell at anyone she could. Every moment of that day, she couldn't help but see the faults in the world around her, from the cracks in the wood that threatened to buckle to the small chips in the plates she was given and the over-seasoned food she refused to eat. Every minute felt like torture for someone who regretted the decision to live. It was a constant battle filled with pain, continuous screaming, and agonizing thoughts. All she wanted to do was sleep and stay in those dreams where her family was still alive, dreams where she could still touch them and tell them that she loved them more times than she could count. The anger and the frustration were fueled by the way she was being treated; all she wanted to do was go help her family.

When night finally fell, she found herself lying down on the floor by the entryway, tears rolling down her cheeks as the anger she had felt all day finally took its toll. When the servant entered the room that night to bring dinner, her eyes once again widened at the scene before her.

Verona quickly scrambled to her knees and begged. "I will do anything I need to do. Please just let me go see my family. I will clean this up myself, I will wrap my own bandages. Just please let me go see them. I just want to see them. I just want my mama." Her sobs shook her body, making her words quiver with despair.

The girl quickly took care of the room without talking to Verona this time; she hung her head low without even glancing at Verona as she begged non-stop without care. As soon as she was done, the servant closed the door with a soft click, leaving Verona alone with nothing but her desperation.

Days passed slowly after that. Verona felt as if she had given up. Anger hadn't worked, and the pleading was unsuccessful. They would never let her see her family. If there was anyone alive, they would have surely perished by now as she was locked in this room, forced to be a prisoner with a never-ending sentence. So, she decided to give up. Once she was done pleading with them, she had pushed herself into the bed and didn't leave it again. Days passed with her curled up into the sheets. Servants came and went, though she never uttered a word. Her eyes never left the window before her. She felt empty inside, she felt dead to the world around her. All she wanted to do was go back out there in that desolate world, crawl into the ashes of her house, and whither away so she could be with them once more. She didn't feel anything. All she wanted was to not live in this plane of existence anymore.

It took a few more days of laying there before she finally accepted that they were gone, and at that moment, she finally broke. Loud, ugly sobs escaped her body as the once bloodied sheets were now dawned with droplets of tears.

One morning, Verona had woken up with the
rising sun, her body forcing her awake for the few
hours it could. She was sitting on her bed, legs pulled
to her chest and arms wrapped around them. She
stared at the wall, trying to fade from reality. The door
creaked softly as someone started to open it, and her
head snapped towards the sound. She let out a guttural
growl of annoyance and anger to whoever dared to
come in. That's when a familiar blonde head slowly
appeared from the other side.

"Good morning, Verona. I'm happy to see that
you're awake." Mariam said softly, fear and hesitation
exuding from her voice.

Verona sighed, turning her head back to the
wall. "I wish I wasn't awake, but more than that, I wish
I wasn't alive. I wish I was down there wrapped in my
mama's arms." Her voice cracked from the pain that
wreaked havoc on her very mind.

Mariam walked into the room, tiptoeing around the broken shards of vases and plates. Carefully, she sat next to Verona and softly placed a hand on her back. Instinctively, Verona leaned in towards her friend as she felt arms wrap around her. That's when Verona broke. As she curled into Mariam, sobs wracked her body, and tears streamed down her face. She had shown nothing but denial and anger these last couple of weeks; she forced herself to feel nothing but the endless torture of the wrath that consumed her every being. Deep down, she knew that she was sorrowful and extraordinarily afraid. Every part of her life vanished before her eyes, and she didn't know what to do anymore. Her parents, the two people who supported her through everything, were gone. She would never see her siblings grow up, would never see them have families of their own, and she would never be able to lean on her twin brothers again for their advice. Everything vanished in those flames, and she was the sole survivor in a world full of pain.

Mariam gently ran a hand through Verona's hair as she tried to calm her grieving friend. "Oh, Verona. I can't imagine how hard it is for you. I will always be here for you. You don't have to do this alone."

Verona wiped the tears away with the palm of her hand. Her bloodshot eyes slowly looked up and met Mariam's. "Some days I feel like I am alone; by my own doing, I'll admit, though other times I feel alone because I am alone now. I watched my mother die, I saw my family dead in the rubble of my home. I lost everyone out there, and only I can carry that burden. The Gods cast me out as an orphan." She softly laughed without a single ounce of humor. "It's such a cruel joke of theirs."

Mariam faced her, features twisted with sadness and a hint of pity. "I can't imagine how it feels to have witnessed that and to see your family that way. Though I can be understanding, and I can be here by your side." A small, sad smile briefly touched her lips before it disappeared another heartbeat later. "Remember that wild and overstated promise I told you the first day we met?"

Verona chuckled hoarsely as she was shot back in time to a bittersweet memory and granted a sweet release from the pain. "You mean that day you chatted my ear off and then promised to be a pain in my ass from now until forever."

Mariam laughed fully now, happiness and love written across her face, evident in her wide smile and the crinkle by her eyes. "Hey now, I'm sure you were glad I rescued you that day. But yes, from now until forever. I plan to keep that promise until the end, no matter the good days or bad, and I will be by your side. I know you lost your family, and I know that you are hurting, but I will help you in any way I can because I love you, Ver, and you are my family."

Verona looked towards the window and out into the world beyond as she chewed her lip. Tears threatened to escape her eyes once again, but she had cried so much, screamed so much already. She was just tired of it all. The pain would never go away, she was sure of it, and she still struggled with it, even now. Verona knew a part of herself would be broken forever; she lost a piece of herself that she would never get back. It would be something that would haunt her forever, but it was her burden to bear. She had to keep that promise she made to her mother. She had to live.

Verona opened her mouth to speak, but as soon as she did, her stomach let out a loud rumble, and her cheeks darkened in embarrassment.

Mariam chuckled, and her face lit up a little more, although the smile did not quite reach her eyes. "I know you haven't eaten much. Let me help you. I can draw up a bath, bring in some of the servants to help you, I have some dresses you can borrow as well, and we can go get something to eat if you would like or eat here if you feel more comfortable."

Verona's body relaxed, eyes crinkled in tenderness, and her lips tilted up as she lifted a hand to stop Mariam from her ongoing rambling. "That sounds good to me. I would enjoy a bath, and we can go to The Wilted Rose to eat."

Mariam's smile widened before she exited the room to find a servant. As Verona waited for someone to arrive, she stood up to stretch her aching limbs. Slowly, she walked over to the window and peered out. Her mind traveled to the others who came with her and suffered the same fate as her. She wondered if they were in torment the same way she was. Her eyebrows furrowed, her mouth twisted in agony, as her mind traveled down a dark path, escorting her into dark and terrifying memories.

The sound of a door creaking snapped her from her thoughts. As a servant walked in, Verona took in a deep breath, composing herself before walking over to the servant. It did not take long before the day turned into a whirlwind before her.

Verona bathed for the first time since the fire. The water had felt wondrous against her aching skin. She knew her body needed this, and with every second that passed, she felt the knots in her muscles loosen and the pain temporarily disappear. She lay there in her peaceful bliss for so long that the water slowly faded to a cool temperature. With a sigh, she pushed herself up, grabbing a towel. It didn't take long for the servant to arrive back in the room and redress her wounds. She had to stand in front of a mirror, and that's when Verona could see it all. She took account of all the burns, scratches, and deep cuts that littered her body. She saw all the burns on her stomach and hands that were pink, mottled patches of skin. She hated how her body looked, all the damage it had taken for no reward at all. She had put herself through all of this and still lost her family. She hated fate and the cards it had dealt her.

As soon as the maid had wrapped the last wound, she carefully slipped on the dress that Mariam had left for her. It was a simple, lightweight blue cotton gown. The sleeves fell three-fourths of the way down her arm, leaving a little skin to show. Though, what did show of her skin was bandaged and made Verona grimace. The gray bodice was carefully cinched and tied behind her back. It wasn't anything fancy in Mariam's terms, but Verona had never worn anything like it before. She was used to her loose hanging dresses that did her figure no justice, along with the rough fabric that always scratched her skin. After a quick brush through her hair, the maid tied it back in a simple braid.

Stepping out of the room, Verona laid her eyes on Mariam, who stood in the hall waiting for her. Mariam turned towards her when the door squeaked open, and her jaw hung loose in amazement. "You look beautiful, Verona."

She tipped her head down with a small amount of embarrassment. A slight blush stained her cheeks as she spoke. "I look okay, however I'm sure it would fit you better. The dress is nice. Thank you, Mariam."

"Of course!" She replied, walking over and looping her arm with Verona's. "Now, let's go get something to eat. I hear there's a pretty famous bard playing today at The Wilted Rose. He's been spoken about throughout Esnia, though we will have to judge his talent for ourselves, won't we?" She winked at Verona.

Verona nodded in agreement, trying to smile but knowing it didn't quite reach her eyes. "I guess we will."

The two walked out of Mariam's house and onto the cobbled streets before them. It didn't take long for the world before Verona to cause her mouth to turn sour. The children who were laughing and playing with a ball stopped and started to whisper as soon as they saw her. They eyed the bandages wrapped around her arms and the scratches on her face, and they knew exactly who she was. A survivor of the fire. The glances her way made her skin crawl. The way the crowd had moved around her with a six-foot gap, like she carried a deadly disease. With the other survivors in this very same town, why weren't they being more accepting of her? Why weren't they being more sympathetic? Why did they treat her like an odd and terrifying sight to see?

Her morning had felt normal to her, it had made her forget, for the most part. With every pair of eyes on her, that veil had lifted as if they saw right through her. They knew what she had gone through, and they molded her into an outcast at that very moment. It made her feel too uncomfortable, too small, too weak. She was helpless in their gaze, and she couldn't breathe. She felt as if she couldn't do anything but fade away from reality to protect herself.

A hand gently landed on her shoulder and snapped her back into reality. "Breathe, Verona." Mariam's voice echoed through her mind, slowly calming her down.

"There's so many people staring. Why are they staring so much?" Verona whispered. She clenched her fists as her nerves frayed, her skin felt too tight, her fingernails dug into her palms, her breath came too quick.

"They don't know how to act. We have never experienced such a traumatic event before." Mariam's hand moved to wrap around her shoulder, pulling her in close. "We're almost to the tavern, I'll make sure we have a private seat. I know Aunt Regina would do that for us. "

Verona nodded, still lost in thought, still feeling shame and embarrassment from their stares. She couldn't live here if that's all it was. It was suffocating already as she remembered every moment of what she had gone through, but feeling those stares of everyone around her left an entirely different impression. It bore into her skin painfully like the fires had only weeks ago. As soon as she shook her head, escaping from her thoughts, she looked up to see the door of The Wilted Rose right in front of them.

With a shaky breath, Verona pushed open the door. It only took a single step for her to regret coming inside. The loud conversations at the crowded tables grew to a hush as everyone turned and stared. The bard's eyes traveled over to her several times, landing solely on the bandages that consumed her arms. Even the tavern maids gave quick and unsure glances over to them. With an arm wrapped around her waist, Mariam used her body to shield Verona from view. She led her towards the furthest table in a darkly lit corner where no one could see them, undoubtedly with the help of her Aunt, who swooped in without a word.

As soon as Verona sat down, she looked right at the table. She didn't want to see their stares; she could already hear the whispers start swirling around her. Her mind felt like it was flipping in circles, controlling the whispers and making them grow louder and louder until they consumed her whole being. She needed to know what they were saying about her. It wasn't until it surrounded her table until the sense of reality crashed down on the tavern. Her mind writhed against her, twisting and spinning lies to her. They whispered calling her an orphan, saying that she had started it, that she had to have started it because she was the only one alive from Felkeirn. They also whispered about something else starting it-- a savage beast, someone had called it. She couldn't focus on anything, she couldn't sit here and listen to their words that lashed out at her. Were they truly saying these gods awful words, or was her mind attacking her, too? Verona's skin felt as if she was burning up, tears welled in her eyes, and her hands shook with anger. She felt her vision fade in and out. With one quick movement, she stood up, knocking over the stool she had been sitting on. Though no one noticed her when, front and center, the town drunk started putting on his show.

Mav had tripped right in front of the stage and spilled ale on the bard's lute, which in turn started a small fight inside of the tavern. The fight erupted into a mass frenzy of flying fists, broken bottles, and shredded barstools. Many had stayed for a good show, though a few, like Verona, snuck out of the tavern. In a haze, she moved to a quiet back alley. Her back hit a slick stone wall, and she slid down it slowly, landing on the cold stone below her. Verona had placed her head between her knees and wrapped her arms around herself. She had to get herself to breathe, had to get out of that place her mind was sending her into. She couldn't do this, it had already been too much. Even stepping out of the house was a struggle, and that thought alone made her feel pathetic.

As Verona sat there, with her eyes closed, she heard soft footsteps come up to her, and a body slid down to sit beside her. Thinking that she knew who it was, she snapped a reply to the person. "I'm fine, Mariam. I just need to breathe for a moment. It was too crowded there."

A masculine chuckle followed her words, along with a lilting seaside accent. "As much as I would love to be a beautiful blonde woman, I, to my dismay, am not."

Her head snapped up at the familiar voice, and her eyes narrowed to slits as she saw who it was that sat next to her. The messy blond-haired man had a split lip and a couple of bruises on his face that were starting to swell. He had looked worse for wear, though it was to be expected for someone who started a fight like that. "Oh, it's just you. That fight wasn't enough for you, so you decided to come over and antagonize me even more?" Her voice dripped with a thick coat of sarcasm.

He rolled his eyes and grumbled. "Shouldn't you be thanking me or something? I only did that for you. I liked that bard too, he's been the only decent one they've hired so far, and there is no way he will be back now."

She wrinkled her nose, and the corner of her lips raised into a lopsided grin. "My savior, how could I ever thank you? My life, and everything with it, belongs to you." The sarcasm had not left her voice yet, though he did humor her, which was a relief to Verona.

"Your taunting apology hurts me so," he said. "although I'm being serious. I know how it is being the one on center stage like that. The one who they all talk about." He paused for a heartbeat before continuing. A thick sheet of somberness blanketed his face. "These people here thrive on that, and I just gave them what they want. They think I jump from bar to bar, spend all my money on drinks, and that I am nothing but a drunk. Though that's what they want to see, so they see it that way. The only time I truly get shitfaced is when the memories become too much. So I know how it is, I truly do." He fully turned to her now, his eyebrows knitted together in sincerity. "I know you may think of me the same way, but I don't want them to devour you the same way they have done to me. You're too good for that. Don't let them get to you. Stand strong and bite back at them."

She mulled over his words as she thought to herself. Would that be how this life would truly become? Nothing but constant pain and fever dreams of her dead family? What would her life truly be if she felt nothing but remorse for not being there in her family's last moments? What would it be if she felt regret for being alive? Verona looked up at him with tear-filled eyes. "Will it ever get better?"

He sighed, giving her a sad smile, his eyes turned down to the cobbled road beneath them, brows knitted, and then he let out a sigh. "The pain will always be there, it's what makes us human. Some days it will get better, you'll be happy, and you won't see that dark cloud for days, months, or, if you are lucky, even years. But you'll have moments where it will hit you in an instant, you'll have days where you won't be able to get out of bed because it will be too much. It'll never go away, we just get better at dealing with it. We need to experience life, witness fear, and know loss for us to be able to fully and truly love a person or to appreciate life. If we couldn't imagine the loss of losing someone, we would never be able to love anyone or live fully ever again."

"Thank you," Verona whispered. She mulled through everything he had said in her mind. It would be the toughest thing she would ever do, coping with the loss of her family. But she knew that they wouldn't want her to live like she had been in such despair and anger. Her mind then wandered to what caused it all. "I just can't comprehend what they were whispering about in there. I thought that it was a natural fire, that something had gone wrong, that an accident might have caused it." Verona took a breath in as her mind flipped in circles, trying to make sense of it all but failing. "Though to think that someone did it intentionally, that they wiped an entire village and maybe even more from our map, is terrifying to think about."

Mav nodded in agreement. "There's something going on here. I will ask around to see if someone else knows anything because if someone or something is doing this, who knows what destruction they plan on bringing us.”

Verona nodded in agreement. She faced back towards the cobbled road, her eyes filming over as she dealt with the horrors in her mind. A few heartbeats later, Verona opened her mouth to speak, to ask him why he was doing this all for her, but before she could, she heard the sound of rushing footsteps coming from the entrance of the alley and whipped her head towards the sound.

There Mariam stood, wide eyes full of panic. “Oh, Verona. I was looking for you. I thought you might have been caught up in that fight, but when it died down and I didn’t see you, I panicked, and I tried looking for you everywhere.” She walked forward but then skittered to a stop as she saw Mav next to her. “Verona, why are you sitting right there? The ground is so dirty, and you’ll ruin your very lovely dress.”

Verona sighed as she shook her head slightly, her brows were furrowed in frustration. “We were just talking, though I think we might be done now. Is it okay if we go home? There’s a lot I need to talk to you about.”

Mariam eyed Mav a bit more before pointing her eyes towards Verona. "Yes, but let's save any type of conversation for home."

Mav let out a huge groan before pushing himself up from the wall. "Of course, let's not talk about this in front of the town fool. I'll go back to my barstool then." He looked down at Verona. "I'll see if I can find out more about what we discussed. You know where to find me." Mav then walked away and out of the alley, leaving the two women alone.

Verona pushed herself up from the cold stone floor and looped arms with Mariam, who still looked at her as if she had grown another head. "We have much to talk about, Ver."

The two women walked through the dank and gloomy alleyways of the Lower Ash District, tension ran through them as they saw the colors start to paint the horizon. This was an area that they did not want to get caught in when the stars graced the sky. The shady district was known for its shopkeeps, bars, and inns during the day; though as soon as the sun set, it was known for a much darker kind of business. The alleyways they were in would fill with traders throughout the Kingdom of Lo'kil, dressed in hooded capes to protect their identity.

Their stalls did not sell bread or handmade weapons. What was on their tables were drugs that could transport you to another world, ale, and mead from faraway lands that were so strong a sip would be the same as ten ales from these taverns, stolen goods, outlawed magic in glass jars, and pelts from unknown beasts. It would not be an area safe for them when the horizon fully engulfed the sun.

They walked towards the farther side of town where Mariam's house sat upon the grassy knoll. Silence plagued the space between them as the tension rose, knowing what was to come. As soon as the door was shut, Mariam turned towards her.

"Now that we are home, can you tell me what that was all about?" Mariam's voice was tinged with bitterness, and hurt dripped off of it in waves as she stared at Verona with knitted brows and weary eyes.

Verona walked over to the table in the middle of the room, pulled a chair out, and sat down. She patted the chair next to her, wordlessly telling Mariam to come and sit down. With hesitant steps and eyes still full of weariness, she slowly moved over to Verona. "Like I said, it's not what it looked like. Well, it kind of was. I guess he saw me panicking in the Wilted Rose from all the attention, and when my seat fell out under me, he knew he had to do something. So he put all the attention on himself, letting me get out of there." Verona paused as her eyes wandered down to her hands and thought of what she had to say next. A few heartbeats passed before her eyes met Mariam's once more and continued. "We talked for a little bit about little things. Most importantly, about what they were whispering in there. I don't know if you heard them, but people there were saying it wasn't an accident."

Mariam nodded, placing her head in her hands. "I tried to ignore them, but yes, I did hear that. But there's nothing we can do about that. Even if it wasn't an accident, I am sure that our kings and queen will put a stop to it as soon as possible. There's no way that the leaders of this land will let their people come to any more harm than they already have." She sighed after she was done speaking, obviously frustrated with the situation at hand.

Verona's mouth twisted into a grimace as she tossed her friend's words around in her mind. There was always something they could do, always a way to solve any problem. She couldn't believe any of the words Mariam spoke to her. Frustration boiled deep in her bones, and with a swift and sudden movement upwards, she stood up. "What do you mean there's nothing we can do? There's everything that we can do about this. There are people out there dying, Mariam.

More will die if no one does a thing about it. We need to find out who it is and stop them! My family needs this. I need this. They were murdered, and there will be more families like mine that will die, too."

Mariam sighed, crossing her arms in her chair. "How do you suppose we would do this? Or is there more I do not know that Mav and you have schemed up in your time together?"

She plopped herself back in the chair with an exaggerated huff. "I know you hate him and all, but he may prove himself useful. I don't have a plan yet, but I believe it is important that we make one. Will you help me, Mariam?"

Mariam stood up and paced the room for what seemed like an eternity. She sat there and watched the emotions flood her friend's face. Seeing them shift to something new every second, Verona watched her with hopeful eyes. She wanted her to say yes and wanted her friend to be with her every step of this journey. Verona knew if she had to, she would do this alone. But she would feel lost without Mariam. She stopped her pacing and turned to look at Verona.

"I will help you, only because you are family to me. I do not like that Mav is involved in this one bit, but if you think he can help, then I trust you." Mariam sighed, with worry still clouding her features.

Verona reached out, grabbing her hand. "Deal. I'd miss your stupid gossip anyway if you did not want to be a part of it all. Though before we do anything, there is something I must do first."

As the world before Verona began to move into motion once more, her heart, which felt broken into a million little shards, pieced itself together again for a moment, and she felt hope for the first time in a very long while.

Chapter Five

Verona kneeled down near the blackened rubble, her head bent low. With one hand on the ground before her and the other on her heart, she chanted the final words to honor those who were being buried. She pounded the heel of her hand hard into the ground as she began. "Oh, mighty ancestors, accept these souls of our own. With a heavy heart, I give them to you. Lead them into the land of the Gods and heal them. So they will serve their favored God in eternal peace." With the last of the chant, their souls were finally free from the world before them. She looked up towards the sky, seeing the sun and the world of the Gods rotating above them. She knew their souls would float up to that very land of paradise instead of going down to Azarath. She shivered at the thought of them being in such a dangerous afterlife. Full of darkness, cold, and unimaginable creatures of the underworld. No one made it out of there once their souls intertwined with its realm.

Verona stood up, shaking the thoughts out of her mind. As she was turning around to leave, something in the rubble caught her eye. Walking into it, she kicked a few burnt ashes away before finding a necklace that survived the fire before her. The necklace was a simple silver chain that held a familiar blue-green stone. She pulled the one out of her pocket and saw that it was the same. It was her mother's necklace, the one that always seemed special to her. She picked it out of the rubble, wiping the black soot from it. The tears welled in her eyes as Verona unclasped the necklace and placed it around her neck to stay there forever.

Just as she turned to walk back to her new home, an odd sight caught her eye. A bright white feather sat in the midst of the rubble. While it was tucked into the soot and charred wood, the feather itself was untouched and just as white as the clouds above her. Something, or someone, was here visiting this gravesite before her. Verona wondered if this made the rumors true, if some vile person could have started the fire. With a grimace, she plucked the feather out of the rubble and walked back, knowing where she needed to go first.

⁂

It didn't take long for Verona to get back to Ashfall. As she walked through the familiar entryway, she knew it was time to go meet Mav. It had been days since they first spoke, and she was brimming with anticipation to know what he found out. The feather she tucked into her pocket felt like a pack of stones with how heavy it weighed on her mind. While it would have looked like an average bird feather to any other person, Verona knew it was no normal feather due to her spending every waking moment outside. The shaft was way too large for even the biggest bird Verona had seen. The barbs of the feather were too rough and strong for a bird to fly. Even the color was pure white and did not fit any birds of the flatlands. This feather did not belong to a bird but something else. Something far more dangerous and unknown to her. The sight of it plagued her mind with worry, and she needed answers as soon as possible.

Her mind was elsewhere as her body, on its own accord, led her where she needed to go. She opened the doors to The Wilted Rose. Ignoring the stares and whispers, she made a beeline straight towards Mav as her mind snapped back to reality.

There he was, slumped into a barstool with a drinking horn full of ale in front of him. His messy blonde hair had fallen in front of his eyes, blocking them from her view. She studied Mav, taking account of every inch of him and his demeanor. He looked better than the last time she had seen him. He seemed more in the moment as he smiled at the man next to him, rather than being overly intoxicated. His clothes were clean of spills or stains and free of any tears or wrinkles. They looked as if he had bought them only days ago. The bruises and swelling that covered his face from the bar fight were now slowly disappearing.

Verona walked over towards him, the corner of her mouth raised up, and she nodded in greeting as his eyes met hers. As soon as he recognized who was next to him, a wicked smile lit his face up in delight. He swung his body to face hers on the stool, legs splayed wide, and rested his elbow on the table as he leaned against it. Verona rolled her eyes at his overconfidence.

Of course, he would act this way only after the heartbeats of her arriving next to him. While her cheeks began to heat at Mav's brazenness, she shook her head to clear her thoughts and trudged ahead.

"Hello, Mav. I hope you have some news for me." Verona climbed onto the stool next to him.

"Well, hello to you too." He wrinkled his nose and rolled his eyes at her. "Thank you for telling me that I look nice. Yes, I did clean up for you. I just knew how you'd love for me to get prettied up for you."

Verona stared back at Mav as he mockingly twisted his hair with a lone finger. Her face was void of any emotion as she slowly closed her eyes, shook her head, and sighed, "Yes, Mav, you're a pretty little princess. Now, let's get to the real problem at hand."

Mav side-eyed her for a few heartbeats, sarcasm thick in his features, before the playfulness dripped off of his face. He eyed the tavern before he moved in close to her, seriousness now gripping his voice tightly. "There has been gossip going around, more on the fact that someone did start the fire. Though no one can agree on who. There's so many names being thrown around that I don't know what could be right or wrong."

"What if it's something else, something more than human?" Verona had a hand in her pocket, feeling the edge of the feather.

Mav looked at her wearily, his eyebrows knit together. His facial expression told her he thought she was saying something insane without him even having to voice it. "What do you mean more than human?"

Verona took a deep breath in before she pulled out the feather and gently placed it on the table before them. Mav picked it up and studied it for a few heartbeats, twirling it around his fingers. His eyes slowly moved over to Verona, confusion set deep into his features.

"You think a bird started these fires?" he asked incredulously.

Verona sighed as she waved a hand toward him, dismissing his disbelief altogether. "Must have been something else then." She plucked the feather from his fingers and pocketed it. "So, if it is true then about someone starting the fires, then what's the plan?"

Mav faced back to his drink, his face void of any emotion as he stared down at the horn before him. It was moments before he spoke again. "I'm sure your lovely friend would like to be a part of this discussion as well. Come back tomorrow with her so she doesn't decapitate me once she finds out you came here alone to talk to me, and we shall discuss what the plan is."

Verona looked at him dubiously. Fury furrowed her brows as her jaw hung loose. "I don't get it. We were supposed to talk about it now, not later. Now. I thought you'd have more answers than confirming what I already know. I figured you'd rather not have her here anyway."

His nose wrinkled, though his features were void of any humor as he looked at her out of the corner of his eyes. "If you'd like to talk about it now, then my best answer is that we go and talk to the lord of this town. If I were honest with you, Verona, I wouldn't have found anything else besides what we had suspicions about. So if you want to know so bad, that is what I think we should do. Felkeirn would land in Ashfall's ruling territory, so if anyone would know something, it is the Lord of Ashfall."

Verona stared at her hands, taking in everything he had said. If it were that easy, then why couldn't they go now? Her answers were so close that her fingertips were brushing against them. Hope and despair danced a fateful ballad in her mind as she was torn between the two feelings. She also felt weary because Mav had acted so cagey towards her. There seemed more than what he wasn't telling her, more that he was trying to hold her back from. Even though these thoughts ran through her mind, she knew she needed to trust him. Besides Mariam, she had no other help, no one else to trust, no one else who would help her in the way that he offered. Though her desperation overruled it all, it was the winning force in a tangled mess of fractured thoughts that knew nothing besides deep and ugly feelings.

With a sigh, Verona stood up and gave him a long look that he refused to meet. "I will be here at dawn tomorrow with Mariam. If you would still like to help me, then I'll be here. If I don't see you, I will take it as a sign. Thank you for helping me this far, Mav. This world should see you as the man you truly are and not the one they think you are." She didn't wait for his reply as she quietly walked out of the tavern and into the cold night air.

The rest of the night was a blur to Verona as all she could do was think of the next morning. She had talked to Mariam at dinner about the plan she and Mav had made. As she had imagined, Mariam was apprehensive, but she agreed to help. Sleep had been fitful for her; she tossed and turned, her dreams full of nightmares that woke her throughout the night.

When dawn finally came, Verona was dressed and waiting for Mariam by the front door. She stared at her bandaged hands that were twisted together while her mind roared in anticipation and a small part of her was nervous about what could happen today. They would talk to the Lord of Ashfall, and she would get the answers she had been looking for all this time. Weeks of devastation led to this morning, and soon, she would be cutting that long, hard string of grief, releasing it from her mind.

The clicking of heels drew Verona from her thoughts as she looked up and saw Mariam drift closer to her in a flowing pink chiffon dress. Her face was etched with concern for what was yet to come.

Arms crossed nervously, Mariam sighed as she stopped right in front of her friend. Her eyes traveled from Verona's face down to the heels, which she felt immensely uncomfortable in. Verona had chosen a forest green silk dress that hugged her body, making that feeling of uncomfortableness grow tenfold. Though she knew that if they were to see the lord today, the two of them would need to look like ladies worth meeting. While her nerves were running rampant, she was pleased that Mariam agreed to join them after all. With a silent nod, Verona followed Mariam out of the house and down the streets to where she hoped Mav was waiting for them at the Wilted Rose.

Eyes were on them as they walked through the doors of the tavern and whispers rose throughout the room as they sat at the same table Mav was occupying. Verona felt elated as she saw him there. She felt hopeful that he would be there this morning, and there he was, sitting in front of them and looking as miserable as a Rilasi's arse. Though as Verona took in the sight before her, she could feel her lips part in shock. There he was sitting, not in his usual outfit of a ragged tunic and baggy pants. He had dressed up in a white tunic embroidered with gilded threads underneath a golden doublet with gleaming filigree designs gracing the edges of the seams. His white linen trousers were tucked into brown boots with golden etching along the cuff. His hair was slicked back, and he was clean cut, though he still had short blonde stubble dusting his face. A decorative golden-hilted sword was buckled to his belt. He looked... Well, Verona couldn't get her mind to process how he looked. If this had been another life, if they both had gone down different paths, this would be the kind of man she would have fawned over on the town streets, hoping he would someday notice a girl like her. She shook her head, trying to clear her mind. These were not good thoughts to have about Mav. Not right now, not ever.

He turned around and looked at them as they approached. "It's only dawn, I forbid you both from making me get up this early ever again. You have to let me sleep in till mid-morning at the very minimum," Mav grumbled in his seat.

Mariam crossed her arms and stared down at him with daggers in her eyes. Her lips were set tightly as she spoke. "I don't know why Verona trusts you at all. If it were my way, you wouldn't be involved. Though since you're here, tell me what you know and how we get to see the Lord of Ashfall."

Mav slowly looked from Verona over to Mariam with an eyebrow cocked. His lips were slightly parted in surprise, though the feeling was quickly replaced with apprehension as he leaned back in his seat. His seaside accent became thicker as tension rose in his voice. "Well, aren't you a pocketful of sunshine? If you had kindly asked why I was so tired, I would have told you that I spent the night talking to everyone who owed me favors and even pulled a few strings to be able to see the Lord of Ashfall right away this morning. Though instead, you decided to be a God's damned arse."

Mariam's piercing gaze did not waiver for a second as he finished talking, her arms still crossed in defiance. Verona found herself giving a tiny smirk at the scene before her, though she knew time was ticking and they had to get the ball rolling for today.

"Calm down, both of you," Verona rolled her eyes, "Thank you, Mav, for getting that meeting with the Lord." She paused for a second as she felt her cheeks warm up a touch. "You do look nice today." A small smile graced her lips as she continued, "Is there anything we need to know before going in?"

Mav continued to eye Mariam for a few heartbeats before his eyes drifted towards Verona's. A small smile appeared on his lips at her compliment, and his eyes turned devilish for a heartbeat before he settled back into his nonchalant position in the chair. He shrugged at her question. "There is not much you need to know. The lord is a busy man, and he will probably rush the meeting, though he is a kind and fair man. Tell him the basics of what you want to know or ask, and he will listen to your concerns."

Verona nodded as she took in every word he said. Nervousness bounced around the walls of her mind as she chewed on her lower lip. She couldn't shake the feeling that something would not work out for her today, though she blamed it on her nerves. When the time came, they stood up and walked out of the tavern. The only sound they heard was the clicking of their heels as they traveled through the empty alleys of Ashfall. Mav followed close behind them, though he did not say a word as he, too, looked mysteriously distracted. As they retreated from the eastern district and towards the southern part of the town, the homes turned from ramshackle houses to massive and luxurious estates, similar to the one owned by Mariam's family. After a handful of minutes, they crested a large hill, inside the valley below was Erebus manor.

Magnificent wooden pillars framed the three-story stone manor. Large windows scattered the face of the house, topped by small and delicately arched decorative window panes. The roof of the house had several angled peaks that were accompanied by multiple large chimneys. Climbing green ivy slithered its way up to the roof in several corners of the stone. An expansive stone path led to the entryway of the manor from the street, framed by neatly trimmed bushes and countless trees.

This was a house Verona's family would have dreamed of having, one that would've been impossible to achieve in their stature, though it was a dream worth having. The thought alone made Verona's stomach sour; she wished they were still here for her to tell them about this. For them to know the adventure she's had these last few days alone. But they weren't here. And if they had been, she wouldn't have stepped foot towards the Lord's manor. Her family was gone, Murdered. And because of that, she pushed forward and walked towards the welcoming door of Erebus Manor.

Verona was the first to be greeted, followed by an impatient Mariam and a nervous Mav. The guards that stood out front nodded at Mav and then stood aside to let them pass. Once they were inside, a small, petite woman with dark skin and night black hair smiled at them.

"Hello, welcome to Erebus Manor. Are you Mav? The one who asked to see the Lord this morning?" she chirped at them with her soft-spoken voice. Her doe eyes were inquisitive as she waited for an answer.

Mav cleared his throat as he made his way to the front. "Yes, I am Mav. We're here to see the Lord of Ashfall for some important matters."

The woman nodded and ushered them through the halls into a set of large double doors. With a curt knock, she opened the doors to a large, expansive room where the Lord of Ashfall sat on a small wooden throne. As their group was led further into the room, Verona studied the man who may soon answer all of her questions. The Lord was a heavier-set man with graying hair and a long, bushy beard. Wrinkles littered his skin and told his age from even this distance. He had a crooked nose, thin lips that were pursed in a tight line, and dark brown eyes that were still waking up from sleep. As they stepped up to him, he took a deep breath in and gave them a slight smile.

"Hello, my name is Oswin, Lord of Ashfall and owner of the Erebus Manor. I believe you must be Mav, the one who asked for this meeting, though I do not know the names of your guests. May I know your names and why you requested this meeting with me today?" the man said, his deep voice carrying through the chambers of the room.

Verona looked nervously at Mav before stepping forward. "My name is Verona, and my friend's name is Mariam. Mav graciously set up the meeting for me. My family was killed in the fires that destroyed Felkeirn and many of the small farming towns surrounding it. I graciously thank you for your kind act of taking in me and all the other refugees, I do not know where I would have gone otherwise. Although whispers have been spreading amongst the town of Ashfall, saying that someone started those fires. I would like to request any information you know about these fires and what is to be done about them." Verona's back was ramrod straight from the nerves that tingled in every limb of her body. Black spots swam in her vision as she held her breath in anticipation of his response.

The man stared down at her for a few heartbeats, his eyes intently watching her, silently judging. He weighed her words, her body language, and the desperation flooding her voice. He sighed and shifted slightly in his seat before breaking eye contact. "I have heard these rumors, but that is all they are at this moment: rumors. Although, many moons ago, a wise man once told me that rumors stem from some half-truths. But I, myself, have been too busy to explore them and see if they are true. I have been doing my best to keep peace amongst my people and also keep the refugees comfortable. My steward was sent to the king a few days ago to raise the problem to him. So, if you truly need answers, he will provide them. Though it may be months before I hear anything back because the king likes to take his time answering me."

Verona felt her whole world shake and then crumble right before her eyes. All she wanted to do was fall to her knees and scream at the man before her. She wanted to reprimand him for being such a coward. He shucked it off to someone higher up than him, someone who would probably get the job done. But that someone was out of Verona's reach. Of course, it would be just her own God's damned luck that this would happen. In her mind, she figured that the Gods deemed her unworthy of having anything even close to a happy life. It was turning out that way far too soon for her liking. With a solemn and grief-stricken expression, she thanked the lord of Ashfall and walked out of Erebus manor. She heard shouting from Mariam and Mav behind her, though her mind roared from anger, disbelief, and every emotion in between. It wasn't until Mav laid a hand on her shoulder that she finally turned and acknowledged her group, far from the shadow of the manor.

Mav sighed, his eyes pinched shut and face twisted with frustration. "You need to listen to me for a minute, Verona."

His words drew out the boiling anger that was simmering beneath her skin. His command was grating against her barely-there control of her emotions. Him telling her to just listen? Oh, he would regret telling her what to do. She promised that. "No, you listen, Mav. You assured me that this would answer all my questions, that the lord would know everything, but that did not sound like everything to me. That sounded like someone who didn't want to even mess with villages being burned and people being slaughtered."

He shook his head before his eyes trailed out to the far distance as if he was trying to control his own patience with her uncontrolled madness. "You're right. It did not sound like he wanted to deal with it at all, though our best bet is to go to the Kingdom of Lo'kil and talk to the king. He may or may not have answers for you there."

She threw up her hands as she paced in front of him. The tears were threatening to escape her eyes now as her anger finally boiled over. "Then what? Get my heart broken over again? End up back at the start of it all? For what cause, Mav? When will it all finally be solved?"

He stepped towards her and gently placed a hand on her cheek, wiping away the lone tear that streaked down her face. "That is the madness of it all, little flame. We try over and over again, hoping for a new result each time. Sometimes, we lose ourselves in it, and sometimes, we slowly piece ourselves back together with the answers we find. Though in the end, it is the trying and fighting for those answers that prove who we really are right here." He placed a finger right on her heart. "Though I have never met them, I know your parents would be proud of who you are proving yourself to be."

Verona smiled at Mav through the tears and then relayed that smile towards Mariam who grabbed her hand, doing her best to comfort her friend. She took a deep breath in and used her free hand to wipe away the tears. In a single heartbeat, she took a deep breath in and steeled her nerves. She knew what she needed to do.

Chapter Six

After the fateful day had come to an end, the three of them had decided to meet up at the tavern to plan their next step. Through the night, sleep had eluded Verona once more as she struggled with nightmares filled with flame. Her tiredness was the reason why she had been running late that morning, as she had slept in and was late to their meeting. There, the two of them were waiting for her to arrive at The Wilted Rose. As she walked in, she saw Mariam and Mav sitting at a table discussing something. There was a map on the table before them; Mav was pointing at key markers on the paper. His face was painted with a stern expression, back bowed as he stared straight towards Mariam. She, on the other hand, was leaning back into her chair, arms crossed and mouth twisted in disgust, with a single eyebrow raised in complete and utter doubt. Verona wanted to laugh at the scene that was laid out before her. She didn't know how long they had been talking, but she knew it was long enough for Mariam to be done with whatever was coming out of his mouth. Verona walked over, knowing it was time to try and ease the tension that was undoubtedly happening before her.

"I see we're all having an amazing time over here, aren't we?" Verona said with a wide smile. She pulled up a chair and joined the pair before her.

Mariam faced her with the same annoyed expression still plastered on her face. "Oh, such a grand time. I would love to spend every waking second talking to this man in front of me."

Mav threw his hands in the air, leaning back into his chair. He let out an exasperated sigh. "She won't listen to anything I say. She says everything that comes out of my mouth is complete arse."

"What is coming out of Mav's mouth?" Verona asked with a wicked smile.

"There is one thing he is *finally* right about, it is complete arse," Mariam rolled her eyes, uncrossing her arms, "He says we should just waltz right into the castle of Lo'kil and talk to the king."

Verona was confused, given the little knowledge she had of the world. She knew a lot about farming, but everything else she had learned only came from Mariam in the few moments they both had the time. So she decided to ask, not knowing why they couldn't do just that. "Why can't we just walk in?"

Mariam sighed, pulling out a piece of paper. "I tried to see if we could do that. I used my father's falcon. He flew hard through the night to get a response back to us by this morning. The court of Lo'kil responded back saying that we need a reservation to talk to the king and that the waitlist is now a year long."

Verona was confused for a second before it dawned on her that Mariam was being serious. "The king of Lo'kil has a year-long waitlist to talk to him? Are you kidding me?"

Mav shrugged. "We could find out who's on the list, pretend to be one of them, and hope that they don't show up."

Mariam gave him a glare, so menacing it even made Verona backup a little. "And what do you think will happen when those people show up, Mav? The king will kick us out or worse! He's killed people for lesser deeds before."

He nodded. "I know he has. I've seen it happen a time or two." Mav looked towards the map quietly examining for a few heartbeats before leaning in. "Okay, so this is how we will do it..."

Everyone leaned in close as Mav went step by step in their delicate plan. The two women listened intently as they learned their parts and what they were tasked to do. After the first time going through it, they went over the plan again and again until there were no flaws and no room for errors. After the sun had set and the tavern started to slowly fill up for the night, they decided to head back home.

<hr>

The world was starting to come alive with life as Verona walked outside. With a steaming beverage in her hands, she sat down on the porch of Mariam's house, watching the sunrise. The scene before her made her fall in love with the world. The sky was shifting from a dark blue to hues of red and pink. The white, puffy clouds that littered the sky were slowly moving above her. She could tell that today would be a clear day with the view before her. She smiled to herself, knowing her mother loved days like this; she always sat outside early and watched the sunrise. When Verona was younger, she had thought her mother was a touch crazy for waking up that early. Though as she was sitting there, she knew her mother had felt serenity and peace during those mornings; Verona herself now. It was life that the Mother of the Wild Nature laid out before her in a beautiful scene: the sounds of the world waking up before her, bird songs growing to life, and the smell of a morning rain show that was yet to come. Verona closed her eyes and took a drink of the cup in her hands. With every sip, she woke up a little more.

Verona heard the door creak open behind her, a yawn soon followed as Mariam joined her, sitting next to her on the steps. "Good morning. You're up early."

She nodded and looked over to Mariam, offering her cup to her. "I know I am. I just wanted to have one more peaceful morning before the chaos starts, and we leave this village for the kingdom of Lo'kil."

Mariam grabbed the cup taking a sip. "I understand. I can't believe that we actually agreed to do this. We really are going to the kingdom. No one in this village has stepped inside there. Well, I don't know about Mav, but who really knows about him anyway."

Verona chuckled a little in agreement. "This is the last day we will be us." Her tone slowed and quieted down to a whisper. She bowed her head, looking towards her hands. "It's terrifying to think that we won't know what will happen out there. We could see chaos, we could walk into a kingdom that's already burnt to the ground, we could get told that we were making it all up in our minds. It could be a disaster. We're just following the words of a rumor, which terrifies me the most. A rumor that is driving me to the brink of disaster."

Mariam handed the drink back to Verona after taking a sip and wrapped her arm around her. "There has to be a leap. There will always be that unyielding, unnatural pit of darkness that makes us not want to take that jump. It's there to truly scare us, it's there to separate the weak from the strong."

"What if I'm too afraid to take that leap?" Verona replied.

Mariam gave a warm smile. "We're all afraid of that leap, it's what makes us human. It's the unknown that scares us the most. Though I know how strong you are. You may not see it, but I do. I see every ounce of strength in your body. You could accomplish anything you can put your mind to. You could move mountains if you wanted to."

"I'd think I would have to be a fifty-foot gigantic human to be able to move mountains." Verona snorted, scrunching up her nose.

Mariam rolled her eyes at her comment. Before she could reply, Mav walked up to them looking as if he had not gotten a wink of sleep. He grumbled a quick good morning to them before walking into Mariam's house. Mariam rolled her eyes even harder at the man who walked right past them before standing up and following him inside. Verona sat there by herself for a few heartbeats, taking in the scene where the beautiful sunrise had been painted before her. With a smile, and a quick thought sent up to her mother, she stood up and walked in after them.

They decided to leave right away, trying not to cause too much suspicion. They seemed to be the only ones in the town up and moving so far, and they wanted to keep it that way. It would be better for no one to see them leave this morning so more rumors wouldn't break out and follow them out of this town. Mav already had a packed bag slung over his shoulder, so it was up to the two women to pack what they needed. Verona walked into Mariam's room; she had a few sets of clothing that were her size for those few times she had to stay the night at her friend's house. She gathered up a few outfits, knowing she would likely have to buy more on the way. Besides clothes, they packed a week's worth of food, money, a couple of tents with furs to lay on, a few water sacks, items to start a fire, and other miscellaneous things they thought they would need along the way and had been slowly buying over the last few days. Verona snuck a pack of playing cards that was sitting on a bookshelf nearby into her bag. The two women discarded their dresses for trousers and long, colored tunics with belts that cinched their waists. After they had packed everything they needed, Mariam locked her house up, and together, the three of them quietly walked through the streets of the village. Mav and Mariam kept an eye out for anyone who would be walking about their day in the town while Verona, who was up in front of them, led them towards the town's arched entryway. They had found their first success as they walked through the exit unnoticed, except for the few guards that were standing watch nearby. Verona breathed a sigh of relief as she took her first step on this next adventure.

Together, the three of them walked through the openness of their world. Spring was just starting before them; the cold, dew-filled morning would soon warm up as they continued on their journey. Besides the sound of their footsteps that moved the loose rocks beneath them, the sound of birdsong and the rustling wind were the only noises they heard. They had been silent for hours on their trip, being too afraid of being spotted by someone from their village. They were on high alert and watched the horizon in front of them. It didn't take long for them to arrive at the first crossroads. The left and right roads led to other small towns, so they continued on straight, heading towards the kingdom of Lo'kil. Verona kept thinking about how far from home they were; besides Ashfall, she never traveled anywhere else. Everything around her was new and exciting, even though she was a little scared of the unknown. Taking in the sights around her, she felt happy, and weirdly to her, she had felt more comfortable in her environment than anywhere else. Smiling to herself, she took in a deep breath, closed her eyes, and relaxed.

"I think we're pretty far away from town, so we can let our guard down a little bit," Verona said once she caught up with the two.

Mariam sighed. "I know, I just want to be careful. You never know who will be out, even this far. Spring has started, and people are celebrating the beginning of new life. You never know how far someone will travel to do just that. Especially with a festival just around the corner."

Verona huffed out a sigh. "I know, I know. It's just too exciting to be quiet out here. There's just so much to see and do. We're true adventurers now, traveling the vast wastelands of our world to vanish the evil among us."

Mav looked at her with an eyebrow cocked upward and a worried expression on his face. "Woah, slow down there, knight in shining armor. We haven't found our damsel in distress quite yet."

Verona rolled her eyes, making sure Mav could see it quite clearly. She stuck her tongue out at him. "Go kiss a rilasi's ass, Mav."

She giggled and ran towards Mariam when Mav pretended to try and tackle her, with his hands raised, snapping his jaws, and snarling something fierce. Her friend rolled her eyes at the two of them as they acted like children for several minutes.

Before Verona saw it, she saw Mariam's face fall, her jaw slacked with horror. She saw Mav shake his head and turn away as his face sobered. She saw the hand Mariam raised, pointing at it. She saw Mariam and Mav try to block her view, but she turned so quickly. She had been curious about what made them look that way. Then she saw it. She felt the punch in her gut that almost made her drop to her knees. Over to the east, the sky was black, not from night, but from smoke as another village burned. Every feeling of that day when it had been her in that moment came flooding back. The tears ran down her cheek, and she didn't know what to do or say. She sat there with Mariam at her side, staring at the destruction before them.

"We have to do something. We have to help them," Verona whispered, her voice cracked in desperation.

Mariam shook her head. "We can't, Verona. It's all gone."

Verona grew angry. She couldn't comprehend why they couldn't. Her mind had brought her back to the day out by her house and all she wanted to do was save her family. She saw the house before her and heard her mother call out for help. As the anger boiled over inside of her; the last thing she wanted was to feel helpless. With a growl of frustration, Verona leaped forward and broke into a sprint. It didn't take long for a pair of strong arms to wrap around her, halting her in a split second. She hated Mav for stopping her. She wanted to be free. She wanted to save them. The tears flowed down her face quickly. With teeth bared, she started to scratch at his arms to try and free herself. Her ears rang with the scream that had spilled from her lips. He had to let her go, she had to go. She had to save them.

"Let me go, Mav. Let me go. I have to save them, my family. I hear her screaming. I need to save her. Let me go!" she cried out.

With his arms still around her, he slowly brought them down to the ground. He placed his head onto her shoulder and took deep breaths hoping to calm her down. She stopped fighting as she gradually woke out of the living nightmare. Her arms dropped but the tears still flowed, even faster now, sobs, wracking her body. She whispered an apology to him as she saw the marks she had left. She couldn't believe how a sight before her would bring her to a point like that.

"Is there anything we can do for those people there?" she whispered to Mav.

She felt him shake his head behind her. "It's too late to get them out of there. All we can hope for is for survivors. Though how we can truly help them is to find out who is doing this and try to stop them."

Verona nodded, she didn't want to agree. She didn't want to stand to the side and watch the flames burn higher. She didn't want to think about all the children in the village, all the families looking for loved ones. Those who were screaming names hoping they weren't trapped or under rubble. Hoping that they were still alive. She wished she could do something, but she couldn't from this far. With a sigh, she turned around to face away from the burning village before her. As she did, a rustle caught her eyes among the tall grass near the village. Several figures moved through the grass, disrupting the meadow. Verona's head whipped back, looking towards the movement, though when she looked back, she saw nothing. She felt as if she could have made it up, or maybe it was other people escaping. They had to be people running from the fire, there was no other option. She sent a quick prayer to the skies above for their safe travels.

Days had passed uneventfully for them, they had seen no other fires or no other refugees. The scenery around them slowly changed between the passing days. The flatlands of the prairies and farming fields merged into the rolling foothills of the south that swarmed with large, shadowing trees. Even though the dense covering of the tree canopy erased most of the sun from view and the landscape wasn't close to the wide open expanse Verona knew and loved, she still found awe in the nature around her. The sound of birdsong floated around in the trees with a continuous melody between them. The smell of freshly opened blossoms wafted through the air, creating an intoxicating scent of spring. Little green buds littered the bare branches of the tree limbs around them, waiting for the right moment to unfurl to big, beautiful leaves. The feeling of being in new places like this was just as exciting to Verona. She thrived on the feelings this newfound adventure had given her so far. She hated the circumstance of what led to it but relished in the thought of being able to do what she loved. The group was following the winding stone path through the trees. Mav and Mariam were in a deep conversation that Verona had moved away from, as she enjoyed the sights around her. It had been like that for a while, until Verona heard an interesting turn in the conversation.

Her head whipped towards the two of them, an eyebrow already raised with an incredulous smile on her lips. "You did what?" she questioned, not believing what was just said in the conversation.

The person in question was Mav, who, to her surprise, was blushing a bright red. "I may have taken a set of underwear from the queen."

Mariam's face had quickly matched Verona's in a split second. "How scandalous Mav. Was it right in front of her? Did she even know? Or did you swoon it off of her with your street charm you so often use at the bars?"

Verona giggled as she watched his face go even brighter. "Oh, don't be quiet now. You never stop talking, and you've already started, so why not keep sharing those wondrous details?"

He blanched in slight horror at the situation he had placed himself in. "I honestly did not know it was hers. I was in the kingdom of M'Ralz at the time, there was a festival going on so I was inside the castle. I had a sort of fling with a local maid, and she was carrying a basket of underwear to a washroom. Thinking it was hers, I was trying to embarrass her by taking a pair. I was going to return it the next time I saw her. She didn't have the heart to tell me who it was until a month after I still had it. Apparently, the queen was livid her favorite set had gone missing. She learned someone had stolen it and had a manhunt going on. Though I was long gone and back to where I was staying in a nearby village. I still have it to this day," a wicked smile lit his face, "it's my lucky charm."

Mariam rolled her eyes. "It doesn't surprise me, it fits your flirtatious ways to steal a woman's underwear from her without asking." She turned to Verona with a wild expression. "Better hide your knickers, Verona. They're not safe around this beast of a man. You might find a pair up and missing one night."

Verona laughed so hard she snorted. "You best watch yours too, Mariam. No one's knickers are safe these days."

Mariam's smile turned wicked. "That would be if I even had any knickers to steal."

Verona had turned a shade of red, equal to what Mav was just a few moments ago. Mav mirrored Mariam's smile, but she rolled her eyes at him and gave him a very special finger in reply, warding him off from trying anything.

The three of them walked more into the forest, taking in the sights around them as the sun slowly shifted down into the horizon. When it came time, they quickly found a suitable clearing to set up camp. Before the sunlight had fully vanished, all the tents had been erected for the night, furs rolled out, and a small fire roared in front of them to cook up a quick meal. While Verona opted to watch the campsite, Mariam left to scavenge for any edible berries, and Mav went to hunt a few small mammals out in the woods. After grabbing her deck of cards, she sat down on a fallen tree and started to shuffle. She wanted to distract herself the best she could since she didn't like being alone in the woods like this. It was getting dark, and the only thing she could see was the fire that was mocking her with its diabolical dance. She tried to keep her eyes away, but it didn't take long for her to get lost in the copper-colored flames before her.

Spacing off, she started to rub the still-healing burns on her body. She could still feel the bite of the hot flames where they had touched her skin, cringing from the way it had felt like her very being was melting off her bones. The fire seemed to whisper to her, to beckon her to come in, to join its dance. Verona went to take a step towards it when a snap of a tree branch brought her quickly back to reality. She shook her head and rubbed her temple. She didn't know what was wrong with her; she had been more than willing to sit in the flames. With worry and shame flooding her emotions, she walked as far away from the fire as she could. Another snap of a branch echoed through the quiet forest. Verona snapped her head up, looking around. It was so dark she couldn't see around the ring of trees the fire had illuminated. A third snap echoed, and Verona's hairs stood on edge. The feelings of worry and shame morphed abruptly into fear. A fourth snap sounded. Verona grabbed anything she could as she reached down for a large tree branch. Rustling sounded amongst the ground foliage; there was something big coming for her. She could tell it was way too big for her to fight. A fifth snap sounded, and the brush by the circle of trees exploded open. Verona covered her face with her arms on instinct. When she didn't feel any attack coming, she placed her hands down to take a peak. There was no man-eating beast in front of her, only Mav, who looked at her like she was the stupidest person living right now.

He placed his hands up with that foolish smile of his, plastered to his lips. "You can put the stick down, I won't harm a lady as sweet as you."

Verona rolled her eyes. "You could have sounded less like a hungry beast, you stumbling twit."

He shrugged, walking towards the fire. "I thought if I made a lot of noise, you'd know it was me."

Verona shook her head in annoyance. Before she could retort anything back, Mariam joined their campsite with a basket of berries. Mav started to cook the six small animals he had managed to catch on the fire, slowly roasting them to perfection. Verona and Mariam got the rest of dinner together. They had a few slices of the bread they brought, the berries, and the meat. It hadn't been anything too exciting for Verona, but she was glad to have something in her stomach. After they ate, they played around with Verona's deck of cards until everyone was tired. It wasn't long until they crawled into their tents with a yawned-out 'good night' and drifted into sleep.

The next morning, Verona woke up to Mariam and Mav talking outside. She stretched her arms and groaned before throwing on her clothes. As she rubbed the sleep from her eyes, she walked out of her tent and over to her other companions. They smiled, handing her the bowl of berries from last night. She ate a few as she looked down at the map they had opened in front of them.

"How many more days do we have left to get to the kingdom of Lo'Kil?" Verona asked.

Mav looked up at her. "We will arrive by mid-day. Then we will need to start our plan as soon as we can."

Verona nodded. She had been a little surprised that they were already this close to the castle, she figured she had lost count of the days they spent walking. Her surprise slowly morphed into nervousness and fear as she thought about the plan that was yet to unfold. She pondered about the part she was about to play and if she could even manage it. It wasn't anything like what she was used to. This really wasn't something she ever thought she would do. With shaky hands, she slowly took down her tent while her mind wandered off to impossible circumstances. It didn't take them long to eradicate their temporary campsite, and soon after, they were back on the road as the sun started to rise.

As they walked through the dense wooded path, Verona saw more of the new world before her. Small animals darted in front of their path, scurrying away in fear. Colorful flowers that radiated vibrant hues littered the mossy forest floor around her. Insects created a chorus in the air joined by the birds that were scattered amongst the branches of the trees. Everything around them was new, and she took in the sights before her. Soon the trees started to become sparse as the path before them grew more open and unfurled into a large expanse of grassland. There was a massive hill in front of them that Verona instantly dreaded as she took in its massive glory. With a groan from Verona in protest, the three of them slowly made the trek up to the peak. As soon as they reached the top, a gasp escaped her lips. There, below them, was a cliff that led down to a large open valley. The grass-filled plains were endless in the scenery before them; the tufts of grass rippled amongst the breeze, creating a whisper in the wind. They would have to cross an endless sea of golden-tan-colored waves to reach their destination. In the middle of it all sat a large, expansive kingdom. Massive stone walls surrounded the main interior of the kingdom, which held the castle, nobleman houses, valuable shops, and other smaller buildings. On the outside of the first wall held nondescript businesses, taverns, and commoner's houses. Around it all was another stone wall that was bigger than the first ring, protecting everything inside the kingdom. Each ring of the stone walls held one gate each, making getting in and out a challenge to those trying to sneak in like them. This kingdom was bigger than anything Verona had seen before, it would have enveloped Mariam's little village tenfold with its size. The stone kingdom radiated power with every inch of its being.

With wide eyes and a slackened jaw, Verona looked over to Mariam and Mav with worry painted all over her face. Before Verona could even mutter a word, Mav gave her a wicked smile.

"Welcome to the kingdom of Lo'Kil. The plan begins now."

Chapter Seven

Hours had passed since Verona and Mariam entered the abandoned carriage that had been left at the base of the valley. They were close to the kingdom, but not enough for any of the soldiers to see them sneak into it. The covered wagon had a broken wheel, several pieces of wood missing, and vines covering it from years of sitting in place. Mav had smuggled them in as soon as they had walked right towards it. His first step of the plan was to grant them entrance through the gates. The kingdom had been locked down tight for a couple of years due to a tragic accident that happened when the last festival was hosted in the kingdom of Lo'kil. A lone assassin paid by someone, still unknown to this day, was sent to kill the king; his mission was to end his reign and leave the kingdom with no heir. Though the assassin had failed and lived his last few moments bleeding out on the cold, hard floor of the throne room. His efforts weren't in vain; the king now had a scar that started above his left eyebrow and ran down past his cheekbone. The king kept the dagger in a glass lockbox. It was displayed in the entryway of the throne room as both an effort to thwart any future attempts on the king's life and a reminder of the end any potential assassins would meet. This mission that they were about to try to accomplish was a dangerous task at hand, one that could leave all three of their heads on a pike.

Verona was visibly nervous. She played with her fingers and moved her hands across her arms as anxiety filled her head. She was worried about what was to come, what would happen if they failed, and what would happen if the king found out they were imposters. This plan of theirs seemed impossible to her. It would take a miracle for them to come out of here alive. At that moment, Verona felt like a fool for ever agreeing to this absurd plan.

Mariam saw the nervousness painted on Verona's face, so she turned to her, giving a soft smile to steady her pacing friend. "It will be alright, Verona. I know how you feel. I ran through this plan several times in my head, running through all the possibilities of what we could do right and what could end up wrong. I wouldn't be here if I didn't think we had a chance. You know how I am. We just have to play it by the books and not let our emotions get to us."

She nodded, exhaling out a long breath filled with all her worries, and trying to make her body relax. "I'm just scared about all the what-ifs that could happen in there, Mariam. There's so much that could go wrong. This king isn't stupid, he will probably find out."

Mariam shrugged. "We just have to give a damn good performance then."

Verona smiled at her words. Before she could say anything else, the canvas fabric of their broken cart was pulled back. The two girls whipped their heads, eyes widened with fear as they looked to see who it was. In the next second, two elegant dresses fit for noble ladies burst into their wagon. Mav followed after them with a smile. With a raised eyebrow, Verona inspected the dresses before her. One was a light blue; the bodice looked tight, with lace fabric lining the edge and small delicate strings crossing around it. The skirt was long and full of layers, pushing it out farther than one's own hips. The other one was a pale pink, the bodice still tight. It was made from chiffon fabric that flowed down in elegant layers. It did not have the large skirt like the other one but a soft waterfall of fabric that hung off the body. Verona knew she would feel more comfortable in the pink one and that it would also look more natural on her. With a nod, Mav slipped away from the wagon to watch for anyone coming and to give the girls more privacy as they dressed. Mariam slipped the blue dress on easily, with the occasional help from Verona to tie the utterly ridiculous amount of laces on the back and front of the dress. With a final cinch and pull of the corset lace, Mariam had her dress on. Verona stepped back and admired her friend; she looked as if she was born to be a lady. Her soft blonde curls bounced off her bare shoulders and flowed towards the edge of the corset. She gave Verona a mock curtsy that was flawless in nature.

Verona smiled at her. "It fits you well, Mariam. You look stunning."

Mariam gave her a wide smile back. "Why thank you. Now it's your turn."

It took a little more effort to get the dress on Verona. When she first looked at it, the fit looked perfect for her; though now, with the corset squeezing every ounce of her body, it felt way too tight. Her breasts looked like they would be spilling out of the top any moment now, even though Mariam was endlessly reassuring her that it was okay and was a normal look for corsets. The blush pink corset was decorated with gilded filigree and golden laces in the front. There were sheer chiffon sleeves that hung off her shoulders and brushed the outside of her arms. The blush pink skirt had multiple layers but still seemed so see-through. Everything about this dress made Verona feel vulnerable and naked. She didn't like the feeling of bare shoulders and barely there dresses. She wanted her tunics and long-sleeved dresses back. She wanted to feel comfortable, and right now, she was far from it. She wiggled around and pulled at the dress, trying to adjust it in any way she could, though Mariam gently slapped her hand for that.

"Don't fidget around, they will notice that. Ladies need to seem comfortable; stand straight and act like you own the court." Mariam lectured her.

Verona sighed, lowering her hands to her side. "I knew this was a bad idea for me. I don't know how to act like any of this. I don't even know how you know or can do it."

Mariam shrugged nonchalantly. "I had practice, and I learned. I wanted to be a lady when I was a child, to have a court life, to try and make princes swoon. It didn't work out for me, as my parents moved from a kingdom to Ashfall when I was just a wee lass. Though I still kept the knowledge with me. You will do fine. Now, let's get out of here. I'm sure Mav is waiting on us."

The two ladies slipped on their heels before stepping out of the wagon. There, standing before them, was a guard in full uniform. Mariam and Verona gasped out loud, moving their hands towards their face before recognizing the man with the messy blonde hair before them. They both sighed in relief and in return, Mav laughed so hard he folded over.

"Guess I scared you both there." He bellowed as laughter still echoed in his voice.

Mariam rolled her eyes in annoyance, breaking the tension between them. "So, are you going to tell us how you got these clothes, or are we just going to be left in the dark?"

Mav gave her a half-smirk, stepping back from Verona. "I know a thing or two about getting some things. It's a good thing I still have access to the kingdom. If I hadn't, the process would have been a lot harder."

Mariam rolled her eyes and looked over to Verona. "In short, he stole them. I bet he stole their knickers, too, in the process. These poor ladies with their missing dresses and knickers."

He threw his hands up in protest, and the two women laughed at his reddened cheeks. "Let's just get on with the plan. You are two very noble ladies visiting Lo'kil from the kingdom of Fel, and I am your escort into the castle. Your ruse for the meeting is that you are asking permission to stay here for the summer with your long-lost cousins. Got it?"

Both women nodded in agreement before starting their walk to the castle door. The women lifted their dresses through the grassy plains to protect them from ripping or getting the hem muddied. As Verona saw they were getting closer to the gate, she breathed in, calming her nerves and placing her mind and body into the role she was about to play. Her spine was set straight, her shoulders placed back; her walk became more precise and ladylike. She combed quickly through her wild hair before folding her hands together near the edge of her corset. She plastered on a large smile as they walked up towards the guards. Mav stood at attention before turning to the guards as they looked towards them in annoyance. There, guarding the gate, were two men in full armor, minus the helms that were laid on the ground next to them. On their hips hung large, sheathed swords, both men keeping their hands on the stone-colored hilt. They were acting as if the day was already painfully long for them as they leaned against the wall and seemed as if they wanted to be anywhere but there.

"State your reasoning for entering the castle," the bored, monotone voice of a guard echoed towards them.

Mav looked towards the guard who talked to them. "I am a hired guard escorting these ladies from the kingdom of Fel to visit family here in Lo'kil." He pulled out a handful of papers from a pouch at his hip. "Here are papers stating my escort, paid services, and letters from family stating their arrival into the kingdom."

The guard reached over, grabbing the papers, he grumbled a bit before he started to read. The tension among the three of them rose with each passing second; their nerves ran hot and fear echoed through all of them. Though their faces remained the cool, unnerved expressions of their roles throughout it. The guard handed back the papers and nodded. As Mav tucked them back into his pouch, a signal was shown to the other guards above them, and the gate began to open. Together, the three of them walked into the first division of the kingdom. It was a shock to Verona, seeing how different it was from the villages and towns she had already seen. While in the other settlements, she saw many of the townsfolk prosper by selling goods and making money. Though in the outer ring of the kingdom, many were lying amongst the stone alleyways; starving and dying with nothing to call their own. They begged those who passed by for money and food to feed themselves, but many who did walk by only looked forward in ignorance. Plenty of the houses Verona saw looked on the verge of collapsing with rotting roofs and missing stones within the walls. She felt sorrow for those around her, for those who had to live in such conditions. She knew her family hadn't been rich by any means, but they still had enough wealth to keep their house in a well enough condition that was far from these.

They walked through streets that had the usual armory, weaponry, tavern, and other establishments that Verona was used to. The people who walked beside them looked towards them with fear and astonishment that ladies like them would even be walking next to them. The eyes of the people and the states of the places around Verona unnerved her to the utmost degree. As they walked the main path, they soon found the second gate into the inner circle. With a quick pace, they walked over to the guards. Mav had flashed his papers to them before they could say any words to them. The guard grabbed the stack and, a second later, gave the papers back, opening the gate. He waved them forward, and with no hesitation, they walked right in. Verona finally exhaled with relief.

She turned to her companions with wide eyes filled with tears that were threatening to escape. "How could a kingdom be like that? Aren't the kings and queen supposed to help their people? There's people starving and dying out there." Her voice had risen up farther than the whisper she intended to. She felt angry about the things she saw in just the entryway to the kingdom.

Mariam hushed her as Mav took the lead, taking them through the main streets. "We ladies do not care about what happens outside of our gate. I do agree with you; it is a tragedy to see a kingdom that should be our savior treat its own people this way. It is sad how the world works in such a cruel manner. If we did not have such limited time, I would try and do anything I could, but we cannot ruin the reputation we have right now."

Verona was trapped in her mind the entire walk; she didn't notice when they came upon a gray house with a stone door. Looking around, confused, she noticed all of the homes surrounding them looked bleak and unnoticeable, like the one before her. The whole kingdom was made from the same dark gray stone and gray-stained wood throughout. Verona did not know if it was a symbol of unity or a sign of reality that told them of their unimportance. Mav knocked on the door in an intricate pattern. After a few heartbeats, the door opened a crack, and a sliver of a face peaked through, staring at them.

"Who is it?" an old voice grumbled at them.

"It's me, Mav, you old fool," Mav echoed back.

The man scowled before opening the door all the way. He shook his head and grumbled, letting them all in. He walked towards the parlor and sat them down before he walked away to get them something to drink.

Mariam looked at Mav, a little suspicious. "Where did you bring us to?"

Mav sighed and leaned back into the chair. "An old friend who owes me a favor."

Verona looked up as the man walked back towards them with a tray of tea and what looked like mead. Verona grabbed a cup of tea with Mariam while Mav, on the other hand, grabbed the other option. The old man sat down near them in a separate chair and stared at them for several heartbeats before speaking again.

"It has been many years since I have seen you, Mav. What matters would bring someone like you with these two ladies to my doorstep? I'm too old for these never-ending troubles you've given me before." His voice crackled.

Mav leaned forward towards the man, his face stern and full of intent. "It's nothing like what was before. I want to call on that favor you owe me."

The man interrupted Mav before he could speak anymore. "I know what your favors usually are, and like I said, I am way too old for that. I told you last time you visited that I am retired from the business."

Mav sighed. He cradled his head in his hands for a few heartbeats before running his hand through his hair in frustration. "I know you are, but this is a serious matter. There's someone killing townsfolk and farmers in the Lo'kil lands. Who knows if it's happening in the other kingdoms, but it's happening here at a too-fast rate. If we don't stop this, people will keep dying."

The man grabbed a cup of mead and took a drink. He stood up and walked slowly towards the window, looking out the window. Verona held her breath as she waited for him to say anything. He turned around. "How do you suppose a man like me can stop that?"

Verona stood up, walked towards the window, and stood beside the man. She looked out towards the scenery, the wall, and what lay behind it. "We, as one person, see things that are out of our control. We see misdeeds, people who are treated unjustly, and murders of innocent people, and think we cannot do anything to help them. Though when you gather a cause, you have people behind you; in the end, a mass of people can be unstoppable. My family was killed in one of those fires. People are saying someone is behind it, and this... this is my cause. I need to find out who did this if no one else will. My family deserves this."

The man let out a sigh and turned to look at them all. "I'm afraid I can't do anything as I did in the past, I am way too old for those wicked adventures. Though I can do anything without getting too heavily involved, I will."

Mav nodded, walking over to the man and clapping him on the back. "I just ask for one simple thing. I need you to get us an audience with the king."

The man laughed in shock at the statement. "You do know what you ask for could be nearly impossible for anyone to achieve."

Mav nodded. "I know it is. I just need forged documents for our meeting, and the proceedings letter forged as well, so it seems as if we are truly on the list."

"I will see what I can do, but you all have stayed far too long. You must go before anyone notices." He led them back to the door, and with a curt goodbye, he closed the door behind them.

The sun was slowly setting on the horizon before them while Verona and her companions made their way over to a more reputable tavern to grab a few rooms and spend the night there. After a quick bite to eat, they each bid each other farewell and drifted off slowly to sleep. Verona had tossed and turned throughout the night; the anxiety of what she was going through and the thought of this fragile plan shattering in front of her was eating her alive. Though not even her anxiety could keep her up for long as sleep slowly dragged her down into its domain. While sleep was peaceful, nightmares still roamed within its lands.

⁂

Verona woke up to a knock on her door feeling groggy from the lack of sleep. Rubbing her eyes, she groaned loudly as the knocking continued.

"I'm coming, just give me a gods damned second," she mumbled.

With barely any grace or balance, she tripped around the room, trying to shove herself into the pink dress once more. Once she was ready, she opened the door to see Mav standing there with that stupid smirk of his as he stared down at her.

"It's great to see you this early in the morning, Mav." She closed the door to her temporary room behind her.

"You look beautiful as always this morning." His smirk plastered there as he led her down the stairs and to the tavern below.

Verona looked away, trying to stop the blush from rising to her cheeks, and spotted Mariam at a table waiting for them. She smiled as she saw Verona, scooting her bowl of berries over for Verona to eat. Verona thanked her and grabbed a few to nibble on while waiting for more food.

"What's the plan for today? Are we able to see him, or are we stuck in this wretched place for another day?" Mariam asked with a sigh.

Mav tried to grab a few berries of his own, but Verona pulled away quickly, sticking out her tongue. He gave her a quick glare before looking towards Mariam. "I met up with him last night and got our papers." He pulled them out and placed them on the table. "We will meet with him a little after midday.

There, we will be able to ask for temporary citizenship inside of the kingdom's walls to continue entering the kingdom to keep seeing family here. That's when you will state your case, Verona, about how your family is dead. We need to do this as painlessly as we can. Most importantly, we cannot blow our cover before we get into that room with the king. Do we understand?"

The two women before him nodded. Food arrived quickly, and they ate in silence, tension and nerves running high. Taking a deep breath, Verona prepared for what was to come.

Chapter Eight

There they were, standing at the entrance of the castle. She couldn't tell if her struggle to get air into her lungs was due to the too-tight pink dress she still wore or all the emotions she felt as if it would crawl out of her throat, and she couldn't stop fidgeting her fingers because of it all. She regretted everything she agreed to up to this point as all the thoughts raced through her mind. All the 'what-ifs' she could think of were running rampant in her mind. She went through all of the possibilities, all the ways the king could find out, how their plan could fail, and how they could die today. She looked over to Mariam, who nudged her with a shoulder. Mariam gave her a glare, and Verona could tell exactly what she was trying to convey. With an exhale, Verona closed her eyes and slowed her heartbeat. She straightened her shoulders, popped out her chin, and painted a wide smile on her face before opening her eyes once more. Mariam nodded in approval and turned towards the guards who talked to Mav. They were looking at the papers for far too long. They had to do something about it.

Mariam raised an eyebrow, her mouth twisting in annoyance. She let out a loud, audible sigh as she started to tap her foot. "What is taking so long, guard? We will be way past our time at this point if they don't hurry up. We will never get to see the king."

Verona echoed Mariam's sigh. "We will never be able to see our family again if we don't meet with the king. Then our noble father will be so upset that he will probably cut the heads off these guards, won't he sister?"

Mariam nodded, her foot still tapping, creating an irritating beat against the stone. "Yes, he will. We were supposed to spend all summer here, but now we probably won't be able to."

The guards grew increasingly irritated, as the women before them uttered their grievances louder and louder. He shoved the papers towards Mav and waved them forward, his face red with indignation.

Mariam blew him a mocking kiss as she walked by, and the guard, in turn, looked as if he wanted to knock her to the ground as he snarled back. Verona held her laugh the best she could as she passed the fuming guards. Together, led by one of the castle guards, they walked through the courtyard. The greenery surrounding the front of the castle was untrimmed and turning brown. Grass was growing between the stone walkway and had grown way too long to even look kept up. Ivy had started to crawl along the castle's stone walls, slowly eroding the rock it touched. Verona was shocked at how unkempt this kingdom really was. It was no wonder why barely anyone wanted to come to the lands of Lo'kil, there was simply no urge to see something so run down. She shook her head as she lowered it, trying to mask her disgust the best she could.

The castle guard led them into the main door and through never-ending and barren hallways that seemed to constantly lead them in circles. Verona's worry grew more and more as her mind raced thinking they had uncovered who they truly were. It wasn't until they were finally led into a great hall, that she let out a sigh of relief. There, in the back of the room, on an elevated platform, sat the king on top of his throne. He looked bored as he rested his head against his fist and slumped down in his chair. Another smaller throne beside his lay empty. Below him was a space for those to stand as they stated their case in front of the king; that too lay empty and waiting for them to step forward. Around the outer edges of the great hall held a bustling castle as servants filled the drinks of the courtiers who wandered about listening to the day's proceedings. While Verona didn't know a thing about this life, she knew enough that those courtiers were only here to capture any rise of power that they could from the king just by being in his midst. She felt sickened by the people who walked these halls. On the outside of their seemingly safe bubble, people worked themselves to death for little pay while these privileged peoples' only worry was to not stain their dresses and nice clothing they had paid a fortune for.

The castle guard that led them here broke off from their group and moved towards the king. He let out an audible sigh before waving them over to enter the main stage. With nerves running rampant between them, they walked towards the king. Two guards moved from the crowd and stood on both sides of the king with their weapons drawn. As Verona and her friends came close enough, the guards' weapons twitched with anticipation, letting them know it was time to stop. As the king saw them, his attention perked and he moved around, sitting more straight and getting rid of the bored expression.

He gave the two women a soft smile. "How can I help you two beautiful ladies today? Anything you ask for, I will give."

Verona moved her eyes to the side and looked at Mariam, barely moving her head. Her friend knew this game all too well, one of deceit and wearing the mask of a stranger. This very game was being played at the tip of a dagger that would pierce their throats any moment now.

If Verona did not know who Mariam was, she would have thought she belonged on the outskirts of this very room, lived in the houses outside of these walls, and had a family just like the one they were about to conjure from their own imagination. Mariam smiled so sweetly to the king in gratitude for his offering and Verona, looking back towards him, did the same. Mav then stepped forward a few heartbeats later.

"Hello, my liege, I am their hired guard escorting them from their homes. I have been assigned to make sure these women are able to continue to visit their family in this kingdom and be able to live here for the next few months inside the walls of your wonderous home. We hope you can grant this request."

The king inched forward in his chair, studying the two women in front of him with intent. A few heartbeats passed and Verona's breath started to pick up, waiting for him to say something. His eyes squinted for a second before he leaned back in his chair. He motioned the two women to come forward. Together, they moved simultaneously and found their place at the foot of the dais; Mariam and Verona both presented a deep and welcoming curtsy.

"It confuses me, a little. I feel like I know my people and they would come to me for anything. I don't see why your family wouldn't say anything to me before you came so we could skip all of this mess." He studied a piece of paper for a second before looking back at them. "It says your family is the Theanos? It is strange to me that they never said that you two were coming to live with them. Especially since I invited them to dine with me here at this very hall a few nights ago."

Verona's stomach dropped at that very moment; something felt wrong, oh so wrong. Her heartbeat started to thump faster in her ears. Her vision felt so blurry. She could see it all fall apart so fast. That sweet smile filled with so many offerings had turned wickedly venomous too quickly. She saw the mask the king wore, drop to show who he truly was. It took two to play a flawless game, and at this very moment, he had outwitted them all.

The king continued, rising from his chair and walking towards the women. "It is also strange that they left that next day to move to the outskirts of M'Ralz, where they had been planning to move since the start of this year. So, tell me who you scoundrels are before I have you hanged for treasonous matters."

She felt every part of their delicate plan fade away before her eyes. She felt something snap in her. The sadness, anger, the darkness that threatened to consume her all came back up. It filled her vision, it consumed her mind; she felt so controlled by it. Her eyes twitched, and her vision blurred. She felt like she was a hostage in her own body, unable to do anything. Verona stepped forward towards the king, everything swelled even more in her as she saw the venom and disgust dripping from the king's gaze. Then, the last thread in her fractured. Her eyes snapped up to meet his, venom dripping in her stare, too.

"My name is Verona of Felkiern. I am the daughter of a farming family, we are the true foundation of your very kingdom, and we are dying. Something out there is killing your own people. My family was one of them. I watched my mother die in front of me. It will not stop, and many more people will die. Villages and towns will collapse, and soon, your kingdom will, too, if you don't do anything. You must stop whatever is happening to your people out there." Her voice rose to a level so loud that the room around her became too quiet. There were so many wide, blank eyes on her.

The king stared furiously at her before taking the few final steps towards her. He grabbed a fistful of her hair, pulling her towards the floor. She gasped out in pain as she was forcefully doubled over. She could see the terrified looks of Mav and Mariam as they watched closely. They could do nothing at this point, their hands were figuratively tied.

"A commoner wretch like you will not tell me what to do. I am the king of this entire kingdom, and you think you have the right to tell me that I am not doing my job correctly? You are nothing to me, you are nothing to even the poorest person in this kingdom. You are an orphaned rascal who deserves nothing but death for doing what you have done inside these walls. You have given me lies, you have shown deceit, and you accuse me of standing by. I should kill you, but that would be far too easy. So, I will let you live and let you think of what you have already gone through. That will cause more suffering than death." He snarled, teeth bared. Spittle flew towards Verona with the ferocity of his anger.

Verona bared her teeth back towards the king; her scalp felt as if it was on fire. "I have done nothing to you, all I do is for the people who suffer in your lands."

He moved closer towards her. "All you speak about are lies and deceit." The king pulled her away, throwing her down on the floor. With a motion of his hands, three guards swooped in from the shadows, taking each of them. In a matter of moments, they were escorted out of the castle and inner circle. Once again, Verona was thrown to the ground on the streets of the poor. She looked around, seeing the townspeople creeping towards them with wide eyes, trying to get anything they could get their hands on. With a gasp, she picked herself up as quickly as she could and ran to escape the crowd that slowly moved inwards. Verona ran as far as she could, fueled by all the anger, sadness, and regret swirling through her. It only took heartbeats to watch the broken houses pass her, then soon the gate, and not long after, she felt the brush of the long golden grass against her waist.

Verona knew she had left her friends behind in the sea of beggars, but she also knew she needed the air and the space; if she looked at her friends now, she would see the disappointment in their faces and eyes.

She knew she had done everything wrong, and they knew it, too. Verona couldn't stand it; that's why she had run away.

She knew she was getting good at that - being the one everyone thought of as strong and determined, but was really weak enough to keep running away from her own problems. Her thoughts suffocated her, feeling so damning that her legs shook and collapsed right under her. The sobs started to wrack her body as they climbed up her throat. She pushed up, slipped off her heels, and walked up the hill towards the tree line. She ripped her dress to her thighs as her skirts started to get caught on fallen branches. She was sick of wearing something so nice. She felt like an imposter in it.

As she entered the thick of the trees, the light faded. Trees surrounded her in a tight formation to the point that they were all she saw. Though she loved the scenery entering it, this time around, she felt so claustrophobic. It felt like the trees were representing her thoughts of self-sabotage that crowded every inch of her mind. Her knees buckled once again, and all she could do was let out a long, pained scream, hoping it would make everything end.

After a few heartbeats of nothingness that echoed through her, she started to hear voices. Looking around, she saw no one near, though her name echoed again through the woods. She recognized that it was Mav and Mariam who called out to her. They seemed worried and scared as they shouted once more. She opened her mouth to call back when another voice echoed with them, something that hissed as it spoke. Something that sounded so guttural and lethal that it made the hairs on her body stand up. Her heart started to beat faster as her mind told her to run, to move, to get out of there as soon as she could, though the fear that ran through her body froze her in place. That lethal voice echoed her name as it came closer and closer. She looked around to get a glimpse of what or who it could be that spoke with such venom, but all she saw were trees.

"What are you? What do you want with me?" Verona whispered, and the tears that formed in her eyes soon blurred her vision.

The voice hissed out a laugh before moving closer. "You asssk too many questionsss, Verona. You mussst stop before you get yoursssself killed, ssstupid girl." The voice wasn't something she heard before; its accent was thick, and it added a prolonged hiss to anything with the letter 's'.

Verona's head whipped to where it seemed like the owner of the voice was, but there was nothing but trees. Her anger started to claw its way into her mind again as her annoyance grew. "I haven't asked any questions, I have been trying to get answers. If you knew what I was doing, then you'd know that much. You're a coward for not showing who you are."

Hot air brushed the back of Verona's ear as the voice laughed. "You want to sssee who I am? Let me ssshow you who I truly am, foolisssh girl."

Chapter Nine

The first thing Verona felt was the shock of it all; it happened so fast she couldn't truly comprehend it all. All she saw was a streak of brown crossing her abdomen. She felt the breath escape her lungs in a gasp; everything at that moment felt as if she was walking through a thick pit of mud. It was funny to her, she had felt no pain until she looked down. Until she truly saw what had been done to her. Blood was streaming out from several jagged lines on her stomach. That's when her world snapped, and everything started rushing in. The pain flowed through her veins like water from a broken dam. She tried to scream, but nothing came through her open mouth as she fell to her knees. Instinctively, she reached for the wound to hold it closed. The blood still trickled through her open fingers, running down like the tears did on her cheeks. The pain was too much, it was unbearable, and she wanted it all to stop. She wanted this to end. She couldn't take it anymore. Verona curled up on the grass, staining it a bright red around her.

"Mama. I don't want to die," Verona whispered. "I don't want to go away now. There's still so much I have to do for you."

Her vision was fading to dreams. Or she was seeing things. She wasn't sure. But shapes of ghosts moved around her; they taunted her, threatened to take her into the veil of Azarath where her soul would remain to await damnation in the City of Smelt. She was terrified of being there, terrified of what they would say about her very soul. She wanted to live. She wanted to survive this. She had more to do and more to accomplish in her life, and this wasn't something that she needed to do. The shapes that hovered around her looked around as voices echoed in the woods. Darker shapes moved towards her, and then they disappeared as two outlines of people kneeled beside her.

Verona took her hand off her wound, trying to bat them away. These beings wouldn't take her. They had to kill her first, and she wasn't dead just yet. Though the beings before she grabbed her hand, her other hand held her wound tight. Verona gritted her teeth in pain. Her body tightened as she felt it everywhere.

"Don't take me to Azarath, please. I don't want to die," she whispered to the beings before her.

A familiar male voice echoed back. "We're not here to take you, little flame. Just stay with us, please. We can't lose you. I can't lose you. Please, Verona, stay with me. We're going to help you, we're going to save you."

"How are we going to save her? We can't go back in, there's no town in sight. We have to do something." A female voice spoke through wracked sobs.

A sigh came from the male as he looked around. "We will go to the coast then."

"The coast is dangerous for us, that's the domain of Death's skull. They control the coast. We will die if we go there, Mav!"

He shook his head. "It's not if you have me with you."

Verona could tell they were talking more, she thought she heard them, though their voices kept fading in and out. She wanted to tell them she was okay, that she couldn't feel anything anymore. But she couldn't talk anymore. Her jaw felt so heavy. She couldn't move any of her limbs. She felt warm as strong arms wrapped around her and picked her up. Her body was limp in his arms as her vision started to fade in and out. Only a couple of heartbeats later, the darkness swallowed her up. Her mind welcomed it, and she stepped into the world of nothingness.

Chapter Ten

Verona blinked as the world came back to her. She didn't know where she was, but she knew she was not laying beneath the forest trees anymore. The once dark sky filled with leaves was now a bright sky that blinded her vision. She felt her body being constantly shuffled and bumped. Verona was confused until she saw the walls of a wagon that she was lying in. The feeling of the hay scratching at her skin was overwhelming and unbearable. She tried to speak, to say anything to anyone who could hear, but her throat and mouth were so dry that nothing escaped. She looked to her other side and saw a sleeping Mav next to her. He must have escorted them the night prior and was finally getting as much sleep as he could. Verona was confused. Why were they in a wagon? They were just at the castle.

Then it happened in a blink; everything came rushing back. Everything that happened that fateful day. She remembered them getting kicked out, remembered running to the field in a rush of emotion, the echo of a strange voice, and then the feeling of claws against her skin. Looking down, she saw the darkened bandage wrapped around her midsection. The once-white fabric was now stained with her blood. Verona rolled over. The pain ebbed through her body, and she clenched her jaw tight. With a single hand, she gently touched Mav's leg, trying to wake him up as softly as she could. She watched as his eyes fluttered open, landing on hers. It took him a few heartbeats of looking into her eyes before he sleepily moved over to her. With wide eyes, he cupped her cheek. He had a painful smile painting his lips as his eyes watered with relief.

He looked past her towards the front of the wagon. "She's awake, Mariam!" he said, astonishment thick in his voice.

The cart slowed to a halt with a whip of what sounded like leather. It didn't take long for a familiar head of blonde hair to pop up next to her, and Verona smiled widely.

Tears ran heavily down Mariam's cheeks as she sat down beside her prone form. "Oh, Verona, I thought we lost you, but I couldn't give up hope. It's so good to see you awake, you must have broken your fever."

Mav placed his hand on her forehead and frowned slightly. "She did slightly. Though we're not out of the woods yet. You're still way too warm, Verona. I should check your bandages. You could use some clean ones."

She nodded as the two went to work, removing the soiled bandages. She had so many questions on her mind, though the first thing she needed was water to even begin speaking. She tried to reach for the pouch that was tied to Mav's side but was unsuccessful after many tries. With a tap on his shoulder, she got his attention and then motioned for the water strapped to his belt. With swift fingers, he quickly unbelted it and handed the pouch over. She drank for what felt like forever. Once she felt like she had enough, she pulled away and gasped for air.

"How long have I been out?" Verona asked, staring at the sky above her.

Mariam looked towards her with sympathy in her eyes. "It's been a couple of days. We've been traveling non-stop to get you the help you need."

The thought of her being out for a couple of days echoed through her mind. It had only felt like moments ago that she was attacked, only felt like a single blink of her eyelids, and then she was here. Though it was exactly as she feared - it had been longer than just a heartbeat.

She looked over to Mariam before her eyes slowly wandered back to the vast openness of the sky above her. "Where are we going then? I don't see any trees, are we somewhere different?" She tried to jest but the fear in her voice was too strong.

Mav cleared his throat as he, once again, paused his task of removing the bandages. "We are traveling to the white coast of Esnia. I have some friends there that will help us, they were the closest option available."

Mariam's mouth twisted, eyebrows furrowed, and nostrils flared. "Oh, how I wish it wasn't the only option."

Verona looked between them, confused. "What do you mean you wish it wasn't our only one?" She asked hesitantly.

Mav sighed and looked towards her with sadness striking his features. He slowly looked down and started on the bandages again. "She wishes there was another option because the friends of mine are the crew of Death's Skull."

Verona's eyes widened in astonishment. "And how are you friends with them?"

He stopped, looking towards her stomach. He stayed still for a few heartbeats before taking a breath in. "That is a story for another time, little flame, but right now, we need to get you to them. Your wound has become severely irritated, it does not look good at all."

He looked towards Mariam with a worried gaze. She nodded, knowing what to do. The blonde-haired girl jumped towards the front, whipped a set of reins, and soon they were moving again but at a hurried pace.

Verona felt the sweat roll down her forehead and onto the hay below her. She grew a little worried, knowing that she was probably getting worse by the moment. As she looked over to Mav, she saw that his worried stare had not disappeared. He placed a hand upon her forehead once more.

"You're heating up again, Verona." His voice was thick with concern.

She rolled her eyes at him, trying to break the tension between them. "It's not like I'm trying to die here. We're almost there, right?"

He nodded, turning his gaze towards the horizon as he drew his hand back. "I'd say less than a day's ride. We will be there sooner than you know. Get some sleep, I'll wake you when we get there."

She nodded, though before she could close her eyes once more, a thought bounced around her mind. One that she could not let go. "Did you really mean it?" she asked, her voice almost a whisper.

He looked at her with a confused gaze. "Did I mean what?"

She turned her head, looking away from him for a few heartbeats. Trying to gather the courage to let it escape her mouth. She then turned and met his gaze. "Did you mean it when you said you said you couldn't lose me?"

He went to place a hand on her cheek, almost as if he were going to let all of his secrets out, but his whole body froze, as if he had broken out of his trance. With clenched eyes, furrowed eyebrows, and lips pulled tight in frustration, he let out a long and painful sigh. Because of that, she knew she wouldn't be getting an answer any time soon.

With a sigh of her own, she rolled over to face the opposite side of the wagon. It didn't take long for her to close her eyes and drift off to sleep. She felt restless as her dreamless sleep merged into nightmares full of sharp claws and dancing flames. They threatened to take her along with everyone else, charred bodies, and collapsed houses. She spent hours tossing back and forth, muttering to herself, trying to make those nightmares go away, but to no avail as they continued their taunting tricks.

Verona's eyes fluttered open to a bright light that illuminated the sky before her. As she lay there, she soaked up the scene before her. The sunrise saturated the wide open sea, painting it in shades of red, orange, and yellow. The sand beneath them was damp with the morning dew. Only a few clouds scattered the sky before her, making it a beautiful morning to witness. She smiled to herself as she realized they finally made it to the coast of Esnia. Verona turned to her other side, seeing Mav once again sleeping. She tapped his leg and watched him startle awake.

"I thought you were supposed to wake me up when we got to the coast, not the other way around." She teased him with a shy smirk.

He rolled his eyes at her as he couldn't help but smile back. "I thought you would still be sleeping by now. Though I'm glad you're awake, the sunrises here are something you can't miss. When I was out there at sea, I'd make sure I would see them every morning."

Verona looked back towards the rising sun. "I would too, if I had the chance."

As the wagon slowed to a halt, they stayed in place for quite a few moments. Verona didn't mind at all as she watched the sun move above the horizon. The colors of the sunrise soon turned to the light blue of the sky. After the show was done, she looked over at the same time Mariam climbed into the wagon.

Her friend looked over Verona with the same worried gaze. She then turned to Mav, and that worried expression soon turned to annoyance. "Well, we went all this way to the coast. Where are your pirate buddies?"

Mav looked towards the horizon and then looked back at them. "Don't you worry, they already know we're here. This is their territory, and they manage it well. That's why no one dares to step foot on this beach because they'll be dead before they get the chance to walk off of it."

Just then, an arrow whistled through the air and landed inches from the wagon, the tip buried deep into the sand. Verona and Mariam looked around, trying to see where it could have come from, but found no one else on the coast. Mav looked towards the horizon once more and shook his head.

"Don't worry; it's only theatrics. If they didn't want us here, they would have made several perfect shots at all three of us. That was them letting us know they saw us and they would be here shortly, " he said with a slight tone of annoyance.

Mariam and Verona looked at each other with worry. Verona thought that they had placed themselves in the deepest hole they could have gotten in. They should have gone to another town and begged to be let back into the castle with the evidence they held etched in her skin. Though here they were on the most dangerous sands in the whole continent of Esnia. She closed her eyes, sending a prayer to the sky before pulling herself up. Both Mariam and Mav helped her sit since they didn't want her to strain herself and rip open her wound. She looked around, taking in the sight of the landscape around her. The beach was surrounded by a grassy plain that sharply ended in a small crag before the stunningly white sand began. She couldn't see far into the tall grass but she knew it stretched on for miles. The beach was thin where they were and seemed empty besides a few large boulders she could see in the distance. Several colorful stones and shells littered the sand. One of those very stones seemed awfully familiar to her with its blue-green swirling color. The sound of the waves coming in created a woosh sound that made her feel comfortable and put her nerves at ease for the moment. She then saw the rilasi that was pulling their wagon. It was such a beautiful beast; its brown fur glowing gold in the early sunrise. It let out a loud huff as it bounced its head in anticipation, wanting to keep moving. With the setup that it was equipped with, the reins, and the attachments to the wagon, Verona knew exactly what happened to get this rilasi.

She eyed both Mav and Mariam with obvious signs that she was not amused plastered on her face. "You stole this from a farmer, didn't you?" When she didn't get a reply, she knew exactly what the answer was. She sighed and continued. "You at least left a few coins to cover a new one, right?"

Mariam nodded, looking sheepishly. "Well, yes, I threw a few coins as he was yelling at us to come back with his rilasi and wagon. It was dark outside, so I don't think he could catch what we looked like. We were desperate, so we did what we had to do." She shoved Mav on the shoulder. "This one didn't want to pay him at all."

Mav didn't take the bait as he stared intently into the distance, so fixed on what was out there that he didn't hear what they said. He then raised his hand and pointed towards the water. The two women turned and looked to see a large black ship sailing towards them. The wood was cracked and worn in some spots, and a couple of the sails were tattered and worn. Though the mainsail looked well taken care of, Verona could tell why. That very mainsail told everyone who they were, with the black fabric and white jawless skull that was painted on with red, glowing orbs in the eye sockets. It was the very sail that made other lesser pirates and the people of Esnia pray for their lives. Verona felt a shiver run down her spine as she looked at the menacing sight that barreled towards them. The closer they got, the closer she could see the five bodies standing in front, watching them intently.

Mariam looked towards Mav with wide eyes. "This could be your last chance, is this what you truly want to do? Do you really want to bring her into this?"

He looked towards Verona with solemn eyes, she could see the regret behind it. "I wish I didn't have to but they're the best chance she has." She watched as all emotion drained from his face and he looked back at the ship. "This time, I will do the talking. It's the only way for us to get out of this alive."

Soon the menacing boat stopped in its tracks half a mile from the beach, a smaller rowboat was lowered into the water and those same five people were making their way towards them.

Verona looked away from the menacing sight before her and towards Mav, stubbornness written over her features. "Take me out of here. I want to stand when I meet them."

He shook his head. "You're too weak to do that. You need to stay where you are."

Her gaze didn't waver. "I want to stand. I want them to know who I am. I don't want people to see me as weak. Especially vicious people like them. Please, just do this one thing for me."

He sighed, caving to her demands. Mav and Mariam quickly helped her out of the wagon and to her feet just as the crew arrived. The five people stepped out of their small boat, one after the other, and onto the white sands below them. Two males and two females stood behind a slender-build male. His skin was tanned to a golden brown from being on the ship for many years. He stood taller than the rest of his crew with a thinner frame, yet still had toned muscles. One side of his hair was shaved almost to the scalp, while the other side fell to his jawline in black strands. He had a couple of scars littering his face, with one crossing his cheekbone and the other crossing his sky-blue eye and ending above his eyebrow. His entire face was covered by a painted-on skull. His nose was crooked, the bridge slightly bigger from being broken over years of abuse. On his neck hung a necklace decorated with beads and several bones. He wore no shirt yet a pair of trousers hung low on hips, tied by a rope.

The pirate smirked towards the group, then eyed Mav for a few heartbeats before speaking. "You know Mav, with the way it ended between us I thought I'd never see your face again, especially after the warning that I gave you."

The pirate's words caused Mav to strain his jaw. "I need help." He looked towards Verona. "She's hurt badly, and I need all the aid I can get. You were my only option, Malakai."

Malakai chuckled softly. "Oh, you humble me so. Though, humor me, Mav. After everything I did for you, everything I gave you when you were at your lowest, what? I get your cruel act in return; why should I help you? I raised you to be the man you are today, but you made me a fool with what you did."

Mav's gaze held pure fury. "I told you time after time when you picked me up, stranded on this very beach. I told you I didn't want to kill anyone. You made me the man I am today, you made me into that killer that I never wanted to be."

A grin graced the pirate's face. "Oh, Mav, I know you secretly enjoyed it, though. You are and will always be one of us. No matter what you tell yourself, I can see it in your eyes that you want it."

Mav looked away. "I will never be the monster you are. I don't want to do this here. Are you going to help us or not?"

Malakai walked over to Verona with a nonchalant gaze and looked at her up and down, humming to himself. "I see the bandage. How did you get hurt, little bird?"

Verona stayed silent for a few heartbeats before shrugging. "I honestly don't know what attacked me. It was so fast; it knew to move where I couldn't see it, but it was always right behind me, talking to me. It had claws sharp enough to do this to me, that's all I know."

A woman walked towards them, her hips swayed as she studied Verona's wound. The sight of the woman threw Verona for a loop. It wasn't that it was a female pirate, she knew a lot of those existed these days, but more so the appearance of the women that stood before her. If Verona hadn't known she had no more siblings, she would have questioned if the woman before her was one of them. She looked like Verona with her red-orange, untamed, and curly hair. A wild amount of freckles splattered across her face. This woman had blue eyes though, so clear that Verona swore that they matched the color of the waters before them. Her face and structure were thinner and her body was more feminine than Verona's and this woman knew how to play it well. Her bust barely stayed inside the dress she wore, making Verona quite a bit jealous. Her face was also painted with the skull that Malakai had, though hers had what looked like a fracture in her skull, painted all the way down to the bridge of her nose.

Malakai twisted his body towards the woman. "What do you think, Joskaline? There's no creature smart enough to talk and do what it did in Esnia."

Joskaline tilted her head, looking closer at the wound. Then she spoke with a thick lilting accent. "There is not, though we have been hearing rumors, Mal. What if they are true?"

Verona's eyes grew wide. She needed to know what they were talking about. "What rumors? What have you heard?"

Malakai sighed and moved away. "That is a story for another time, little bird. Your time is running out, and we need to get you healed. You won't be well enough to do anything about them if you die in a few days." His eyes wandered from Verona's to Mav's. "We will heal her, Mav. We will talk as soon as we get her settled in."

Mav nodded in agreement. "Anything for her." He softly said in defiance. They gathered what they needed from the wagon. Verona hobbled over to the Rilasi that pulled their wagon. She placed her forehead against its and closed her eyes.

With a soft tone, she began to whisper. "Thank you for the ride, my friend. You rode fast and hard and I am grateful for you saving my life. In thanks, I give you freedom. I hope to see you again, my friend. Ride fast with the wind."

She took the reins off, giving the Rilasi a soft slap on the rear. She watched as it ran, stomping its paws into the dirt, and bobbing its head in a thank you back. It roared a sound of happiness as it disappeared into the tall grass. Verona sent a prayer to the gods hoping they would give the proud beast nothing but a happy life.

Verona collapsed into the sand below her, feeling all her strength ebb from her body. Mav and Mariam rushed over to her side with worry in their eyes. Mariam placed Verona's head on her lap, brushing the auburn strands out of her face. Mav looked at her, his face scrunched up with worry. He then looked over to the crew as they watched intently from where they stood.

"We need to leave now." He demanded.

Malakai had an eyebrow raised in surprise of being demanded something, though he nodded, knowing how serious the situation was. The crew walked back towards the small boat while Mav picked Verona up gently. With a quick pace, Mav walked towards the crew with Mariam hot on his heels. Together, the two crews paddled towards the ominous ship that was soon to be her savior.

Chapter Eleven

Verona was carried onto the ship. The wood below Mav creaked with their combined weight as he walked forward. The crew around them stopped and stared with wild gazes both at the stranger and an old friend boarding the boat together. Some carried heated gazes, some hope, and the other small handful of people didn't care seeing Mav walking amongst them once again. From memory, he carried her to a door on the main level of the ship.

When he opened the door, Verona looked around taking in the sight of the room. Laying center in the middle of the room was an old mahogany wood desk stained in a rich dark red with elegant filigree carved amongst every corner. Scars and knicks covered the top of it from knives being forcibly wedged into it from anger. Scattered on top of the desk in a messy array were maps, read letters, inks, quills, and a couple of nearly burnt-out lanterns. Pushed into the desk was a large wooden chair that matched the style of the wood and filigree and in front of the desk was an identical wooden chair. Underneath them was an ornate rug of dark midnight blue and gold wool threaded into a complex pattern of burning flowers and filigree. Two large windows took up almost an entire wall framed by large billowing gilded curtains. Above the window, a large silver sword with an ornate swirling metal handle was set proudly on the wall. The other two walls held two sets of doorways and a handful of bookshelves that were covered in novels, journals, and trinkets.

With a quick glance around the room, she wondered whose room this could be; though Mav did not stop for her to ask as he walked to the doorway on the left.

As he opened the door, she took in the sight before her. In the middle of the room lay a large red-stained mahogany four-poster bed. The sheer white curtains that were supposed to be tied down around the posters of the bed were billowing in the wind from the open window. White cream sheets were made neatly on top of the large expanse of bed. Twin nightstands stood on each side of the bed, matching the design of the bed frame. Underneath the bed was a twin wool rug to the one that was under the desk. Looking around the room, the walls were decorated with swords, artwork from around the world, maps of far out lands, and other items that Verona could not comprehend what they could be. There were also a couple more bookshelves in the bedroom, though they only held books. Mav gently sat her down on the bed and pulled the blankets over her.

She felt small in such a luxurious room; besides Mariam's house, tents, and the rundown inns and taverns, she had never had a room to herself like this. She wondered if someone would be angry at her for taking their place of refuge. "Whose room is this?" she said softly.

He chuckled lightly. "No one will be at the door with a pitchfork trying to get you out of this room. This was my room, and it hasn't been used much since then, so it's free for you to use."

Verona's cheeks reddened at the thought of sleeping in Mav's room. Though he saw the thoughts racing behind her eyes and, with a wicked laugh, assured her that he would be sleeping in the belly of the ship with the crew or in the study attached to this room. She relaxed deeper into the bed as the tension escaped her body.

He sighed, his expression changing as he looked over her like a worried mother would. "I have to talk to Malakai soon, but I will get a healer in here before then. He will probably want to talk to you after he talks to me. I just want to warn you. He doesn't take generously to helping strangers, so he will want something from this."

She swallowed loudly, looking around nervously before looking back at him. "And what will he want from me?" she asked cautiously.

"He may be a bastard to me, but he won't harm you. He will take your consideration in mind, but he's a man who wants what he wants." He said with a heavy tone.

The two of them talked for a little longer before Mav stepped out and fetched a healer. She took some time to close her eyes for just a few minutes, drifting off into a dreamless nap. Though it didn't take long for a small voice and nimble fingers to wake her up. Verona looked to see a tiny, dark-skinned woman with silky black hair that was braided into many long braids. Those brains were decorated with small golden hoops in several places. Her sea blue eyes, flecked with gray, were focused on quickly undoing her bandages with skilled hands as she sat on a wooden stool. A woven basket sat on the nightstand beside her, filled with fresh bandages, herbs, and anything else she would need to heal the wounded girl before her.

"Oh, I am truly sorry to wake you, miss. I was trying my best not to." She had a thick accent to her voice, one Verona never heard before.

Verona rubbed the sleep from her eyes. "It's fine, I should be up for this anyways. I'm sure it would make it a lot easier for you."

The woman smiled. "That it would, though I've done my fair share of treating battle wounds on unconscious men here on this ship. It wouldn't be as much of a challenge as you'd think."

Verona propped her head up with a hand, looking at the woman with curiosity. "How long have you been on this ship, and how did you end up here?"

The woman chuckled sweetly as she finished unwrapping her wound. "It's quite the story. When I was younger, I lived among one of the lower tribes of Nomad's Lane. One day I was out throwing a net to catch fish for food when I saw a ship on the horizon. Many of my people screamed and hid, others left the island completely; though me being as young as I was didn't know who they were, so I stood and watched.

When they came in and saw only a young girl with a basket of fish, they decided to camp at the island for a few days. Well, my people tried to come back, and when they noticed me among them, they offered me in payment for them to leave. At the time, I was already trained in many things, including healing, so the captain took me in as their new healer, and I've been with them ever since."

Verona raised an eyebrow at the gentle story. She thought it would have been more of a kidnapping, rather than an offer. "Do you ever wish to be back home?"

The woman shrugged as she started to put a salve of some kind on the wound after cleaning it. "When I was younger, I was homesick for many days, though now I can't remember much of home. This ragtag crew of pirates is my family now. I've seen, experienced, and lived so much more than I would have if I lived back with my tribe. I do enjoy it here, they're not as bad as Mav will tell you. He likes to make things more than they truly are."

A small smile lit Verona's face. "I do have to agree with you on that one."

The woman laughed as she coated the rest of the salve on. It was green with flecks of red and Verona thought it could be some blend of herbs to help her heal. Once the healer was done, she quickly wrapped a clean bandage around Verona's midsection and tied it tight. With a smile she stood up and packed her items away with the soiled bandages.

"You should get some rest. I will check to see how your wound is doing tonight. You do have an infection, but it's easily treatable, and I'll get you better here soon." She turned to the door to leave.

"Wait!" Verona vocalized before the healer could step out. "I forgot to ask what your name was."

The woman held that same sweet smile on her face. "My name is Atalia."

Walking out, she softly shut the door. As much as Verona wanted to fall asleep, she could only toss and turn in the foreign bed. She closed her eyes tightly as she thought of falling asleep in hopes that it would work. After several minutes of trying, she huffed out in frustration and stared at the ceiling above her. Once that was boring for her, she looked over to read the spines of the books that sat on the bookshelf near her. Many of the books were stories of history, some were stories of fantastical sea battles, and others were bookkeeping notes. It wasn't until she heard a click of a door and steps in the office, that she turned away from the books. The door to the bedroom was slightly cracked, so she heard two familiar male voices talking.

It was Mav and Malakai. She heard two chairs being pulled across the wood floor and a sigh as they both sat down. The sound of rustling papers took up the silence between them. Verona held her breath as she craned her head towards the room and listened as best as she could. A few heartbeats of deafening silence followed before one of them coughed slightly before speaking.

"What do you want to talk about, Malakai?" Mav asked with irritation tinged his voice.

"Out of every option, why come to me to help her?" The captain asked.

A rustle of clothing against the chair told Verona he shrugged. "Like I said, you were the closest option. Why would I risk her life to avoid you"

The captain sighed. "I told you to never come back in front of the whole crew, you walking on this boat jeopardizes me. They're already talking about it. Who knows, they may try to challenge me as they always do. I know you're smart enough to know I never meant it, you'll always be my brother, and I'll always help you. Though you must have known you would have risked me by coming here, so why did you do it?"

"I know it was a risk to you, but I calculated it, and bringing her here outweighed anything else. In the end, if they try to take over this ship, I will always stand by your side. As we always said, we're brothers until a sword kills us both." Mav chuckled lightly.

The captain laughed. "Ah yes, that stupid saying." Silence followed for a few heartbeats. "What's so special about her, Mav? You've never cared this much about anyone."

Mav sighed, shifting in his chair uncomfortably. "She just reminds me a lot of myself. I'm just trying to help her."

"So you think helping her will help you with the demons of your past? If that's the case, then you should just let the poor girl go."

Mav grumbled. "It's not that, I just can't stand the thought of leaving her. I know I have my demons, but so does she. If I can never heal mine, that would be okay because in the end, I did everything I did to help heal hers, and dammit, I will die on that hill breathing my last breath."

Malakai chuckled loudly before he stood up and clapped Mav on the shoulder. "Oh my boy, I know that feeling all too well. Come with me. I need your help with the usual things around here. Just because you're not my crewmate doesn't mean you get to be a lazy drunkard around here."

Verona heard two sets of footsteps walk out, and the door softly shutting closely after. Verona let out a sigh of relief, knowing they were gone. Her mind raced with everything she heard as she fell back into the bed. His feelings toward her confused her. She heard everything he said, and it was clear as day to her, though he hadn't even uttered a word like that to her yet. Even more confusing was her own feelings. She liked him, he was nice to be around, and she had felt something for him. Though, what did it feel like to truly like someone in that way? Verona didn't know, she never knew the feeling because her only job in life was the farm, and her father didn't want her to be near any boys that could talk to her. She never got that experience and life that Mariam had, so Verona only knew of such things from the words that fell out of her friend's mouth as she blushed about her guy of the week. It drove her crazy, thinking about all of this, and she didn't want to worry about it any longer. She let out a frustrated sigh and closed her eyes, finally feeling a blanket of tiredness drape itself over her body. It only took a few seconds before the door to the bedroom creaked open again. Verona opened one eye to peer at her new visitor, annoyance was painted quite thick on her face.

Mariam looked at her with surprise. "I thought you'd be sleeping, Mav said the healer told him you were. Though I'm glad you're awake. I was just going to sit here and read while I waited for you to wake up, but now I don't have to anymore."

Verona raised an eyebrow, disbelief fell across her features. "You're rambling, Mariam, why are you rambling?"

Mariam sighed as she plopped down on the bed beside Verona. "I am, aren't I? I just feel weird here. I'm so used to my town and my normal mundane life of being at home, walking through the markets and talking to our friends. Though now, I'm pretending I'm a lady, talking to kings, running through woods hiding from creatures, and now on a pirate ship that I thought were just tales to scare children. I just feel so out of place. I don't mind the experience; what I don't like is the men out there calling me a beautiful damsel."

The feeling of annoyance and disbelief disappeared from Verona only to be replaced by humor. A laugh shook her body after Mariam stopped talking. It took a few moments for her to stop as she wiped the tears from her eyes.

"I can't believe they call you that," Verona said, still chuckling.

Mariam rolled her eyes. "Unfortunately, they do, but that is beside the point. I was also told to tell you dinner is almost done, so let's go head there and talk on our way."

Verona's eyes widened. She couldn't believe dinner was almost done, that meant the day was ending, and she didn't know where the time went. It felt like she only just arrived on the ship. Though she shook the worry from her mind only knowing it was something too small to even think about. Slowly, she pushed herself out of the bed and walked towards the door where Mariam was waiting for her. Together the two of them walked out of the office and onto the main deck. Some of the crewmates looked at them with wonder, though most of them were too busy working to pay them any mind. They mopped the deck, pulled rope, glassed the horizon in front of them, and did every task that needed to be done in order to keep this ship running smoothly. Verona looked out onto the horizon as she stepped towards the railing. They had moved far away from Esnia, so far that she could not see the shore anymore. The sun blended in with the horizon as they traveled west. Verona watched the sky give a final slow dance of beautiful colors as the sun sunk deep into the horizon. The sky slowly faded to black as the crewmate that was once mopping the deck was now running around lighting the many lanterns. Verona watched him in confusion as another crewmate walked towards her. The man looked familiar, and it took her a moment to recognize that he was one of them down on the beach. He had a messy mop of short blonde hair that stuck up in every which way looking as if he just rolled out of bed. On the sides of his head, his hair was shaved. He had a boyish look on his face as if he had yet to reach maturity, though something else about him looked familiar. He had a wide set of greenish-brown eyes and a wide set of lips. His nose turned upwards at the tip. He was thin yet muscular like the captain and shared a similar height.

The man looked towards the horizon at the sliver of remaining light. "Once it gets dark out here in the ocean, you can't see an arm's length from your own face. We keep as many lanterns lit on board, though it can only help so much." He turned towards the two women. "I'm afraid I have not introduced myself yet. I am Daelyn, co-captain of Death's Skull and brother to Malakai."

Mariam looked at him with an inquisitive look. "So you're named after our Elden God of storms, weather, and thieves. Seems fitting for a pirate to be named after such a God. I bet you quite live up to the name."

Daelyn looked surprised for a second before smiling at her. "I'm glad someone knows. Though, yes, my mother thought it would be a good idea to name me after the Elden God, Daekelyn, as I was born on this very ship." Daelyn looked towards the crowd that was filing below the ship, then back at the two ladies. "Could I escort you two ladies down to our mess hall? We will be eating shortly."

Verona nodded and so Daelyn led the two women down the stairs that sat by the Captain's quarters. The stairs led down to the belly of the ship, where Verona heard men talking loudly and laughter soon following. The walls were illuminated by the flickering flames inside the lanterns that were scattered amongst the long tables taking up most of the small room. Men and women were seen sitting at many of the chairs that framed the tables as they drank from the curved horns, frothy liquid spilling from the edges. At the very end of the room, on a stage, sat a couple of musicians playing an upbeat melody on several instruments. Verona looked around to try and find a familiar face amongst the crowd, a wave of a hand caught her attention as she saw Atalia smile widely at her. Verona smiled back and started to walk towards her before a large set of hands grabbed her shoulders and stopped her. Verona whipped around and found herself inches from Mav's face. She blushed and stepped back, looking down towards her feet.

"Hello there, " he said softly with a crooked grin. The captain would like us all to join him tonight, so c'mon follow me." With a quick glance between Mariam and her, he led them to a table in the back of the room.

There, by the musicians, was a solo table that sat only a handful of people. Verona saw that at that table those very same five people were already sitting there. She already met Captain Malakai and his wife Joskaline, and she just met Daelyn. There were just two left of this crew that she had yet to meet. Mav pulled out two chairs for Mariam and Verona, once they sat down, he moved to sit at the empty chair between Malakai and Verona. Even though she squirmed a little at the thought of him being so near, she kept herself busy with the conversation around her. The two pirate women who sat next to each other chatted and laughed, Verona leaned in as she was a little curious about the second woman whom she hadn't met yet.

Verona let out a little cough, clearing her throat as she heard a lapse in conversation between the ladies. "Excuse me, but I don't think I've met you yet." Verona brought out her hand in greeting. "My name is Verona. What's yours?"

The woman fully turned to Verona, and she saw how she truly looked. The woman smiled with grace and sat with even more as her posture reminded Verona of the nobles at the kingdom court. The woman had wind-blown wavy hair that was so blonde it could have been white. The top was pulled into a ponytail in the back, and two braids hung in a loose curve on each side behind her ears going towards the back. The rest of her hair hung in loose waves, it ended right between her jawline and shoulders. She had a wide set of golden brown eyes framed by long lashes and perfectly arched eyebrows. Her nose was perked at the end, giving her a childish look. She had sharp cheekbones that led to a full set of lips. Her face was a perfect heart shape, making her utterly beautiful to Verona. This woman also had a white mask painted on her face, though it was just a band across her eyes with small circles around the top and bottom.

The woman brought out her hand, shaking hers. "Hello, Verona." Her voice was thick and soothing to Verona, with a hint of an old accent. "My name is Kalil. How are you adjusting to such a life? I know for me it took a little while."

Verona couldn't help but smile. "It is quite different, but I don't mind the experience; it's something I wouldn't mind if I got trapped here." Verona chuckled. "If you don't mind me asking, how did you find yourself amongst the crew?"

Verona saw Joskaline smirk as she leaned back into her chair, crossing her arms. "This is one of my favorite stories."

Kalil gave her friend a wide smile before looking back at Verona. "I won't go into too much detail, but I was a princess in a faraway land, and Malakai thought it would be funny to kidnap a princess. Though he didn't expect me to want to stay. So, when he tried to drop me back off after my father gave him 50 tons of gold in exchange for my safe return, he couldn't move me an inch off the ship. So we took the gold and ran. Whenever we have to meet with any royals, I'm the one they send since I have the experience, and it helps to have a royal talk to another royal. People have named me the lost princess from my lands."

Verona looked at her with wide eyes. "That's quite the story you have there. I can imagine that had to have been quite the lifestyle change you had to make."

Kalil shrugged. "It was quite easy actually, I didn't like the life I was born into, so I changed it. Even though you may think you are stuck with what you're born in, it's your life; you can do whatever you want with it. Don't let anyone tell you otherwise."

The conversation slowly died out as the cooks started to bring out large plates of roasted meat with vegetables, and other plates of delicious-looking food. Verona's mouth watered at the food, which made her stomach grumble. It had been a while since she had a meal that wasn't small portions of roasted wildlife, berries, and bread. She felt so hungry, so as soon as she got her plate; she focused on her food and ate, savoring each bite she could. Not long after, a woman with a dress and apron came over to her with a horned cup in her hand.

"Some of the crew thought you'd like a cup for yourself," the woman said softly.

Verona looked at her with surprise. Swallowing her food, she quickly wiped her mouth before talking. "Thank you for bringing it to me, though I have to ask, what is it?"

The woman set it down with a smile. "It is a drink from the floating islands down south. It is strong like mead though it's sweet and fruity. If you're like me, you'll love it."

Verona thanked her as she walked away. As she took a sip of the drink, she tasted the hint of sweet, yet tart fruits, and the smallest hint of the mead. She loved the drink more than she thought she would. As Verona laid back in her chair she watched the crowd around her. Some of the crew were still eating while most of them, like her, were done and now started talking amongst themselves once again. As time went on they started to get more rowdy, laughing more, and overall having a great time down in the belly of the ship. The music picked up speed with the tune changing. A man took the hand of the lady beside her and brought her towards the musicians. They started to dance in a way she had never seen before, he was picking her up, swinging her, and tossed her in the air a couple times. It was such a different dance than the ballroom kind she knew the royals and nobles did, though to Verona this seemed like something she would enjoy a lot more. She smiled, watching more couples join them and start to dance the same way. Daelyn walked over to Mariam and asked for her hand, with a nod of her head and a smile they joined the dance floor. Verona laughed to herself as she watched Mariam have the time of her life.

"You know you don't have to just watch. You could join them," Mav said as he was inches behind her.

Verona let out a tiny gasp as she turned towards him, a slight blush crept across her cheeks as she looked at him. She shook her head, clearing her mind then spoke. "Oh really? I don't think anyone would ask me, and even if they did, I wouldn't know how to do that anyway."

Mav walked to the front of her and held out his hand. "I would always ask you in a heartbeat. Let me show you how."

Her blush crept back tenfold as she placed her hand in his. Together, the two of them danced the night away. She laughed as he twirled her, tossed her in the air, and caught her. In that moment she felt carefree, she felt like herself, utterly content. She knew they had so much to do, they had words to discuss with the captain, murderers to find, and there was so much responsibility with this mission they took upon themselves. Though for now, in that moment, she soaked up every second she had before her.

Verona gasped for air as the music slowed to a stop, getting ready to play again. Her stomach cramped, and she winced before straightening herself. The pain that was creeping up was feeling uncomfortable. She opened her mouth to say something, though before she could, she felt Mav place a hand on her cheek, gently brushing her cheekbone with his thumb. She closed her mouth and looked up at him with wide eyes.

"There's something that I've wanted to tell you for a while now, Verona," he said, his voice thick with emotion.

Her blush colored her cheeks as his free hand landed on the small of her back and pulled her close to him. Her eyes widened before she winced again as the pain flared up once more. Gritting her teeth, she kept herself from making any noise. She looked towards Mav. His mouth was moving, but she couldn't understand what he was saying. She squinted her eyes in confusion, trying to focus on understanding his words. Beads of sweat rolled down her temples as she gritted her teeth. She looked towards his lips, and as his eyes closed, he started to move towards her. She was about to say something to him as she felt her world drop, and her body along with it. Darkness consumed her seconds after she understood what had happened.

Chapter Twelve

Verona blinked a few times, clearing her vision, seeing everyone surrounding her with worried looks painted heavily on their faces. She grew annoyed for a quick second before realizing what had happened, she passed out right in front of Mav, right as he was... A voice broke her from her thoughts as she saw a familiar head of black hair rush towards her.

"Get out of my way!" Atalia said as loudly as she could.

To Verona's surprise, everyone listened to the small healer and moved out of the way. Atalia rushed to her side, looking her over quickly before moving to the bandage. Mav knelt beside them, holding her head and slowly brushing strands of hair away from her face. Verona tried to mutter that she was fine, but they didn't budge one bit.

Atalia looked over to Mav with a solemn expression. "It's the wound, let's get her upstairs for some fresh air and then to the cabin to get her bandages changed. You need to take it easier, Verona. Wounds don't heal in moments."

Mav nodded and gently picked her up, cradling her against his chest as he carried her from the belly of the ship up towards the deck. Verona closed her eyes, feeling the cold gusts of wind against her face. As soon as she opened her eyes, she gasped in amazement at what she saw. The ship around them was so dark she could barely see anything besides where the lanterns illuminated several points. Though what really took her breath away was the sky. Streaks of green, red, pink, and purple rippled across the sky in a slow, melodic dance, flowing gracefully in slow patterned waves. She had seen this before, it always happened during the summer though it was so strong here, so vibrant, and beautiful that it took Verona's breath away.

She looked over toward Mav and smiled when she saw he was just as mesmerized. "It's beautiful."

He looked down at her and smiled. "It is most definitely a beautiful sight; this is my favorite time of year, seeing spring turn to summer. Though we can watch it another night, getting you better is more important."

Mav and Atalia walked over to his old room, opening the doors until they got to the bedroom. After she was set on the bed, Atalia got to work removing the bandages, putting more salve on, and placing new bandages back on.

She patted Verona's cheek softly. "I'm going to leave you here, get some rest." She looked at Mav with a pointed look. "You better leave her alone here soon so she can do just that."

He gave her an uneven smirk and nodded. "Yes, ma'am."

Atalia laughed softly, the stress and worry that once held her tight had now slowly ebbed as she knew Verona was a little better. She walked away from the room gently shutting the door behind her. Mav's features softened as he looked at her. He went back to slowly moving his hand through her hair, brushing the strands from her face. Sleep fell heavily upon her as she relaxed and her eyes started to feel heavy. She looked towards Mav, trying to talk to him but he shook his head.

"Go to sleep, Verona, you need it," he whispered.

She nodded, feeling that she needed it after a long day like today. The warm, soft bed helped her drift off to sleep as the darkness finally overtook her. It didn't take long for her dreams of dancing and laughing to turn into nightmares of loss, mocking flames, and tearing flesh. She tossed and turned leading to a restless night's sleep.

⸻ ❧ ⸻

Days had turned to weeks for Verona on that ship. Slowly, her wound started to heal, though it was not all the way healed yet; she was getting better, and with it, her strength returned too. She did enjoy her time on the ship amongst the people she had now called her friends. She watched Mariam spend more time with Daelyn, and knowing her friend was happy made her happy. She was beginning to feel that happiness, too, for the first time in a very long while as she and Mav were drawing close to each other. He doted on her faithfully, though they still danced around the words of actually saying their feelings to each other. Through her time on the ship, she slowly grew comfortable enough to forget everything she was fighting for, everything that she wanted to find out and change. Some days she remembered, some days it drove her into a panic; though on those days she pushed the feeling away. She forced herself to forget. Today was one of those days. As she stood out on the deck watching the sunrise, she thought about her mother, she thought about the towns out there burning, and the people who were losing their lives as she was here having the time of her life. That thought alone felt like a slap to the face for her. She shivered both at what she was feeling and from the cold morning air against her skin. She had brought a blanket with her this morning, and she pulled it tighter against her body. Footsteps sounded behind her, but she still watched the sun in front of her.

"I'd say it's a beautiful sight, but I'm questioning why you're out so early," Mav said behind her, sleep still thick in his voice.

She shrugged before turning towards him. His blonde hair was a mess from sleep, poking every way it could. He rubbed his eyes before giving her a soft smile as he saw her looking at him. Her heart clenched tighter at the sight before her, he had proved himself to be everything to her these last couple of days, from the constant doting and helping her feel better, to the soft touches when she fell asleep. Being on this ship had changed everything for the better; she finally felt happy for once in what felt like a very long while. A part of her wanted to stay here, to explore what that kiss would have been like if she had not fainted, to feel free amongst the people here like Kalil did, and to enjoy a long life here with the people she truly loved. Mav had done so much for her since the moment they met, he had changed his life for the better to help her chaotic one. Everything he had done, sacrificed, and risked was all for her. All for nothing in return. Her mind rolled through her feelings for him before moving on to a thought more daunting, a thought she had been pushing down for days now. A thought of fire, murder, and outrage. Verona had been shoving it down for way too long. She had work to do, though maybe when this was all over, Mav and her could spend the rest of their lives watching the sun rise from this very ship.

Verona sighed, her words were just a rough whisper on the breeze before them. "I guess I couldn't sleep for any longer. I just have a lot going on in my mind."

He walked towards the railing, standing so close to her that she felt the side of his hip brush hers. "About what?" he asked softly.

"I've forgotten everything since we arrived on this ship. I forgot what I was trying to do, what I was trying to find out. The worst part is that I've felt so happy being here, I felt so happy forgetting about it. I feel like I let my family and many more down by doing that. I can't do it any longer. I have to go back to shore." She bowed her head as the tears once more threatened to escape though this time, she could not stop them from spilling over on her cheeks.

He sighed, shaking his head slightly. "What is so terrible about feeling happy for once in a long time? I feel happy being here on this ship with you and everyone else, so why decide to go back to being miserable?"

She sniffled as she looked up at him, trying to compose herself but failing. "You don't get it, Mav. You never will. I lost my family out there, and now I'm sitting here doing nothing. I feel pathetic for doing nothing here."

Anger rolled over his features. Her eyes widened as she watched the carefree Mav change into a stranger right before her eyes. "You don't think I understand, Verona? Oh, I understand it quite well. I watched my parents get cut down right in front of me. I saw the rest of my family murdered. My sister lay in my bed scared, screaming for me as she was pierced with a sword through the heart. I was only a few seconds late and I couldn't save them in time; that haunts me every day. It took me a while to get over it, but I did, and I moved on. I fell in love, and I watched her die in my arms by the very same people. So don't you dare tell me that I don't get it."

She looked at him eyes wide, jaw slack. She didn't know what to say to that, how to even respond. So she said the only thing she knew how. "I'm sorry, Mav. I didn't mean it like that."

He sighed as he bowed his head, eyes closed shut. His knuckles were white from gripping the ship railing too tight. He was silent for a few heartbeats before opening his eyes and looking at the water. "I know you didn't, but I know what it's like. So if it's bothering you, you have to decide what you want to do. Be happy and move on, or figure out what happened and do something about it."

She nodded her head. She knew she only had one choice, and that choice was simple. She couldn't stand by in all this chaos, she couldn't choose to be happy even though she knew that's what her family would want for her. Though that's not what she wanted for herself, maybe in a distant future she would be; though that future was not today.

Her eyes snapped into focus as she shook herself from her thoughts. Eyes meeting him, she saw his demons clouding his own eyes. Without a thought, she wrapped her arms around him, tucking her face into his neck and closing her eyes. Instinctively he wrapped his arms around her, pulling her into him tighter as he buried his face into her hair. "I am sorry for the words I said, I did not truly mean them, I am just upset at myself. I am sorry for what you went through, that must have been so hard to live through. If you ever need to talk to someone about it when the feelings get too much, I am here for you."

He gave her a soft yet sad smile before placing a light kiss on her forehead. "Thank you, little flame. You are too good for this world."

They stayed in that hug for a few more heartbeats before she knew it was time to do what she needed to do. With a smile, she walked away from him and towards the captain's quarter. After a few short knocks, the door opened to Malakai standing there with a smile.

"What can I do for you, Verona?" he asked with a slight tone of surprise.

Determination was painted heavily on her face. "I'm ready to talk now."

He nodded, waving to her to come in. Before he could close the door after her, a hand stopped him, and in walked Mav. She sat down on one of the chairs in front of the desk, and Mav did the same. He gave her a quick, reassuring smile before turning towards Malakai as he spoke.

"It's a surprise to see you here Mav, though I guess I should have expected that." He didn't try to cover the annoyance that dripped from his voice as his eyes darted back and forth between Mav and her, eyebrow cocked

She shrugged in nonchalance. "He's fine here, though I need to talk to you about going back to the coast. I've healed up, thanks to you and your healer, and I can't thank you enough for your generosity. Though I have a mission to complete, I have deaths to uncover."

The captain leaned forward in his seat, resting his chin on his curled fist. "I've been waiting for this conversation. I thought it would never happen as I watched your friends and you become comfortable here. Thought I'd be getting a few new crewmates here." He chuckled. "Though I'm glad it has come time, there are things we must discuss."

Verona nodded. "I know you have a price, so let's talk."

"I do, though I'll start with what I know. I know your family died, and many others are dying by fire as well. I know you talked to the king of Lo'kil, but he doesn't have a clue what is going on. So, to me, it seems like these are clear signs of skilled killers among us if they are working unseen. I have heard word from other pirates on this sea that they have seen unmarked and unknown ships pass in my territory. I have seen them, but there have been too many ships and they are too heavily armed for me to get close. My land is in as much danger as your homeland is, and if Esnia falls, we lose our food, necessities, and so much more. So my price is knowledge. I want to know what you find out, and if this becomes something bigger, I want to help you with that battle."

Verona sat there thinking about the price he had given. She expected something heavier, like a life in return for saving hers, not something as simple as knowledge. It surprised her quite a bit, though. From her short time on the ship, she truly expected this captain to be as fair as he was now. It was a simple price she could pay.

With a reach of her hand, she shook his in agreement. "It is a done deal. How would you like us to send word back to you on the ship?"

He smiled. "It will not be easy, but I will send you with one of mine to be there in person. To not upset your friend too much," His grin grew wider, "I'll send you with my brother. He has done this a time or two, so he will know his role quite well. Once the crew wakes up we will tell them of the plan to head back. We are quite close so it will take only until mid-day to see the very same shore we picked you up from."

With a final thanks, the two of them walked out of the room. Verona walked down to the lower deck and to the rooms where she was moved so she could pack the rest of her items to leave. Mav had followed her down as well, though he had nothing to say to her as worry flooded his face so clearly. He sat down on her bed as she began packing her things. His silence grated at her nerves, so with a sigh, she stopped packing, crossed her arms, and leaned against the dresser.

"If you have something to say, might as well get it out, Mav." The words came out in a sigh, sounding almost defeated.

His eyes danced as he looked at her with concern. "Is this truly what you want, Verona? This may turn to bloodshed, someone may die in this in the end -- we all may die! Whatever this opponent that we are going against tore you open as just a simple warning. There are many more of them out there, and I don't know if four of us will be able to stop them." He looked down at his feet and anxiously chewed on his lip.

"You don't need to be worried for me, Mav. If you don't want to do this, you can stay here. The crew wouldn't mind and you can have your life back now that everything seems back to normal here."

Verona turned around to grab what was left from the dresser when she heard footsteps as he came closer to her. His hands wrapped around her waist, feeling massive against her hips as he twirled her around to face him. In that moment, all she could do was let out a gasp as he drew in closer, backing her against the wall. He leaned in so close she felt his warm breath brush against her cheeks. His arms trapped her in as he placed each hand on either side of her head against the wall. His eyes were clouded with fierce emotion as his eyelids drooped.

"That's where you're wrong, darlin'. I'll always be worried about you." His voice was gruff, filled with a foreign emotion that Verona couldn't figure out what it could be.

He cupped her cheek and pulled her in close as their bodies collided. Verona bit her lip as a small sound escaped her. His other hand cupped the small of her back as his fingers dug in hard. He closed his eyes and leaned in as Verona started to do the same. She was done fighting this feeling for him, done not wanting to experience this. She wanted to open herself to him. To wrap her whole being around him, to lay claim on every inch of his being.

Just as their lips were about to collide, her door slammed open, bouncing against the wall, and made them both jump apart.

A familiar melodic voice filled up the quiet space. "I heard we're docking with Daelyn today...! Oh, did I? Did I interrupt something?" she asked, her eyes wide.

Verona muttered a soft 'no' as her cheeks heated up a bright red. On the other hand, Mav bared his teeth in frustration as he chucked the pillow that was once on the bed, now connected with Mariam's face. Mariam maniacally laughed after the soft hit, and with a wicked grin, she looked between the two of them.

"I'd say carry on, but we should discuss what happens next," Mariam giggled.

Both Mariam and Verona sat on the bed while Mav stood on the other side of the room, leaning against the desk. His arms were crossed, and a dark shadow filled with frustration cast over his features.

Verona looked towards him, trying to see if he would look at her but all he did was stare at the floor. She sighed and then turned towards Mariam.

"Yes, we will be docking with Daelyn. He will serve as the captain's right-hand man in gathering information on what is going on. So, we will be continuing what we have been doing and finding it out. If this turns out to be something more, the captain will be on our side."

Mariam looked at her with concern. "Something... more?" Her voice wavered

Verona nodded, looking to the side of her room. She fell deep into her mind as the worry of what was yet to come surfaced. She thought of her life, what she had done, and what was yet to be accomplished. She thought of Mav and indulged in the life she could have with him if she decided to just be happy. She thought of Mariam and the amazing life she built for herself, the very one Verona took her away from. The doubt of everything she was doing rose with each thought. She felt foolish even trying to accomplish this. She was stuck where she was now, the plan she once had when she entered Lo'Kil was gone now. She didn't know what to tell them both, she couldn't come up with anything, not even a lie to tell them. She thought she could have done this, she thought she could have been this wild adventurer and figured out every trouble there was in this world. Though right now, at this moment, she was nowhere near that. She was no one, and that single thought suffocated her more than anything. She couldn't even sneak into a castle to get help, so how could she defeat this monstrous evil that wreaked havoc on her homelands?

Verona tried to take a breath in as the tears clogged her throat. She couldn't do this anymore. She moved her head, looking down at her lap before a hand waved in front of her face, catching her attention.

"Verona, are you okay?" Mariam whispered with a tone of worry heavy in her voice. "What are we going to do next?"

As soon as she looked up, seeing the worried faces of both Mariam and Mav, the tears finally fell. "I don't know what we're going to do next. I don't know what to do from this point. I've failed everyone before, so how can we keep going if I don't know where to go next?"

Mariam wrapped her friend in a tight hug before pulling away and looking straight through Verona and into her soul. "You have not failed anyone, Verona of Felkeirn. When you think you have failed, you have only failed yourself by giving up. We all fall at our hardest times, but the strongest will pull themselves up again and keep fighting. So let them see you fall, Verona. Let them see you fail over and over again. But do not let them see you quit. You are the strongest person I know, so show yourself that."

Verona wiped her tears before standing up. She would follow those few simple rules, she stashed those words away close to her heart. They could see her fall, but they would not see her quit. She felt a surge of determination flow through her veins as she looked at her desk, seeing all the papers lying there.

She braced her hands against the desk before looking back to her friends sitting on the bed. "We need to figure out what to do next before we get to the shore. I know we can figure out that much between us, so I need your help."

They nodded as they discussed where they could get answers next. Verona looked back at the papers, focusing as hard as she could. She wished she knew someone who would know a lot about the world. Someone who traveled among the lands, and knew it by heart, someone who would also know something about what was going on. Verona sighed, knowing that she knew only the two other people in the room she was in, and they knew as much as she did. She turned around, leaning against the desk, ready to jump into their conversation when she placed her hand in her pocket. Something bumped against her hand, a long-forgotten stone that she had received when her parents were alive. A stone that was given to her by Calder, the adventurer. The very adventurer who traveled the lands was going to M'ralz.

Verona looked at the group as she pulled out the blue-green stone and held it out in front of her. With a wicked smile in answer to the two confused gazes looking at her, she finally spoke.

"We're heading to M'Ralz to chase after a certain adventurer." Laughter echoed thick in her voice as she was ready to see a certain face once more.

Chapter Thirteen

The four of them had docked on the beach midday. The crew waved goodbye when the ship sailed, but not before they were given weeks of food, water, and other items to survive. The captain had also held his brother tightly for a long time. Mav told her afterward that they had not been apart since the death of their parents; that very death created the strong bond they had to this day. As the ship left, the four of them walked into the woods to begin their journey to the kingdom of M'Ralz. With a map, they figured they would travel for a week, stopping once to see the Valley of the Gods. Verona had been excited about that. She remembered when she was a child, her mother would tell her bedtime stories about that certain valley. She thought her mother was making up stories until she talked to Calder. Now, she was even more sure her mother had been there, and she couldn't wait to step in her mother's footsteps. Verona was curious about which god she would align herself under, but that would be a decision for when they got there. What she needed to focus on right now was how to get there.

The forest around them was thicker than anything she had experienced before. The thick canopy blocked out the sun, and it reminded her so much of her last moments in woods like this. She flinched from the memory of that moment before moving closer to Mav, her body shaking slightly from fear. He noticed all too quickly, throwing an arm around her.

He leaned down, his lips brushing her ear slightly as they walked. Then he started to whisper. His breath tickled her cheek, but she shivered from something else entirely. "They cannot hurt you here, Verona. They will have to get to us three first, and I will fight with every ounce of my strength before I let them have you."

With a smile to him and a breath of relief passing through her lips, she felt a little less scared. Though she kept herself pressed close against Mav as they walked deeper into the woods. Feeling a little calmer, she took in her surroundings. The dark trunks of the trees were twisted with climbing vines, ones that she had not seen before. Beautiful flowers were scattered on the grassy floor underneath their feet. The flowers were all different. Masses of little white flowers swallowed most of the space. Scattered amongst them were dark purple bell-shaped flowers that grew in a bush with large green-white leaves. Next to those was a different kind of flower that grew in a column of many little petals right on top of each other. In many places around the forest floor, large groups of these flowery columns grew together. Off the path were large bushes that grew bright red berries, the same ones they had seen in the forest surrounding Lo'Kil. Though here, there were many more than what they had seen before. Mariam kept picking them by the handfuls, sharing them with Daelyn who looked surprised by their sweet taste; that sight had made Verona smile slightly.

A twig snapped, making Verona jump. She and Mav were on edge as they fell to a crouch and watched the trees around them, waiting for something to attack them. Though the only thing that appeared near them, nibbling on the berry branches, was a very common creature among these lands. The creature had four legs ending in cloven hoofs, short brown fur, a short round, snout with four eyes that looked around with square pupils. The beautiful set of curling horns branched off in several places, ending in sharp ends. Its tail flicked in anticipation as its nose flared, sensing everything around it.

Verona's mouth hung wide at the sight of the magnificent creature. She turned to Mav. "It's beautiful."

He nodded, still looking at it. "It's a young male madalak. They are good to eat and would last a while with the meat they have on them. Though we do not need to hunt it."

Verona looked at the full packs that sat on each of their backs and agreed internally. There was no use killing such a beautiful and innocent animal right now when they did not need to. A twig snapped behind them as the other two caught up, the madalak looked up towards the sound before running off into the woods. Verona let out a breath that she didn't know she had been holding. She stood up, looking towards the woods and trying to see if more of them were out there despite the sound of laughter between Mariam and Daelyn scaring off anything within a mile radius of them with how loud they were. Verona looked back at them and then towards Mav with a raised brow. He rolled his eyes in return with a smirk gracing his lips.

The four of them continued their trek through the woods with no problems that first day and set up a campsite for the night. The night air was getting warmer as the days passed so Verona fell asleep on top of the soft furs in her tent since she didn't need the warmth of them anymore.

The days passed on their journey to M'Ralz without a hitch. It had taken a few days to leave the woods and step into endless grasslands. Verona felt better stepping into this side of the land. The horizon was as far as her eyes could see, and nothing could remain hidden. The long golden grass moved like the waves of the sea from the wind blowing around them, the sound of the swooshing grass in the flatlands echoed the waves hitting the boat. Being here made Verona feel a little homesick for that life she could've had out there on the seas. She closed her eyes and took a breath in, though instead of the smell of salt, it smelled of dirt and springtime air. The grass tickled her arms and legs as they walked through. She lifted her hands, coasting her fingertips against the wispy ends as they walked pretending her hands were small little ships upon an eternal sea.

She looked over to see Mav looking at her with his intense gaze. She gave him a soft smile, her eyes closed, head tilted towards the warm sun, as she whispered. "If we don't find what we want in the end, I will still be glad we did this to see sights like this."

"There's so much beauty in this world that I hope to show you more of." He said reverently, his eyes full of so much emotion as he watched her with rapt attention.

She smiled at him, almost drunk with the emotions she was feeling at that moment. "I hope we do just that."

It only took a day for the grasslands to turn into rolling hills and then soon after into a small grouping of mountains on the cusp of the horizon. From what she knew, the Valley of the Gods was nestled right into that grouping of mountains they were just so happening to be walking towards. She felt excited knowing she would finally see a sight she always wanted to see, but a part of her felt oddly nervous at the thought of it. She was worried it wouldn't live up to her mother's wonderful stories. Although, in the end, the determination won as they saw large stone pillars break the horizon in front of them. A line of those pillars bordered a gravel path that led right under a stone archway. On each side, lying next to the base of the arch, were two small pots filled with a never-ending flame. Beside those pots were chests of gold, swords, jewelry, and other trinkets left to the gods as offerings.

Verona watched as Daelyn offered one of the many gold rings that ordained his hand, Mariam tossed a silver necklace, and finally, Mav tossed a dagger into the chest.

Verona felt a wave of panic crawl up her throat as she stared at the chest. She looked up to see Mav staring at her. "I don't think I have anything to offer. I don't have gold, silver, or any weapons."

He gave her a soft smile of reassurance. "Then toss some berries in. They will take that as well."

With a breath of relief, she opened her bag, threw a handful of berries into the chest, and walked through the gateway and into the Valley of the Gods.

Verona gasped in amazement as she looked at the scenery around her. The path they walked on led into the valley that was surrounded by a crescent-shaped mountain range. On each mountain face was a god carved from the stone. Each of them protruded from the rocks in a simple pose of prayer. The carvings were absolutely massive, making Verona feel so small standing in the midst of them. She looked at each one of them, so finely carved. She had never seen a god before, but she could tell the carving held a lot of their likeness.

They had humanistic faces with flattened noses and jutting chins. Their ears were long and ended in a sharp, drooping point, jutting cheekbones framed their faces well. Horns grew from their brows and usually curved around towards their jaw, fracturing off in many places with other points leading to dull tips. Floating between each of their horns was an orb; each one was unique with its own color and fractured differently, showing the years the Gods had already lived. At the very end of the path, in the middle of the crescent-shaped mountain range, was a waterfall that ran from the top of a mountain and ended at the base of the valley floor, pooling into a small pond. Verona walked along the path, mesmerized by all the statues of the gods.

Staring at them, she remembered a single memory of when her mother had sat her and her siblings down and taught them the name of each god and what they were the gods of. Though after years of not keeping up with memorizing them, Verona now only knew four of the seven gods. Azakel was the ruler of all gods and the bringer of justice. Valencia was the goddess of new beginnings, secret lovers, and the bringer of spring. Daekelyn, of course, was the god of storms and thieves. Then there was Varsfel, the goddess of war and death. Those four were the ones that always interested her the most, and now she had to choose which one she would pledge her allegiance to.

Many did choose Azakel because of him being all-powerful, though she didn't quite have a connection to him. As she thought about her decision, she watched the others. Daelyn went to Daekelyn, and so did Mariam. Mav chose Daekelyn and Azakel. It didn't take long for her to decide as she chose her allegiance to both Valencia and Varsfel. When it was her turn she knelt by each of the goddesses, whispering her pledge of fealty with her gaze up to the sky. As she stood up from Varsfel, she was met with shocked expressions from those who did not expect her to choose that goddess. With a shrug and a sheepish expression, she walked towards the group.

Mav raised an eyebrow at her. "You pledged to Varsfel?"

Verona shrugged nonchalantly. "Just thinking about the future is all. We can't be too careful, right?"

Mav stuttered for a heartbeat before looking concerned. With a sigh, he finally talked. "I guess we can't. I just don't know how I feel about this war idea. Why are we jumping straight into it? Who knows, maybe it's all a misunderstanding or work of nature."

Her expression turned stone cold. "We jump to it because a 'misunderstanding or a work of nature' didn't almost disembowel me."

Mav grew silent at her words, his face solemn with an edge of anger that built up like a storm behind his eyes. "I'm sorry, " he whispered. "If I could do anything at all to reverse what was done to you, I would give everything I had to do just that."

Verona sighed, looking down towards the ground as she walked at a slow pace. "I know you would have, Mav. Though what is done, is done. It gave us insight, and we should take that as a sliver of hope."

He gave her a reassuring smile as they joined back together with Mariam and Daelyn. Together they all walked out of the Valley of the Gods, and back towards the kingdom of M'Ralz.

⁓⁕⁓

As the sun was setting, they had stopped for the night in a flat, open valley. The strong winds were rushing across the plains, making Verona shiver, so they decided to set up their tents tonight instead of sleeping on just their furs. Daelyn and Mav helped the women set up theirs first before working on their own. Once they were all done, they sat before the roaring fire and cooked food. Verona was quiet that night, too in her mind to enjoy the conversation that ebbed around her. Mav had noticed and elbowed her gently in the side.

"Everything okay?" he asked quietly.

She nodded, giving him a half smile. "It is, I guess I'm just tired. I think I might climb in my tent for the night."

He gave her a gentle smile. "We all are." He looked to the horizon, seeing the sun disappear. "We should all retire for the night. We only have a couple of days left until we get to M'Ralz, and we should have an early start tomorrow morning."

They all agreed, saying goodnight to each other before climbing into their own tents.

Her body felt tired, exhausted even. She knew she couldn't take another step. As soon as Verona lay in her furs, she knew she wouldn't be able to fall asleep. Her mind raced as fast as it could, thinking about anything and everything. It frustrated her to no end. With a defeated sigh that escaped her lips, she sat up, annoyed with her own mind. She needed to do something to calm her mind down, something to make her fall asleep. With a single reckless thought, she had a wicked idea in mind.

Quickly, she slipped a nightgown over her head and pulled it on before walking out of the tent. The wind still howled fiercely, making her shiver once more as she walked over to Mav's. As she knelt down at the opening, she didn't know what to do. She couldn't knock, maybe she could just whisper. Just as she was about to say something, a voice sounded from inside the tent.

"Verona?" Mav asked. Confusion and hesitation echoed through his voice. "What are you doing over here? I thought you were going to sleep."

She sighed as her shoulders dropped and relaxed. "I can't fall asleep. Could I come in?"

She heard rustling around from him moving before the tent opened up. Verona crawled in, and then she saw him. Her jaw slackened at the sight of him lying there with nothing but a pair of underwear on. He smirked at her obvious staring, and she blushed in return.

She looked towards the side of the tent. "I didn't know you didn't have anything on."

He chuckled. "Well, I do have something on, but I can change that for you."

Verona gasped, raising her hands. "It's okay! We can keep it like this!"

He laughed even louder at her. "So Verona, what are you really here for then if it isn't to see me naked?" He looked at her fully; she was sitting there in just a nightgown that had now inched up her thighs.

She felt the heat rush back to her cheeks as she stared at her hands for a few heartbeats, gathering up the courage to accomplish the idea that had brought her out of her tent. With a final inhale, she stared at him with a mixture of determination and want.

"I came here to do this," she said, getting so close to him that their breath intertwined together. She placed a hand on the back of his neck and pulled him in. Their lips connected hard as they finally kissed for the first time. He groaned into her mouth as he moved his lips against hers. He bit her bottom lip softly as he leaned away. Leaving her gasping and breathless.

"Finally, " he said, his voice deeper and rougher. His pupils were blown up wide; they were so black Verona could barely see any color.

"Please," she begged.

He gave her what she wanted as he pulled her onto his lap, connecting their lips once more. The heat built up intensely between them as they continued to kiss with fury. She didn't want it to stop, she wanted to do this all night and more. She wanted so much more as she sat there. He had one hand gripping the back of her neck while the other gripped her waist pulling her in closer to him. He groaned at the movement from her. His lips trailed down to her jaw, slowly moving to her neck. His hand started to trail down her throat, to her collarbone, then to her chest before her hand lashed out, stopping his exploring path. Her body was feeling electric, every nerve was on its edge. She couldn't catch her breath, though it felt wonderous in every single way.

He groaned once more. "You don't know how long I've wanted to do this, Verona. It feels like an eternity, waiting for this moment."

"Please," she whispered.

"What do you want me to do, Verona?" His eyes filled with primal need.

"Please." She groaned out once more. Her mind was so fuzzy she couldn't think of anything to say, so her lips moved on their own. "Please distract me."

Mav paused, stiffening beneath her before pulling away. The hurt echoed deep into his eyes as he stared at her. "Is that all you want from me? To just be a distraction to you? I'm a damned idiot. Of course, that's what you wanted." He growled the words out.

He picked her up, moving her off of him. "Mav, wait!" She snapped back into reality as she cried out. "I didn't mean it like that, I swear."

"Of course, you meant those words, Verona. That's all anyone ever wants from me, to be a distraction because no one truly wants me after they see the damaged parts." He sneered at her, the anger showing clearly on his features.

"Please listen to me, Mav!" she begged, her voice full of desperation. Tears filled her eyes, threatening to spill.

"Get out of here. I don't want to see you for the rest of the night. So just go, Verona," he snapped, turning away from her.

The tears finally fell as she climbed out of his tent. She ran as fast as she could, the tears blurring her vision. She passed her tent and the others as she ran towards the woods. Her thighs ached, but she shut any feeling down, suffocating everything that threatened to escape her mind and force her to feel.

She didn't want it to happen like this, she wanted it to be different. She wanted to be as far as she could from that damned tent. The low branches snagged her nightgown as she entered the tree line, tearing at the thin fabric and creating holes. She felt the thorns of various bushes scratch at her skin, though she kept going. She continued to run, even after falling several times, breaking the skin open on her palms and knees. She ran to escape the feelings and hurt that his words caused when he yelled for her to leave. She wanted to forget, but she couldn't. She fell one last time before staying there, knelt down on the ground, feeling the blood trickle from her open cuts. Her head was bowed as the tears ran down her cheeks. She wanted to yell, to scream it all away. Just as she was about to let everything out with a guttural scream, voices echoed through the woods and caught her attention. Voices that didn't sound human, voices that sounded like a hiss of words, voices that reminded her of another time in the forest. Verona snapped her neck to where they were coming from; they had to be so close to her. Slowly, she pulled herself up and walked to the sound as quietly as she could.

As she got close, a fire lit up the darkness around a small campsite. The tents were oddly shaped and made out of thick logs and tropical leaves that Verona had never seen before. Around the campfire, she saw several human-like creatures. Beautiful feathers donned their bodies that varied in colors and patterns. Some were gray and white, some were all white, and some were colorful patterns of reds, orange, and blues.

Their faces were human-like, though their nose, chin, and cheekbones were sharper. There was skin on their face, though starting around the upper part of the forehead and rounding down to their jawline, that skin started to fade to feathers and shaped into a crest of feathers at the crown of their head. Several large primary feathers stuck out farther than the rest on that very crest. Their hands and feet held large claws, and Verona recognized them instantly as the creatures that attacked her. She shivered as she placed a hand on her lower abdomen. She knew she had to hear what they were saying. If these were the things that had been starting the fires, she had to stop them.

"Why don't we go now?" One of them hissed. "They would be all asleep by now, more people would die in the fire."

The one with the large feathers turned to the one that talked. "We don't go now, Tekala. No one would live to spread the fear, and what fun would that be? She did tell us that is our mission anyway."

The one named Tekala sighed in frustration. "But the town is only a couple of miles away, I want to go now."

The one who seemed like the leader hissed at Tekala, annoyance thick in its voice. "Fine, if you want to do it now, then let's go and get it over with."

Verona slowly walked away from the camp, her eyes wide with fear. They were going to strike another town tonight. She couldn't stand by on this one, she couldn't watch innocent people die again from these monsters. She knew what needed to be done. She needed to stop them. So with a final push of her tired muscles, she ran to her own campsite to be the savior of a town.

Chapter Fourteen

Verona skittered to the line of tents that were void of any sound. She had to get them all up, she had to make sure that they would be with her. They needed them to be there because Verona feared she couldn't do this alone. As Verona panicked, she ran into her tent, trading her torn nightgown for a tunic, pants, and boots. After jumping out of her tent and slipping on her last boot, she ran to the others and began slapping the walls of each tent. She tried to get them up as silently as she could because she didn't know where this other town was. It could be down the hill from them, and these monsters could be walking straight towards them. Rustling came from each tent as all three of them emerged with sleep-stricken eyes and tangled hair. They all looked at her incredulously, seeing her out of breath and wide-eyed from panic.

Mariam, who now stood beside her, gently touched her arm as worried filled her eyes. "What's the matter, Verona?"

Verona looked at each of their faces; Mariam and Daelyn looked concerned while Mav looked away from her with fury still painted on his features. She choked down the feelings of regret and turned to Mariam and Daelyn.

"I know what is burning down the villages, and they are striking another one tonight. We need to find what village it is and get the people out before they're all dead," she said, panic thick in her voice.

When all three of them looked at her with that same slightly unbelieving look, she let out a sigh of annoyance. "Mav, get your map and find what town is nearby. Daelyn, get the tents down and packed. Mariam, help him and make sure we're ready to get going as soon as we find out what town it is."

Mariam and Daelyn nodded, getting right to work. Mav shook his head and dragged his feet to his tent. Verona followed him with her arms crossed, becoming increasingly annoyed with his attitude with each step.

"You can feel however you want about me for however long you want, but we have people to save, so shove it with your childish feelings for the moment and go get that god's damned map," she snapped at him.

He turned on his heels, his face boiling with anger. He opened his mouth, about to snap back, before he sighed and closed his eyes. "I'm not going to do this right now, Verona. I will get the map and do as you told me to do, but other than that, I'm not dealing with you."

Hurt flickered over her face for a heartbeat before she put on a mask of indifference. "The faster you can do it, the more lives we save, Mav."

He climbed into his tent without a word and retrieved the map. He walked over to the still-burning fire, placed the map on the ground, and looked over it to find the town they needed to save. After a few moments of looking, he placed a finger on the map, right on a small village.

Without moving his eyes from the map, he spoke. "This is the one."

Verona whipped around, looking to see that Mariam and Daelyn had finished packing everything in their tent site. She gave them a curt nod before reaching down and grabbing the map. She gave it a quick cursory glance once more. With a point to the north, she looked at everyone.

"That's where we need to go. It's a little under a mile from where we are now. We need to leave now if we want to stand a chance of saving those people." She said as she threw her sack over her shoulders. Verona looked towards Mav, then her gaze moved to Daelyn and the swords that hung from various parts of him. "Can I have one?"

He reached behind his back, unbuckling one of them and handing the sword and sheath to her. "It is yours. I don't mind it that much, too light for me," he said with a small smile.

Verona studied the sword before her. The hilt and blade were both the same worn-down silver color. Its pommel was heart-shaped and filled with filigree-like designs around the two empty spaces that were tear-drop shaped. The grip of the hilt reminded her of chainmail and the guard curved towards the blade in an elegant pattern with more filigree carved into it. An ancient language was etched directly on the fuller of the blade. It was beautiful, the weight felt perfect for her as she flipped it around in her hands.

"Have you named it?" she asked in awe.

"No, it didn't work for me, so I did not believe that I should be the one to give it such an honor. Now that it seems to be yours, what shall we call such a mighty blade?" Daelyn asked with a crooked smile.

She looked down at the blade reverently before looking up to meet his gaze with steel determination. "Her name shall be Fury, and she shall be an oath to the forgotten. A protector of the lives these monsters are trying to take, and a heartrender to those who stand in my way."

He gave her a wicked smile and she returned it before looking towards the north. She quickly buckled the sword to herself and then, with barely a thought, she took off running toward danger.

It had not taken them long at all to reach the top of a large hill that overlooked a small village with wooden walls surrounding it all. It was bigger than Verona's home village, but it wouldn't have come close to Mariam's town. It had a few dozen houses, some buildings that looked like small shops near the center, and little market stands in the middle of a garden. Most of the town seemed desolate and run-down, with the broken roofs and torn walls of various houses. She felt bad for this community that was barely holding itself together and was now about to become even more chaotic.

Verona threw her pack down on top of the hill as she turned to her friends. "We need to split up to cover more ground. Try to get as many people to flee this village as you can. If anyone can help get others out, let them, but women and children need to escape no matter what."

Without any confirmation from the others, Verona took a running start, then slid down the hill on her hip. The gravel and rocks tore up her skin as she accelerated down the slope. She wanted to wince and stop herself, but she had to get down there as quickly as possible. She heard noises akin to falling rocks, so she knew the others were coming as well, though she didn't turn around to look. As she came to a slow stop at the base of the hill, she pushed herself up and went back to a full sprint. In the all-consuming darkness around her, she could hear the predatory screeching that echoed in the night; while it was distant, the sound grew nearer and nearer to her with every step she took. She pushed her muscles almost to their breaking point as she ran under the wooden archway that served as the town's entryway. She heard pounding footsteps behind her as her friends caught up to her. She pointed and yelled at them to start with that part of town. Verona ran to the first building she could see knocking furiously. It felt like too long before a sleepy-eyed woman holding a child answered the door. Her husband joined her as Verona explained the situation.

The man didn't want to leave his family's side as he led them out of the town with a sword gripped tight in a set of white knuckles.

She took a little time to watch them go toward safety before moving to the next house and repeating the process. More people had joined those evacuating, but men with the will to help and nothing to lose had joined her mission of getting everybody awake and toward safety. Screams were starting to echo through the town as house after house was being awoken in the dead of night. Some were stirring awake from the commotion and fear that hung thickly in the air. The townspeople's eyes were wide with terror as they ran through the streets holding screaming babes, still in their nightclothes. Verona stood there for a second, looking around, her breath catching in her throat. Even though Verona was doing everything in her power, she still felt helpless as terror dug deep into her bones.

Verona had made it through half of the town before that high-pitched screeching started to echo within the town walls. She shivered with fear and anticipation, knowing what was about to come. She looked around, fear slightly tinting her eyes as she looked for the monsters among them. The town was still so dark, except for the dull light of lanterns coming through the windows of several houses. The town had an eerie feeling to it, knowing death was walking among them, waiting for an opportunity to strike. She broke into another run, trying to escape the beasts. Verona looked over to her right as she spotted an alley, skittering into it with a sharp turn. The screeching turned to howling as it came from everywhere. It sounded like there were dozens more than what she saw in that campsite, and it drove fear hard into her bones. The hairs on her arms stood up as she shivered from the silent ache of dread. It took every ounce of strength she had to push the feeling down deep. Closing her eyes, she swallowed hard. She took a few steps back, feeling her back collide with the brick wall of the alley, slowly sliding down and tucking her knees into her chest. Verona opened her eyes and looked at her open hands. She felt the fear try to push its way up and into her soul. With an exhale, she pushed it back down for the final time, as she slid a mask on her fear-driven expression and turned it into determination.

"They have taken everything from me, but they cannot hurt me. It's my turn to show them what it's like to feel that," she snarled to herself.

Pushing herself up, she stood and drew out her sword, Fury. She ran out of the alley and ended up in the middle of the town square. Empty market stalls surrounded her, and she looked around, trying to think of the next place she should go. She wanted to find these vile creatures. She wanted to get rid of them all, wanted to show them what every one of these people was feeling. She wanted to show them the fear she felt back in the woods as her abdomen was opened wide. The determination she felt turned to anger as she let out a primal scream. She heard a nearby howl, so she turned and ran to it with a snarl on her face when, at that moment, flames erupted to her left. They blinded her for a few moments as she covered her face with an arm. Verona stumbled backward, tripping on uneven stone and falling towards the cold hard surface. Her vision slowly came back to her as she saw the beast named Tekala run away, howling with laughter. As she sat there, she watched the house in stunned silence. Her jaw hung loose and eyes wide with shock. It didn't take long for the fire to engulf the house in a wild inferno, and with the overwhelming crackle of flames, screams joined in as well. Tears streaked her face as she mourned for whoever was inside there. She mourned for a life she couldn't save. She sobbed, placing the blame on her shoulder for being just a few minutes too late If she wasn't so wrapped up in getting to the beasts. If she had been focused on saving these people still, she could have saved one more. Though she knew there would be more than just this one life lost tonight, she couldn't stand the thought of it. Her palms started to tingle, she felt the burns on her skin feel as if they were on fire once more. Verona was stuck in time as she was transported to that place, the very same place where she crawled over her burned house, the same place where she watched her mother die. It played in her mind over and over again as she lay there. She was reliving it endlessly, and she couldn't stop it.

A pair of hands broke her from her thoughts as she mindlessly stared up at Mariam. "We need to get out of here, Verona! We rescued all we could. Get up, please!" Mariam pulled Verona up as she saw the house burning next to them. "We saved almost all of them, Verona. They all owe their lives to your actions."

Verona looked over to Mariam, tears still running down her cheeks. "I was only a minute late, Mariam."

Mariam pulled her into a hug. "If you had been there a minute earlier, it could have been your life as well. We have to get out of here before it's too late."

Verona wiped the tears away as she pushed herself up, grabbing the sword with a loose fist. Silently, she walked towards the entrance of the town. They quickened their pace as the fire began to spread around them, engulfing the town in its hunger to devour everything in its path. The howling and screeching slowly died away as the sun began to rise, joining the fire with its unending light.

As they passed through the same gate they had entered only hours ago, she saw the grief-stricken faces of the townsfolk who had lost everything in one night. Some were screaming out names, hoping to find loved ones. Others were huddled together, hugging their families, and a few were on their knees, begging for mercy from the gods.

She knew the mass of feelings before her with such intimacy that her heart ached for each one of them standing there. Fury clawed its way through her body with such force she couldn't help but feel it fully. She stared at the sword that hung loosely in her hand as she made a promise for it to act as vengeance for these very people. With a twist of her wrist, she moved the sword towards the ground, and with a solid push, she pierced the ground with a thud. She walked a few paces to stand in front of the townsfolk. A few of them noticed her and stared, waiting for what was to come.

"Many of you don't know me. My name is Verona of Felkeirn. I am a farmer's daughter. I am like you. Poor and meaningless to those who live inside the kingdom walls. Yet, we are people, too. We have the same skin, same blood, same features as those who live in peace, and yet here we are, being killed and slaughtered like frightened livestock. We have to stick together and warn the other towns of the dangers yet to come. These feathered beasts are targeting the weak, though together, we can stand united! Together, we can defeat this evil that plagues our land! Go, find another town as a safe haven, warn them of the evil that lurks in our woods, and prepare to stand united, for we will defeat this evil."

Standing there with the wind blowing through her hair and her clothes tattered and soot-stained, she created a picture of wild beauty. She stood there proud and determined. Verona knew she had so much to change in this world, and that it was going to take time. Though she was on the path of changing the future, she knew it. If someone had told her younger self that her life would lead to this moment, she would have been shocked, but she would be proud of who she was becoming. These people before her looked up to her for answers, for help, and for leadership, so that's who she would be to them.

As the townspeople slowly dispersed to head to other towns, many thanked her and her friends for helping them, she saw the helplessness in their eyes but also saw gratefulness. She sympathized with each one, knowing how this situation had felt. She knew the pain that they would go through would last for weeks, and for some, that pain would never go away. She hoped for the best for them as she watched the final person disappear into the horizon. Verona turned to her friends knowing what they had to do next. It was time to go to the Kingdom of M'Ralz. It was time to create a plan of action. It was time to finally change the course of the future. These beasts had the upper hand in how this game was being played, though Verona knew it was time for the tables to turn.

Verona turned to her friends and saw each one of them with hope-filled gazes and faces full of determination. She knew what needed to be done now, she saw the road ahead clear as day and she was ready to continue on.

Slowly, Verona walked over to Fury, who was still pierced in the ground, and with a hard tug upward, she pulled it free and slid it back into its sheath. "We will still need to go to the Kingdom of M'Ralz. There, we will gather the allies we need to defeat these beasts once and for all."

With a final turn to the east, she began the last leg of the journey to get to the beautiful Kingdom of M'Ralz. With anxiousness running amok in her mind, she was more than ready to finally get the answers she needed.

Chapter Fifteen

It had only taken a couple of days for Verona and her crew to arrive at the main gates of M'Ralz. Even though it had been quite the uneventful past couple of days, she still had not gotten used to the cold shoulder Mav had given her since that night in his tent. That same night she had let her mind take over, the night she let those damned words slip from her mouth. She wished she could take it all back. There was a part of her that wished she hadn't walked inside that tent, though there was another part of her that still felt the press of his lips against hers every time she closed her eyes and relished the feeling over and over again. It wasn't like she didn't try to talk to him. She tried over and over again to make him talk to her. Though if it wasn't a command or something about their journey, he would just walk away from her without a word. It drove her crazy to no end. She wanted to rip her hair out or even slug him in the head with the back of her sword every time he just walked away. But she kept her cool the best she could, it wasn't time to focus on such silly romance, she had a mission to complete, beasts to slay, and a family to avenge.

The lands surrounding the Kingdom of M'Ralz were never-ending rolling hills of prairie land. Dry grass, small colorful flowers, and endless clear skies took up most of the landscape. There were a few trees that dotted the landscape, but not enough to create any semblance of a wooded scenery. The lands were so flat that when they arrived all they had seen were the large, looming, stone walls that surrounded the kingdom entirely. Parts of the castle had stuck up amongst the top of the wall, yet it was not enough to create any picture of how it really looked.

As they made their way towards the main entrance of the kingdom, they noticed two guards standing post on either side of the entryway. Their armor was clean and newer, unlike the guards she had seen at the Kingdom of Lo'Kil. They also seemed happy with the job they were doing as they joyfully chatted amongst themselves. As the crew came closer to them, they stood straight welcoming them to the Kingdom of M'Ralz.

Verona looked at them, slightly confused. "I don't need any proof that I live in these walls, or have something showing I need to enter? Anyone can come into the kingdom?"

The guard looked puzzled for a second before realizing they were not from these parts of Esnia. "No, my lady. The queen believes anyone can come and go as they please in this kingdom. She welcomes guests and throws festivals to entice anyone to enter the kingdom. We actually have our spring festival going on right now, it's something you truly can't miss."

Verona thanked the guard for his kindness as the group walked into the front entrance of the kingdom. She was awestruck with her jaw hanging loosely as she took in the sight before her. A little part of her thought that M'Ralz would be the same as Lo'Kil was with its ramshackle poor quarter, homeless people on the street, and barren walls that framed the inner heart of the kingdom. This one, however, had blown her away already with just one look. She couldn't see an inner wall that stood as a silent division between the rich and poor. Every house she saw was in perfect condition; they were colorful and unique. Even the ones that faced the outer wall were bigger than Verona's family house, complete with sound structures and beautifully furnished interiors. There was no one begging in the streets for money or sleeping in the alleys. Everyone she could see was wearing tidy and beautiful clothing, and they were genuinely happy as they talked to one another.

Intricate lanterns hung on thick ropes that swooped across the alleys and roads. Flags dawned the corners with pink flowers stitched into them as they waved in the silent breeze. Flower petals littered the stone pathways as it all symbolized the ongoing festival. A tone of excitement ran through Verona as she looked at the kingdom before her. She couldn't help it at all as a giddy laugh escaped her lips.

Mariam looked at her with an eyebrow raised. "A little excited for a festival?"

Happiness burst from every pore of Verona as she turned to Mariam. "Oh, I am excited for everything here. I'm excited to step foot in this kingdom, to experience this festival, but most of all, I'm excited to find him, to find Calder."

Mariam looked at her in silence for a few heartbeats. "And how are we going to find a single man in a kingdom full of people?" she asked incredulously.

Verona placed both hands on her hips. "Well, it can't be too hard to find a man in full armor around here, can't it?"

Verona looked around, seeing the multitude of guards swarming the streets in full armor and realizing that her statement was far from the truth. Finding Calder among the various guards that patrolled the city would be rather difficult. She thought hard as she dove into her memory. She wished he had given her a clue where he would be here in this city. Verona knew he said he would be here for the festival, though that was all the information she had received at the time. Cursing under her breath, she looked back at Mariam with a twisted expression, knowing this would be more difficult than expected.

Verona lifted her head high, determination running thick in her veins, and then walked into the kingdom. She passed shops she had seen before with the usual storefronts of tannery, swords, armor, and general goods like food and supplies. Though there were also some she rarely saw: beautiful amulets of colorful gemstones and rings with delicate designs, a shop with flowers from faraway islands, a stand with tropical fruits on display, and finally, a shop with dresses on display fit for a queen. There was another place deep in the alley that Verona didn't linger to look at, a place with women in scandalous clothing who walked up to men and hung onto them. The men looked at the women so ravishingly that she was surprised they were not undressed at that point. They were so close that it brought up memories of the night in the tent. A blush crept up her cheeks faster than anything before as she coughed to herself, looking away from the scene in the alley. It was then, when she crossed the street, walking away from that dark alley, when she stumbled upon a shop from which a delicious smell wafted. The door of the building was open, the smell so warm and sweet that Verona couldn't help but take a peek inside. There, on the display, sat many baked goods that made her mouth water just by seeing them. She made a mental note of where this shop was as she ran to catch up with her friends.

As she caught up to them, they stood on the outer edge of the main square of the kingdom, and once again, as she surveyed the scene, she was left breathless. Out in the middle of the square, the market stands had been replaced with a stunning garden. In the midst of it were numerous flowers with different shapes, petals, colors, and foliage. None were alike. Mixed among the flowers were bushes trimmed in different shapes of beasts, crowns, castles, and a mix of people and races. All this foliage was broken up by a stone walking path that created a maze amongst it all. On one side of the garden, the large bushes and foliage turned into smaller nondescript bushes, large flowering magnolia trees, and weeping willows that wrapped around a large clear pond. On the farther side of the pond, rocks were piled up, creating a delicate waterfall, pooling into the pond below it. Small aquatic creatures swam in the water, and some danced amongst the flowering lily pads that littered the surface of the water. Scattered amongst other parts of the kingdom, one could find more magnolia trees and weeping willows. This area had stolen Verona's heart with just one glance.

Though what surprised Verona the most was the ethnicity of the people who walked through the streets. It wasn't just humans that walked by her. There were a handful of godlings that walked past. Many people stopped and stared as they watched the group of half-human half-gods laughing amongst themselves. The godlings looked more like their god ancestors as they had smaller pointed ears, curved horns, and god-like features that dawned on their faces. When gods walked among them here in Esnia and were more than just the seven, they had found lovers amongst humans and created the godlings. These offspring were worshiped as much as their god ancestors were. They also were protected heavily inside the stone walls that surrounded this kingdom from the old clan of god killers that walked in search of them.

Following the nobles were people of a race Verona had never seen before. The female had beast-like horns that grew from her dark-skinned forehead. Her ears were long, drooping down and ending in a point. Her black hair was short and braided back on both sides into a small mohawk. A set of scars on the left side of her face started above her eyebrow and ended below her eye. Jewelry hung from several parts of her body; several cuffs decorated her horns connected by a chain. A handful of studs were on the lobe of her ear with chains bridging them in a delicate arch, a small gold hoop pierced the septum of her nose, and several gold chains hung from her neck. A set of thick cuffs was snug on her wrists; they were connected by a silver chain the noble held as he pulled the women along. What shocked Verona the most was the pair of cloven hoofs where human feet should have been.

Verona looked over to Mariam, nodding over the woman being dragged. "What is that?" she asked curiously.

Mariam looked over, her expression turning hesitantly as she whispered. "Their kind is called Zarraki, they are from Nomad's Lane. They try to come to Esnia in search of a better life, but they are often chained and used as servants. If the rumors are true, they know how to wield the old magic, and those cuffs she has on her wrists somehow stop her from using it."

Verona shivered at the thought of them being servants. If she could find the power to change the world, one thing she would do was to take away any servants.

She turned away from the noble and servant, staring past the garden. A single trail led out of the center of the kingdom straight towards the castle that loomed largely in the background. It was another beauty on its own with spiraling towers, walls of glass, and a large keep that stood like a giant amongst the other buildings in the kingdom. She knew that exact castle was where they needed to be, but first, they needed to find Calder, and after that, they needed to find a way to speak to the queen. Before they tried to accomplish that, the most important task of all was finding a place to stay, and along with that, enjoy the kingdom around them with the festivities that were yet to begin.

It had taken some time to find a place to stay for that night, many of the taverns and inns were filled with guests coming in to see the festival. It had taken them several times asking about rooms when finally they had found a handful of available ones for the night. The rooms they reserved in the tavern weren't something they would have picked if anything else was available. It was quite the letdown of an establishment, especially given the kingdom it was in. The inside looked outdated, run-down, and hanging on by a thread. She heard the small buzz of a few insects flying around her head. Swatting them away, she looked at Mariam with a raised eyebrow.

"Is this really where we want to stay for tonight? There's nothing better out there?" Verona whispered.

Mariam shook her head. "Unfortunately, there isn't. We are here just for a night or two, and then we will be out. At least we won't be spending much of our time here, that's for sure."

Verona let out a frustrated sigh as she walked towards the stairs and to her room. With a thud, she tossed her bag onto the floor and flopped onto the bed. She grimaced at the uncomfortable feeling of the bed underneath her; it felt so lumpy and itchy. She would have had a better time sleeping on the floor tonight rather than on this sorry excuse for a bed. Slowly sitting up, she surveyed the barren room as she drifted into her mind. She thought of how she could find Calder. Verona knew he would be out tonight, but so would everyone else with the festivities going on. As she struggled to come up with a plan, her only hope was to go out tonight to explore the kingdom and hope for a sliver of luck in her quest to find him. After walking out of her room, she bounded down the stairs and found the barmaid who was wiping down the counters.

"Excuse me, miss," she spoke as she climbed onto a wooden stool. "I am not from this kingdom, so I don't know what the festivities are like tonight. Would you know by chance?"

The barmaid looked frustrated from being held up at her job. "Yes, I do know. There will be a hunting party and archery at midday, though tonight we have a band coming and the celebration will be in the heart of the kingdom."

Verona thanked her before walking up the stairs. She looked out the window to see the sun still high in the sky. She would have to wait quite a few hours for the celebration to commence, but she couldn't just sit around. After entering her room, she quickly swapped her tunic and pants for a simple dress and then bounded down the stairs to explore the kingdom.

Verona ran through the streets of people, passing shop after shop and taking in the breathtaking sights around her. Murals were painted on the open walls of buildings and houses facing the street. One mural had the night sky amongst a sea of mountains, and dancing among the stars was the colorful summer aurora. Another mural was a tribute to the gods featuring all seven of them facing toward the viewer, their ornamental robes draping over their frames as they stood in prayer. Though Verona's favorite one she had stumbled upon so far was a painting of a rilasi captured mid-sprint in a field of wildflowers, wind dancing amongst its thick mane. She had stopped and stared for a while, looking at the beautiful painting before her.

After walking around for a while, she noticed a crowd gathering in the heart of the kingdom. As she walked closer, she saw several armed men in full armor atop golden rilasis. Many of the women her age were swooning at the men, reaching out with outstretched arms at the fine men before them. The one in front held a flag dawning the crest of the kingdom, which was a group of magnolia flowers behind a silver sword. Verona figured that this was the send-off for the hunting party. They would come back later in the day, hopefully with a bounty of meat in tow.

As she looked around, not caring much for this part of the festival, she noticed a particular shop. It was the same shop that smelled like baked goods and everything else that scented the air so wonderfully. As her mouth watered, she walked quickly to the shop to get more of a look at what was inside. The shelves were filled with all kinds of delectable goods that were more than what her mind could imagine. There was a single shelf filled with colorful bite-sized treats that could transport your mind to another world. Another shelf had cakes; the smaller ones were on the top and were quite plain compared to the larger and more intricately designed ones on the bottom. The shelf next to it had an endless amount of chocolate goods. Lastly, the final one held a mix of baked goods that came in various shapes and sizes.

Staring at the glass with hunger dancing in her eyes, she wished she had any amount of money, even just a small amount to get the tiniest of treats. As she sighed, disappointment slowly washed over her. Just as she was about to turn and walk out, a voice caught her attention.

"It would be such a disappointment to travel all this way and not taste the unique and magnificent treats that M'Ralz has to offer," a male voice echoed behind her.

Verona stiffened, feeling confused at the familiarity of the voice before she gasped and whipped around to the man who she came to this kingdom for. A smile lit her face up so fully that her cheeks hurt instantly.

"I didn't think I would be able to find you!" she said hurriedly.

Calder stood before her, lacking his armor and dawned in normal civilian clothing. His sword was the only weapon that hung loosely from a belt on his waist. The smile that had spread across his face was just as wide as hers. "I'm not surprised you were trying. When we parted ways, I almost came back to try to find you after I heard about the fires. Though I knew if you were going to look for me, I would have to be where I said I would be."

Tears threatened to escape her eyes as he mentioned the fires. "There is so much I need to tell you, Calder. I have some friends who have had quite the adventure with me so far, and I think it would be best to have them there when we talk, but I need your knowledge to figure something out."

His face fell into a solemn expression mixed with worry as he saw her watery eyes. "If there's anything I can do, I will do it with all my power. I have a private home nearby. Once you have your friends in tow, meet me here at sundown, and then we will go there to talk."

Verona nodded, she couldn't help but wrap her arms around this new friend of hers. Even though she had only shared a few hours with this man, she knew she could place her life in his hands. He made her feel comfortable and safe just being in his presence. With a quick goodbye, Verona ran back to her friends. The sun was getting lower, and she had barely any time to convince them, so she prayed that they would trust her to do this. She had no choice, no second plan. Calder was her lifeline and she was grabbing onto it with all her might. She laughed to herself, feeling like a maniac among the growing crowd that surrounded her. She felt like something, just once, was going in her favor. She could feel the tide shift; it was a slow shift, but now she could feel the power, as if it was time to grab the reins. And so she would grab them with every ounce of effort she could muster. It was time for her to avenge her family.

Chapter Sixteen

Verona pleaded with Mariam, Mav, and Daelyn several times before they agreed to come with her and meet Calder. They were very cautious at the start, and for a good reason. He was a stranger to them and someone they didn't know if they could trust. It didn't help her case at all either when she had told them that she had only met him once. Though after telling them over and over again that he would be their key, they finally reluctantly agreed. Together, the four of them waited tensely, eating supper on the main floor of the tavern in silence as they watched the sun merge with the horizon. Both nervousness and excitement were felt throughout the table, though Verona knew she was the only one who was truly thrilled.

As soon as the sky was painted with hues of purples and reds, they walked towards the sweets shop. Mariam, whose face was plastered with worry, huddled close to Daelyn. Together, they whispered to themselves in a hushed and stern tone; Verona knew that their nerves had not settled down yet. Mav, on the other hand, had his arms crossed, brows furrowed, and lips pulled taut as he still refused to look her in the eyes. She could feel the anger and regret boil off of him in waves as he walked further back into their pack. She desperately needed to talk to him again, needed all this silence and anger to disappear. Though she knew as much as she wanted to plead, to ask for forgiveness, to scream at him and shake him to no end, it would have to be him to make that move. He would need to come to terms with what happened and take that leap and Verona finally accepted that fact.

With a sigh, Verona turned around to see the sweets shop just down the road. Her breath caught in her throat as the excitement and anticipation covered her in a thick blanket, her pace quickened as she made her way over. As the group drew closer, she could see him. Standing out in the crowd with freshly cleaned silver armor and the same sword hanging loosely on his hip was Calder. He looked worried as he scanned the faces passing him, but when his eyes landed on a familiar mess of red hair, his shoulders relaxed, and a small smile graced his lips. Verona's pace quickened for the few seconds it took to reach the shop and Calder. With barely any hesitation, he pulled her into a tight hug.

"For a little bit there I thought you wouldn't come. I admit I was quite a bit worried," he said sheepishly as he rubbed the back of his head.

She gave him a reassuring smile. "Even if I had not convinced them to come with me, I still would have come by myself. This is a matter that is important to me, and I couldn't imagine myself not doing everything in my power to solve this."

He nodded, looking at the faces behind her, studying them. His eyes narrowed at Mav's face. In return, Mav did the same. Verona looked between the two men, confused. Before she could ask what it was all about, Calder told them to follow him and then walked towards their destination.

Calder led them through the inner streets of the kingdom. As they walked further, Verona could see the castle loom closer and closer with each step. Her mind whirled furiously with thoughts of where they would end up. She was getting increasingly nervous as she thought about how they would soon be inside the castle, she was nowhere near dressed accordingly to be inside those walls. Though when they had stopped at a small cottage on the outskirts of the castle grounds, she had let out a sigh of relief.

Quietly, the five of them stepped inside once Calder had unlocked the door. Verona looked around as she was the last one to step inside. The inside looked cozy in a homely way. The front door opened into a small living room with a fireplace sitting in the middle of the far wall that was framed by large gray stones. Two wooden chairs were placed by the fireplace with a fur rug underneath them. Large wooden bookcases lined the left and right walls filled with books and other miscellaneous items. In the corner by the fireplace was a second set of armor that a hay-filled dummy was adorned with; Verona had yet to see Calder wear that one. On the right wall were two closed doors leading to other rooms, and on the left was only one. A round table sat in the middle of the room with a basket of fruit on top and two more chairs placed by it. Large wooden beams ran across the ceiling, and in the middle of the room, hanging down, was a large antler chandelier with lit wax candles pierced by the points. Several other candles were scattered around the room on bookcases and the table.

Calder walked into one of the rooms on the right and came back seconds later with another chair in hand. After bringing the chair into the room and placing it by the table, he then grabbed the two chairs by the fireplace. When he was done setting the table up, he waved his hand, motioning them all to sit down. Calder leaned against the wall that was nearest to the table after they all sat down. He stood there in silence, looking between them all. Verona felt as if her throat was constricted, as if her breath could not escape with how thick the tension was filling up the room. Her nerves ran high as anxiety felt like a hot knife against her skin. She looked between all of them as well, and she nervously started to chew on her bottom lip.

Calder sighed as he looked towards the ground, shoulders slumping slightly. "I can tell most of you don't want to be in this room. I can also tell that you have been through Azarath and back with this trip you've been on. I hear there is trouble going on, but I haven't been told what this trouble is. I am an adventurer by trade, and I think I may have answers to your questions, but in order to do so, I want to know everything. I met Verona many weeks ago, and I want to pick up where we left off."

With a nod and her nervous eyes bouncing around the room, Verona sighed and then started to tell her story. She started with all the faces she saw walking back from the village and finding her family dead. She spoke of the three starting this wild quest, of their failed plan in the castle, and her almost getting gutted. She smiled as she told of her time on the boat, and how she loved it there. Her smile dropped as she got to the part about finding the creature. She skipped the part about why she ran into the woods in the first place, but her eyes met with Mav's for a second. Verona spoke highly of her team saving the town and finished with them arriving at M'Ralz. She let out a small breath as she finished talking. Verona felt a small relief as she had the chance to finally tell someone about what she had gone through. Calder had walked over to her halfway through and had placed a hand on her shoulder with a sad smile.

"I understand what you have been through and how tough your journey has been so far, I hope I can be of any help and ease some of that pain as well." Calder knelt before her as he held one of her hands in his.

Their eyes held each other's gaze for a handful of heartbeats before she looked down towards their hands. With a shaky breath in, she forced every feeling she had down to the deepest part of her mind. "Does anything make sense in my story? What vicious beast would kill for fun, would burn countless families alive in their own home?"

His lips tightened to a thin line as he stood and started to pace. His arms were crossed behind his back, mindlessly playing with pieces of his armor, and his eyes were clouded and deep in thought. Verona impatiently watched him from her seat as she tapped her fingers on the table. Her eyebrows furrowed in confusion as she watched his head snap towards one of the bookshelves before quickly walking over to it. He pulled out a large dusty leather-bound book, its pages worn, torn, and folded in many places. Verona read the cover, and her expression showed even more confusion.

She looked over to him hesitantly. "I don't quite understand how a book of Esnia's history has answers to our problem."

A small smile tugged on his lips but fell when he became absorbed with flipping through the pages. "It may seem like that, though time again has proven that history has and will repeat itself and if I'm right about what you are talking about, we are in the midst of a very horrible repeat of our bloody history."

Fear rattled her bones as she comprehended his words. She'd had a feeling for the longest time that this would be something bloody that would scar their history, but she didn't know that this wouldn't be the first time. "If these creatures have been here before, then why don't we know what to watch out for or how to stop them? Why are we letting them run rampant throughout our lands?"

Calder stopped at a page, studying it for a second before sighing. "We don't know much about them because in their history, we are the monsters."

All four of their heads snapped towards Calder, shock was written plain as day on every face before him. "What?" Verona stuttered and quickly stood up, walking towards Calder and the book. She studied the page, looking at the words before her again and again. She couldn't believe it when she saw the image and read the words on the paper. She could see everything before her, but she didn't want to believe it. Quietly, she walked back to her seat in stunned silence and sat down on her chair with clouded eyes. Her friends looked at her with concern before looking back to Calder.

Mariam looked slightly upset as she crossed her arms. "Are you going to tell us or not? What is going on here?"

Calder sighed as he brought the book over to the small table where everyone was sitting. With a thud, the book lay open before them right on the page that answered so many questions.

"These creatures you ask about call themselves the Telana. They are as humanoid, intelligent, and dangerous as any of us, if not more so. They have beast-like tendencies and features. They live off the land on the island of Ro'L amongst the wild beasts that respect them fiercely. They are a force to be reckoned with, and if these are the creatures you have encountered, then it will take an army to stop only a dozen of them."

Mav studied the book, reading the description over and over again. "So what motive do they have? Or are they creatures of war who get off on killing innocents?"

Calder walked back to his original spot on the wall, leaning against it. "When I say history repeats itself, I truly mean it. Before we colonized Esnia, the Telana called these lands their home. When we became greedy and desperate for more land, we kicked them out of their home, forcing them to live on unknown lands with ferocious beasts sentencing them to their deaths. It was only time until they remembered, until they demanded back what was so rightfully theirs. So now they are here, repeating history once more."

The room around them grew quiet as it dawned upon them all what they were up against.

There was no way this small ragtag group of misfits would be able to defeat monstrous beasts that were out for revenge and spilled blood. It was a vendetta that was written in the very soil that they were standing on, the same soil their ancestors had stained with so much blood.

Verona placed her head in her hands. She didn't know what she believed in anymore; it had started as the simple task of finding her family's murderer and avenging them. Though at this point, if she did avenge them, would she be walking the same steps her ancestors did, supporting senseless murders? If she didn't avenge them for the sake of a grudge that was hundreds of years old, would she be supporting the pointless spilling of innocent blood? The blood of those who didn't know what happened all those years ago, those who were getting murdered at this very moment? She felt like her hands were tied behind her back so tight that she didn't know what to do anymore.

The tears that were welling up in her eyes from frustration spilled down her cheeks and dripped slowly into her balled-up fists that were pressed so tightly against her face. Her nails were digging so fiercely into her palm, and pain was the only thing she wanted to feel. It was the only thing that felt real at this moment. Her limbs felt so numb as rage roiled through her; it was overtaking her so quickly. With a crack that only her mind felt, she burst upward in a single fast move, knocking the chair over underneath her. A scream clawed its way out of her as she looked up at the wooden beams above her. A single thought echoed painfully through her mind: there was nothing they could do. There was nothing they could do. There was nothing they could do. She collapsed onto the floor below her, a heap of a sobbing mess as she repeated the thoughts out loud. She muttered them to herself as she lay there.

A set of footsteps echoed through the silence as someone walked over to her, a large set of hands wrapped around her. Verona looked up, seeing a face through her blurry vision, the one she was expecting the least. There, standing before her, was Mav who had pity plastered so clearly across his face. His pity stung more than his anger; he didn't want him to pity her.

"It's going to be alright, Verona," he whispered softly in her ear. "We will come up with a plan to fix this madness. I promise you that."

Verona shook her head as she sniffled softly. "There's nothing we can do. I am not strong enough to change fate itself. I think my journey ends here on this day."

Another set of footsteps walked closer to them. "The only person who would know that would be the all-seeing. I would not give up hope, Verona. Even though the journey ahead is dark and full of death, it does not mean there isn't a sliver of hope and light there. You must *be* that sliver of hope and light to those who need it the most. There are people out there who need you, Verona. Just as much as you need to set this right."

She took a large breath in, looked up at Calder, and nodded. She then moved her gaze to Mav, Mariam, and Daelyn. "I do not know where to go from here. I am lost, and I am afraid. Though just because I feel alone in this world does not mean that I truly am. This moment is the one where I need every one of you the most. I need all the help I can get from here on out if we intend to change the future, if we want to make Esnia a better place for future generations. It is time to make our stand."

Chapter Seventeen

They had all gone to bed that night feeling tired and overwhelmed. Thoughts of everything that happened and all that she learned these last couple of months ran rampant through Verona's mind. This circle of events was drawing to a close, and she felt it deep in her veins; it was about time for her to right the wrong in this world. But it would take time. Especially for someone as little and unknown as Verona of Felkeirn was, though soon -- if they would do what they were talking about -- everyone would know who she was, and that terrified her.

She tossed and turned all night with everything going way too fast in her mind and before she knew it, the sun was peeking through her window. It had taken her a long time to wake up and throw on her clothing. By the time she left her little room and walked slowly down the stairs with blurred and tired vision, she had found out she was the last one to arrive. She grabbed a cup of a warm liquid before walking to the table.

As she sat down with her hands wrapped around the cup, she gave her friends around the table a sleepy smile. "What's the plan for today?" she mumbled to everyone, setting the cup down and rubbing her eyes.

Mariam looked over at her with wide eyes and a raised eyebrow. "You look horrible, Ver. Did you get any sleep last night?"

She looked up at them. She thought she saw a look of worry flash in Mav's eyes, though when she blinked, it was gone, and that mask of boredom was placed on his face. She didn't let the hurt echo onto her own as she looked towards Mariam.

Verona gave her friend a small smile. "I couldn't sleep that well, but I should be fine, especially having this with me now." She lifted the cup in her hands up to them.

Mariam shook her head, a sigh escaping her lips. "Well, the plan for today... if I remember right,

Calder said we were going to meet someone called the all-seeing?"

That perked Verona up more quickly than the warm cup. She remembered hearing Calder say something about them, which made Verona curious. They had magic in lands where magic was banned. She needed to witness them for a few heartbeats to ebb her curiosity.

"When are we going to see them?" Verona asked excitedly.

Mariam leaned back in her seat, looking out the window to the rising sun before her eyes met Verona's. "We're leaving here soon to meet him, then he will lead us to them."

Verona nodded. After those few words, everything else was a blur. She ate a quick breakfast before the four of them left to meet Calder, who gave Verona a quick hug before leading them through cramped alleyways that led closer to the castle. These quiet, dank alleyways were unlike the main streets of the kingdom. They weren't colorful or lit up with lanterns; they were dark, wet, and had people lingering in the shadows watching their every move. Calder had nodded to them in greeting, though all Verona could do was stare as she passed, feeling a chill run down her spine. As she was nervously looking around at her surroundings, she didn't notice when Calder stopped before a large stone door, causing her to screech to a halt right behind him. Her jaw dropped in awe as she studied the door. She couldn't help herself as she walked straight up to it.

Verona brushed her hand against the gray door, the rough texture scraped against her fingertips. That feeling alone told her that it was made from stone, and roughly carved at that. Etched into the slab on the top were words from the old language curved in what seemed like an arch. Below it was each god and goddess roughly carved in, though well enough she could pick out who they all were. They seemed like they were all looking at the map of the universe that sat in the midst of them all. The atlas held so much detail of various solar systems with a multitude of planets, many of them Verona did not know herself. If her life had been different and she had been born into a rich family, she would have been given an education of things as simple as the planets that surrounded them, though her education only reached the level of how to run a farm. A part of her wished she could have learned more, could have been born into a family that taught her such things. She wanted to know more than what she was given. Her thirst for knowledge was starving. The twinge of regret startled and confused her, but she shoved it down quickly as the feeling of guilt arose to take its place.

She looked over to her friend clad in silver armor, who was also studying the door. "You'd be the one to know what this door says, right?."

He nodded at her question, as he studied the door along with her. "It's quite the mural. There's so much in just this picture alone that I could talk about this all day. Though we don't have the time for that," He said with a small smile. "But the words say, 'those who are worthy of the all-seeing eyes shall place their hand upon our door and enter for our wisdom.' So I guess we place our hand upon the eye in the center?" the adventurer said to the group.

Mav raised an eyebrow at him in question. "Do you know who would be worthy enough, or should we all just try to place our hands upon the door one after another?" he said with a little bit of mockery.

Calder turned towards Verona. "I don't think we need to do that because I know who the door will open up for."

Verona's eyes widened as she took a step back with disbelief and a little bit of fear mixed in her gaze. "Me?" She took another step back. "Why me? I'm no one."

He gave her a comforting look. "There's no one else here who would be more worthy of their time. It's you, Verona, who is making waves in our history."

She swallowed hard. She never thought through what she was doing now, and she never thought what she had been doing would change anything. Though she would be a fool to believe that. Of course, she had to know that what she was doing would change not only her own life but everything along with it. She, a simple farm girl, was a catalyst of war. A war so big that it would probably fracture kingdoms and history. A war that would most likely end the simple peace that their world had known for so long. So, of course, she would be worthy, for she was the harbinger of war. She was the lady of death. And so she placed her hand in the middle of the door.

It seemed like an eternity that she kept her hand placed there upon the door, though it didn't take long for what sounded like gears clicking inside the stone, shifting and moving to unlock it. After a brief pause of silence, the door opened slightly.

Cautiously, Verona heaved open the heavy stone door with strained arms. She had never seen a door like this one; it was rare for anyone to have anything like it. Something like this was hard to make and even harder to place in a house, making it worth more than she could ever achieve in her lifetime.

The door groaned as it scraped against the stone floor, but she finally managed to open it. As she walked in, she surveyed the room around her. The main room was simple, with a plush chaise on one side of the room and a rug covering most of the floor. The walls themselves held paintings of the universe and of the gods. More plush seating was scattered on the left side of the room for those who needed to wait to see the all-seeing. Pillars covered in art made of gold surrounded the seats. Several of them were simple pitchers, though others were more extravagant designs like daggers and busts of important kings and queens. Heavy smoke that smelled of jasmine, redwood, and pine filled the room. Right in the middle of the far end stood a thin, frail woman behind the wooden counter. She gave the group a wide smile that seemed absent of any emotion. As Verona stepped closer, she could see the woman's eyes were fogged over and milky as if she was blind.

"Welcome to the all-seeing. They welcome you, Verona, and your friends as well. They ask for you to take a seat as they prepare for your visit," the woman said. Her voice sounded like it came from several voices and one at the same time.

Verona stiffened, they knew she was here without even seeing her, unless they were watching from another room. Though she wondered how they even knew her name.

Calder leaned towards her. "Do you think the all-seeing are real now?"

She shook her head, trying to clear her thoughts and looked to Calder, giving him a weary glance as she walked over to the seating. "I don't know what I believe, but that woman," she said, her voice going to a whisper, "Looks like she died and they brought her back to life. Are they controlling her? Can they have that power? They would be dead if they did, wouldn't they?"

Calder shrugged. "They say any of the ones with eyes like that are willing servants to them. They believe the all-seeing are gods so they devote their life to the cause, helping them throughout the continents. I don't know what power they have -- definitely some kind of mind trick. Though it is pure power, the royal decree made them untouchable when they used them in their court many years ago."

Verona looked at him with a puzzled look. Sliding a hand through her curly red locks, she poked through her memory of the small amount of history she knew to see if she remembered anything like it.

"The royal court used the all-seeing? I thought they hated any form of magic, They created their own force to abolish all magic."

He nodded in agreement. "Yes, they did, though the seers were protected for some reason. Maybe they just needed some reassurance that they wouldn't be killed by other magic users in the future." He smiled coyly.

Verona shuddered at the thought of magic being in these lands freely. She knew that it was a power people were being killed for, a cause that those who wanted it gone would hunt someone down for years just to rid this world of them. It was the cause of their latest war in the lands of Esnia. Two centuries ago, there had been plenty of those who carried wonderful gifts: some could summon weather, such as rain, lightning, and even sun; some could heal both physical and mental wounds; and some could help gardens of food grow and make soil plentiful. The people saw them as the children of the gods; they worshiped them throughout the lands and even had celebrations in the cities when one came to stay. Though Verona knew with good there was also evil. Power had to be balanced. There were those with the gift of war, death, and destruction. Many could raise the dead, kill on command, and summon the darkest shadow. They, too, had their own group of worshippers who saw them as death incarnate, they believed they could kill the gods. So when they drew too much power, too much of a following, all magic was erased from the world to stop anything like a god culling from ever happening again.

Verona shivered at the thoughts she was lost in, so deep in her mind she didn't hear the woman call her name. As soon as Mav elbowed her in the side, she snapped her head towards him, clearing her clouded head with the snap of her neck. She was about to growl out words of annoyance at his very sharp elbow, but then she heard the woman again.

"Verona, you may now enter the room. They are ready for you and are awaiting your presence," she spoke, followed by a tight-lipped smile.

Verona gave her a curt nod. "Thank you. Can I bring my friends in with me? I would feel so much better with them alongside me." She blushed a little with the admitted truth.

The woman's smile softened just a touch at Verona's words. "Ah yes, they will allow them to join you, they are expecting them as well. They have words they must tell them too, pieces of their own puzzles to hear as well."

The four of them looked at each other with weary looks.

Verona looked back at them with a look of confidence; she reached out both of her hands to them. Mav grumbled some small words of protest before uncrossing his arms and reaching a hand out. Calder grabbed her hand with a warm, loving smile. Mariam stood behind them with Daelyn's arm slung over her shoulders. Looking at them, going from one face to the other, she smiled softly. She leaned her head down for a second, gathering her breath and feeling the well of tears prick her eyes. Looking back up, the tears were bursting, threatening to explode as she saw the love in all of their faces.

She felt her bottom lip quiver as the words tumbled from her lips. "Whatever happens in that room, whatever is said about my future, our future... I want you to know that I love all of you with all of my heart. I'm so glad that I met each one of you and that you came with me through this wild journey with no hesitation at all. I started this journey thinking that I had no family left, thinking that they died in that fire. But along the way, I found a new one, forged by a stronger bond. I would do anything for every one of you. I hope whatever comes, whatever the outcome will be, I hope that we all pull through it and live." Her smile blossomed as the tears rolled down her cheek, hitting the floor. A small laugh escaped her lips as a thought rolled through her mind. "Every one of you better survive till the end, because we need to grow old together. I need to see you all gray-haired, holding canes so I can finally kick all of your old wrinkly arses."

"Oh, my sweet child," Calder said. The way he looked down at her carried so much warmth, love, and memories that they shared together in such a short time. "There's no way you could get rid of us that easily. There's nothing you could do that would scare me off. I am here for you and always will be, little one. There's so much more that I have to teach you about and show you. But Verona, I am glad that I found you. You're my family."

Mav rolled his eyes. "I think he said it all." His usually cocky grin slowly came to the surface. "We're not going anywhere, we're here till the end and then some."

Mariam looked to Daelyn with nothing but love and then looked towards Verona with that love showing tenfold. "From now until forever, Verona. Nothing will stop that."

Daelyn nuzzled Mariam's cheek. He echoed her words to Verona with a smile on his face.

She took a deep breath in, looking at them all with a shaky smile, wiping the tears away with the back of her hand. Exhaling, she steadied herself and faced the door with such determination it seemed like a familiar hug. A feeling that was once shaky, distant, and unfamiliar was now like a second skin to her. She was no longer that scared girl in that room wanting nothing except to join her family in death. At some point, her mission had become not only about them. It had ebbed into a cause for everyone who had lost their lives to this mysterious killing force. She saw what she needed to become and rose from the ashes of her grief. Verona became the voice to the voiceless, she became the light to the lost, and she became the unstoppable force that demanded to bring down this unknown corruption. This woman was now a force to be reckoned with, and she was damned sure she would show the world what she was capable of doing.

With a solid breath and a gaze full of steel, she walked into the room with a stride so sure no one would have guessed she was walking into the unknown.

As the door opened to them, waves of smoke bellowed out towards their feet. They were so thick that the dark room in front of them seemed a bright white. After a few heartbeats, the smoke settled and the room came into focus. This room wasn't as intricate as the waiting room with all its carved walls and art decorating the room. It was a simple dark blue painted room accented with gold trimming. The floor was covered by a dark blue and gold woven rug and on top of it sat three cushions for them to sit on. Verona was surprised by the simplicity of it all, though she knew that there was more she couldn't see, she honestly thought that it would have been more spectacular for those who held magic in their veins.

The mist before her swelled and shifted around as three figures moved towards them. Verona looked up, shaking herself from her thoughts and watching as the figures became more visible. As they broke from the mist, Verona could see them in all their glory: they were human. She could tell that much, though they weren't like any human she had seen before. They moved with such grace as if they had hundreds of years of life to perfect such movements. The two males on each side were thin and wiry, they held themselves with a little nervousness. Between them was a female, her body sensually shaped by thick curves. Her confidence was strong as she swayed her hips with each step. The skin on all of them was not tan or dark like Verona's group, they did not even have a lighter skin tone like Verona; their skin was like the color of porcelain clay akin to the gods. They wore very little to cover themselves, though it seemed natural to them. The two men wore white loincloths, while the female wore a white cloth wrapped around her chest several times and a few panels of white cloth between her hips connected by a gold chain. She also had gold cuffs on her legs, several on her arms, and a chain around her neck. All three of them wore a red cloth around their eyes, blindfolding them. The woman faced them and gave them all a red-lipped smile, dripping with her sensual touch.

As she spoke, her voice had a calming, feminine tone that drew them all into her. "Hello, darlings. I have been waiting so impatiently for this moment. It is time we finally talk, Verona of Felkiern. I know I seem way too excited, but I have seen your past, your present, and the woman you are yet to become. I wish I could express the feelings I have for your future self, but I can not say too much. So I will say what I can."

Verona swallowed the heavy lump in her throat and closed her eyes, feeling the pressure on her shoulders. With a deep breath in, she summoned all the courage she needed and opened her eyes once more. "So I guess I will live longer than a couple more months then, huh?" she said shakily with a joking tone.

The woman laughed with that sultry voice. "There are many more months in your future, Verona of Felkeirn, and very exciting ones as well."

Verona smiled softly. "Are you able to tell me much about what is to come?"

The woman frowned slightly, looking lost in thought. "I wish I could say more, though the laws are holding me back. What I can say is that nothing is as it seems, Verona of Felkeirn. Trust your heart, because that will always be right, she is in your heart leading you with every step you take."

Verona reached to her chest, feeling the necklace that hung there right on her heart. Tears pricked her eyes as she smiled, feeling the love bloom through her as she thought of her mother.

The woman turned to Mariam with a sad smile. "Don't be afraid tonight, little one. It will happen fast, but you will feel loved."

She then turned to Daelyn with the same expression on her face. "Destruction paves your future, but do not let it consume you."

She then looked towards Mav, eyeing him for a moment before looking between him and Verona. She blushed, knowing the woman knew of that moment in the tent. With a tight set of lips, the woman looked as if she was lost in thought. "Forgiveness is what you need to break the chains that bind you to your past. You are not alone. Lean on those who hold you tight. Trust them, for they are the ones who hold your key to Salvation."

She then turned to Calder with a warm smile one would give a friend. "It's too early to give you anything else, Calder. I will see you in a few more weeks."

She looked at the five of them. Silence echoed through the room for a few heartbeats. "The queen knows who you are and that you are in her kingdom. She sends an invitation to come to the castle tonight. Not everything is what it seems to be. Trust yourselves tonight. Listen to your heart and mind, for it will be the truest thing amongst those halls."

Unease filled the veins of Verona and her crew; they all looked between themselves with worry plastered on each of their faces. Though what concerned Verona the most was the recent invitation. The queen knew who they were and wanted to talk to them. Verona would be lying very clearly if she said she wasn't nervous at all. She was going to be face-to-face with another royal, and she didn't want it to be anything like the last time. Her mind was also gnawing on the thought that tonight would be nothing but dangerous and she didn't know what to do with that knowledge.

With an audible swallow, she thanked the woman before her.

She smiled that sickeningly sweet and flirtatious smile at Verona. "I will see you again, Verona of Felkeirn. I cannot wait to tell you what I can when that day comes."

The smoke that bellowed lightly around the ethereal figures grew thicker as it wrapped around their bodies, making them disappear into the white mist.

After they left the magical stone room and walked back into the alleyway, it felt like hitting a brick wall. Every inch was filled with magic, so much so that it had started to intertwine with her very being. It felt like a drug running through her system, and stepping back into a world without it made her skin itch, her fingers twitch, and her teeth start to grind. They all walked back to Calder's small cabin to talk about what was to come, but lying by the front door were five golden papers with elegant handwriting. Those had to be the invitation the woman was talking about.

There was a royal celebration being held at the castle tonight for the festival, and the five of them were among the very few who were invited to be there. Verona's face blanched as she read the words over and over again. She wasn't going to make a fool of herself this time. She needed more than a stolen dress, desperation, and her anger. Most important of all, she needed more than a fragile plan. She needed confidence, grace, and just a little more luck to survive through the night.

With the little coin she mucked up, she and Mariam walked to a shop to buy a couple of elegant gowns for the festivities that night. The clothes they had been wearing from their adventure were now worn, stained, and torn. They were nowhere near suitable to be in the company of the queen and her royal guests.

That's how Verona found herself amid an endless sea of colorful dresses being suffocated by all the layers of silk. It didn't take long for Mariam to pull out a dress with a wicked grin. The sight of it made Verona stop breathing for a heartbeat; it was nothing short of beautiful. The colors mimicked the sunset with its oranges, yellows, reds, and even dark blues blending together in a jaw-dropping display of fabric. The silk and tulle were thin, sheer, and draped over the frame loosely. A large slit in the skirt traveled up to the upper thigh. What looked like sleeves draped loosely over the arms, leaving the shoulders bare. It seemed scandalous to wear such a dress, but Mariam would pull it off quite well, and Verona wouldn't doubt that Daelyn would have quite an interest in such a scandalous piece. Verona smiled at Mariam and nodded. With a cheerful giggle in response, Mariam walked away to buy the dress.

Verona spent a little more time looking for the perfect dress for herself. There were too many to choose from, way too many to even look through. Every dress that was there on display was unique in its own way. She almost thought about giving up until she found a deep red dress hidden in the back. The top was a normal corset with a ribbon tied in the back. This dress had no sleeves and bared everything above her chest. The skirt was large and thick with layers that fanned out at her waist. She loved the dark red and knew this dress was the one she would wear.

It wasn't long before both women were walking out of the store. The shop owners' workers would deliver the dresses to Calder's house later in the day. So, while they waited for them to arrive, they headed back to begin the lengthy process of getting ready for tonight.

As they walked through the door, the three men were crowded around the table talking. They smiled and waved at the women as they entered the house and paused their conversation. Verona gave them a worried look, but Calder walked towards them.

"I suppose you two would love to freshen up for tonight. You are more than welcome to use my private room on the right, and I also have a guest chamber on the left for the others to use, " he said with a small smile.

"Thank you. We won't take long, it's only a few hours until we have to leave." Verona's nerves were shaken as she thought of it again, though she didn't let it show.

She quickly walked to his room, entered the bathing chamber, and poured the already waiting hot water into the tub. Quickly, she stripped down and stepped into the scalding water. Her eyes rolled back, and an exhale crossed her lips as she relaxed into the bath. The hot water soothed her aching muscles as she lay there with her eyes closed. She felt the time pass by as she lazily lay there in the cooling water. It wasn't long until a knock on the door told her it was time to step out. With a towel wrapped around her body, she opened the door to find her dress ready for her. She smiled and got to work getting the dress on. Halfway through, a maid entered the room and helped her tie the back. In no time at all, she was ready. Her hair was brushed and dried, makeup was applied to her face, her dress was properly tied tight, and now all she had to do was wait. She did not like to wait, all she wanted to do was pace the room anxiously. With a huff of breath, she sat down on the bed. That's when the door to the room creaked open, making Verona jump off the bed. There, in the doorway, was Mav. He looked as shocked as ever as he stood in place staring at her.

"I didn't realize you were still in here. I'll find somewhere else to go, then, " he mumbled, dropping his gaze to the floor.

Verona sighed as she crossed her arms. "Wait, Mav. I was just about to leave, so you can have this room. It's nice that you've finally decided to talk to me again." Her lips were drawn tight in a scowl.

He looked back up at her face, his eyebrows knit tightly together in frustration. "A lot was going through my head. There always is, Verona. You know how much of a mess I am from my past. I just couldn't handle what you said to me, and when that woman said to let go, I knew the right thing to do was forgive you."

Verona took a few steps forward. Her eyes were full of sadness. "You have forgiven me, but you have yet to let me in, Mav. There's much that I don't know about you and your past. If you would just let me in, I would still be there for you."

Mav filled the gap between them. He was so close to her she could feel his breath against her skin. "There's so much I want to tell you, so much I need to tell you. Though our mission has to come first." He closed his eyes, his face twisting as if he was in pain. "And, Verona. I want more than you just being here for me, I want everything from you. You, Verona, are my answer. The one I've been looking for, the one I've been wishing on stars for. You're the one that makes this crazy life just make a little more sense. You're the one that I've spent years looking for, and I would be crazy to let you go again. I was a fool that night, and I have regretted it every night since then. I would try to go to sleep, but when I closed my eyes, I saw that moment behind my eyelids. I won't wrong you again, Verona."

She looked up at him, her eyes full of tears threatening to escape. She was relishing the moment before her, though she couldn't help but mourn for it too. "Mav, there's a part of me that's afraid that I'm too broken to love. I feel like I've been through hell and back again in only a few months, and I've been so focused on our cause that I feel like my brain is solely full of revenge and nothing else. There's nothing that I wouldn't do to be with my parents once more. I feel like nothing makes sense in this world anymore, except for you"

He reached an arm around her waist, pulling her into a hug. "I was an outcast in my family of nobleborns, that's how I found myself on Death's Skull. I felt those same emotions, though I felt them even more when I saw my entire family get murdered right in front of me. My sister was the only one I was close enough with to write to. However, on that fateful night when I heard her call my name in her final moments, my heart died with her. I wanted nothing more than revenge; my whole life mission was to find those men. It took a while, but I finally healed my heart, and after those words that woman spoke today, I know that I need to face my fears." His eyes wandered down to her lips. Heat simmered in his gaze before those wanton eyes met her. "I learned that I am not afraid to burn, so douse me in your fire, little flame."

They locked eyes for a few heartbeats. Her lips parted, and that was all the invitation he needed as he leaned in and kissed her.

The rest of the time flew by with Mav occupying her mind. She relished the quiet moment they had in that room; she couldn't help but smile thinking about that kiss. It was all that consumed her mind, and before she knew it, they were leaving the house, dressed up and ready to meet the queen. Her mind was buzzing with so much happiness that she couldn't focus on the nervousness that once invaded her every thought.

Together, the group came to a large set of wooden doors being guarded by two men wearing a special set of armor that was fully black and trimmed with golden edges. Calder, who was in front, handed over five invitations to the guards. They quickly looked over them before opening the doors. The first thing they saw was the courtyard filled with beautiful greenery, flowers, trees, and wildlife; split by a stone path that ran all the way to the castle. A small pond filled with flowering lily pads was nestled into the corner between a bed of magnolia trees. Splashes came from the water as many small creatures played on the edge of the pond. The crew slowly walked down the path, taking in the sights. They suddenly came to a halt as they came to a set of stairs. Verona's eyes followed them and landed on a woman who stood there at the top. She knew by the look of her that she was none other than the queen of M'Ralz. She wore a dark blue flowing gown that hung loosely on her figure. An inch of fabric held the dress up on her shoulders. Small silver speckles scattered across her dress made it look like the winter night sky. Her hands were laced together as she looked down at them with a warm and inviting look.

"Hello, my darlings, " the woman said with a smile. Her voice was intoxicating and sultry. Welcome to my home."

Chapter Eighteen

The events that followed after meeting the queen were a whirlwind for Verona. She couldn't wrap her mind around the idea of standing there and talking to her. The queen of M'Ralz was one of the most talked-about royals for her kindness and for being so down to earth. She was loved by so many, and she embodied every positive word that was spoken about her. When she wrapped her hands around Verona's, she felt every nerve calm in her body, and the anxious feeling rushed out of her bloodstream. She even found herself swooning over this beautiful queen.

She couldn't stop her eyes from roaming over her features. Her face was a perfect heart shape, framed by beautiful flowing locks of strawberry blonde curls that didn't have a single hair out of place. Her lips were tinted a silver color to match her starlit dress, though they were full and had a pronounced cupid's bow. The tip of her nose was daintily curved upwards. Thin, manicured eyebrows framed a wide set of doe-eyes with dark, full lashes. Her eyes were the color of an iced-over lake that was frozen in time. Verona could tell there was so much emotion behind those eyes. A thick coating of red blush was powdered across her high cheekbones, evening out her pale skin. She was a petite woman, much shorter than anyone in their party, though her thin frame made her movements elegant in every way they could.

She looked up at them, smiled with her perfectly white teeth, and started to talk to them once again. Verona couldn't focus on anything she said as she was pulled into a lull by the queen's intoxicating voice. Verona had blushed fiercely as they walked away from the queen and into the castle. She awoke from her stupor once she was away from the queen, and shame slowly crawled up the back of her neck.

More guests were pouring in from behind them, so they slowly followed them. The walls were a pearlescent type of stone that sparkled with twinkling lanterns running down every hallway. Paintings of pets, the queen, her friends, and her family were scattered amongst the walls. Banners hung from the high wooden beams that crossed the ceiling. Below their feet on the stone floor was a large, intricately woven rug with a colorful and complicated pattern. The chatter of conversations grew louder as they came upon a large entryway framed by wooden doors. A set of wide stairs led down to a massive ballroom. Wooden arches framed the ceiling above them, holding several glass chandeliers and countless wax candles adorning each perch. More banners hung from the empty spaces with painted golden leaves embellishing the wooden beams and walls that surrounded them. The light of the flame bouncing off the filigree created a gilded shimmer in the air around them. Wooden tables surrounded the outside of the room, leaving a clear area in the middle where many couples were already dancing in their elegant clothes and prime posture.

Verona took a deep breath of relief as she noticed no one was staring at them. Many were too absorbed in their conversations or enveloped in their own little bubbles on the dance floor to even notice her companions and her arriving at the top of the stairs.

She slowly looked over to Mav and Mariam, her uncertainty painted so plainly across her features. In return, they both gave her a reassuring smile, and

Mav reached across to grab her hand. She gave him a curt nod, and together, hand in hand, they walked down the stairs. Mariam and Daelyn followed suit, with Calder following behind them, a wide smile painted on his face.

The sound of her heels against the stairs echoed in her mind, calming her. With one last deep breath in, she looked toward the crowd and steeled herself. Being here was the catalyst, the moment that would change everything, and she was ready for it all to start. With a deep smile that shone bright with excitement, she pulled Mav onto the dance floor and let the night carry her away.

Everything from that moment on felt like a blur to her. She danced, had way too many glasses of the sparkly liquid that was being passed out by the wandering servants, and ate way too many fruits that sat out on the outer tables. She watched Mariam and Daelyn have fun dancing together, though they had danced the way only pirates would, and from that, they had received many looks, but they were too stuck in their own world to even care what anyone else thought.

As time slowly ticked toward midnight and the room became darker, many guests had left. However, those who were left escaped to the courtyard and continued dancing underneath the shifting lights that streaked across the night sky. Verona and her crew decided to stay in the empty ballroom, tired from tonight's events. As they sat beside the table full of fruit, slowly picking at it, a woman with a dark blue gown full of stars walked over to them. They all grew silent as the queen stood before them with that elegant smile framed perfectly by her features.

"It certainly looks like you all had fun tonight." Her smile widened to a grin, showing her perfect teeth. "I am glad. Though this is where our business truly starts. When you are ready to retire from the festivities of the night, let one of my guards know. I would love to talk to you shortly before you retire to your rooms."

Verona perked up at the last words. "Our rooms?" she asked softly.

The queen nodded. "You are my esteemed guests of the night, so because of that, I have a wing set out for you and your friends to stay in so it will be easier to do business in the morning."

Verona's eyebrows were knitted together in confusion. "Can I ask why? I just don't understand how our ragtag group could ever be an esteemed guest of a king or queen."

The queen stepped closer to them, placing a hand on Verona's shoulder. "Word travels fast in this part of Esnia. I have heard of the great deed you have done for the town outside this kingdom's walls, and I wanted to thank you for your heroic efforts. For that, I invited you to my ball and reserved a wing in my castle for everyone to stay and enjoy my hospitality as my thanks to you. Though it is also a selfish reason of mine because I would like to aid you in this fight you have so heroically involved yourself with."

Verona looked towards her friends with wide eyes, not knowing what to say back. Calder stood up with a hand on his heart, and his head bowed. "We give you all of our thanks for your invitation and hospitality. We would gladly accept our rooms for the night."

The queen gave that wide smile to them again. "Great. I will see you all here shortly."

She walked out of the ballroom gracefully with several guards trailing after her. Verona watched her with wide eyes and mixed emotions swirling wildly underneath her skin. She slowly turned toward her friends, her mind racing.

Daelyn looked around at them, with an eyebrow raised and his arms crossed. "Why does my skin crawl around her? I don't like staying here. Something doesn't feel right about this place."

Calder huffed out a sigh. "I have heard nothing but good things about our queen. I don't think we have anything to fear from her. My father was close friends with her parents, and I watched her brothers and her grow up."

Mariam looked at Calder, confused. "Who are your parents?"

Calder side-eyed her. "That's a story for another time."

Mav pursed his lips in thought as he, too, crossed his arms. "I agree with Daelyn. I don't feel great around that woman. She gives me the creeps. Though, a castle has to be a better place to stay than the dump we're staying at. My bed feels like rocks."

Verona looked at them all. "She's the best thing we have to get a winning hand in this fight, so I think we need to stay here."

Mav looked over to her with a nod. "If that is what you want, then that is what we will do."

Verona looked around the room for a few heartbeats, taking in the magnificent sight before her. "I can't lie," she started, still slightly turned away from her friends. "There is something that feels off here. I don't like how I feel, though I can't give this up. She may know something, and I couldn't forgive myself if I walked out now without trying it."

Mariam walked over, placing both hands on her shoulders. "Then we will stay. We will always be with you every step you take."

Verona smiled, placing a hand above hers. She then turned to Mav and grabbed his hand. "I don't want to miss dancing under this beautiful night sky. So let's make her wait for just a few moments."

Mav smiled softly as he took her hand. Together, they walked out into the courtyard and danced among the swirling colors and twinkling lights of the night stars. The only sounds that echoed her mind were the sweet nothings he whispered to her, promises of an endless future filled with many more nights like this one.

Later that night, when they could barely hold their eyes open, they finally walked to a guard and asked to retire for the night. The guard led them through corridor after corridor, going deeper into the castle when they finally stopped at a set of intricately carved wooden doors with golden filigree. The guard that had led them this far knocked on the door. He waited for a faint voice telling him to go ahead before opening the door and letting them in.

Together, they all walked into the large room. Verona looked around, taking in the sights before her. Even though it was a very large room for her own standards, it seemed very homey and familiar to her at the same time. A large fireplace lined the outer wall with a fire roaring steadily inside its small cage. Shelves that were filled with countless books lined another wall. Verona felt the pull to walk over and run her fingers across all the different spines. She wished she could spend hours in this room. Though what caught her attention was the woman lounging in the middle of the room on a silk settee. There was the queen, who had exchanged her dress of a starry night sky for a silken pink robe and held a large novel in her hand. She peeked over the top of the book and eyed them for a heartbeat before placing it on the table nearest to her. She smiled widely as she motioned to them to sit on the several couches around her.

"I hope you all had a wonderful time tonight," she said as she shifted to sit straight up. She waited for them all to sit down before continuing. "There is much more I would like to discuss about our hopeful future alliance together, though it is late at night, and we will have much more time to discuss this in the morning. I figured since you were deemed the savior of one of my towns, you know exactly what is plaguing Esnia. I would love for your friends and you to join me and help me vanquish this evil foe. I know it's quite the task to ask from you, so I will let you sleep on it, but please take as much of my hospitality as you need. I will have my guards show you to each of your rooms. All I ask of you is to please stay in your rooms tonight. I have had some bad guests show up in the middle of the night recently, and I want my guards to be fully aware of any movement that is not my guests' or my own."

They had all looked between each other, wariness was in many of their gazes, though Verona gave them all a pleading look. Mav let out a sigh and nodded, turning away from everyone.

Verona looked towards the queen and smiled. "We would love to meet you in the morning to discuss our possible alliance with you, though, like you said, we are very tired and would love to think about it tonight. We are staying the night here, and we will respect your rules."

The queen nodded, almost as if a sense of relief had washed over her. She waved her hand, and a set of guards walked into the room. There was one for each of them. Together, they all stood up, and Verona wished the queen a good night as she left. They each followed their guards as they were led through a new set of corridors. Her friends fell back a step, Mariam pulling on her arm so she could join them.

"I don't like this at all," Mariam whispered. "Something doesn't seem right. Why are there break-ins in this castle, and why do we have to stay in our rooms because of it?"

Calder hummed to himself lightly. "I didn't hear anything about break-ins. I don't know why anyone would try to break into the castle, no one has any ill feelings towards the queen."

Daelyn side-eyed them all. "Either the queen is trying to cover something up, or something sinister is happening behind the scenes. I think we need to dig a little deeper."

Mav nodded with full agreement, his arms crossed tightly, and his jaw clenched from nerves running high. "There's something not right going on here and I don't like it one bit that we have to stay in our rooms. I feel like a caged Rilasi."

Verona sighed, running a hand through her hair in frustration. "I can feel it, too, but I don't want to lose this chance. Let's obey her rules and stay in for the night. Nothing will happen to us."

Mav, Mariam, and Daelyn looked ready to continue arguing. Just then, the guards stopped in front of a dead-end hallway, and their arguments fell silent. The guards motioned to each of them separately and led them to rooms where they would spend the night alone. Verona looked at them all, pleading with every ounce she could muster with just a single look.

She then wished them all a good night and stepped into her room.

She let out a sigh of content, seeing the large bed in the middle of the room. A lit fireplace took up a large expanse of the outer wall, and next to it sat a steaming bathtub. On the left wall, a couple of bookcases were filled with endless novels. She knew exactly what she was going to do first; she stripped off her dress and stepped into the bath. She sat in content silence, and she felt the time tick by along with the aching muscles of the events of the day. The countless nights she had spent on the hard ground made her back ache, though sitting there in the steaming water made it all go away. She couldn't tell if it was minutes or hours that had passed sitting there in the tub, though when the water had gone cold, she stepped out, throwing on the robe that was laid out on her bed.

With a book in hand, she snuggled into the large bed that was full of pillows and blankets. Her mind drifted off as she read, thinking of the room next door where Mav was sleeping for the night. She wondered what he could be doing at this moment. The curiosity was almost enough for her to get up and knock on his door, but she knew she couldn't leave this room. It didn't take long for the dark blanket of sleep to envelop her.

A loud thud followed by hushed whispers made her bolt awake. She clutched her chest as her heart raced furiously. Her mind felt jumbled as she thought the intruders were in their halls. Verona quietly walked to her door, clutching her robe tightly to her body. Taking a deep breath and holding it, she opened her door. That's when she saw the figures of none other than Daelyn and Mariam at the end of the hall. They each took a different direction, and Verona felt infuriated as she watched them disappear into the darkness.

They didn't listen to her. They didn't stay in their rooms, and now they would be the ones who got them all in trouble. With an exhale of breath that was full of anger, she stormed after Mariam. She tried to catch up to her, but there were so many hallways. She ducked down one only to not find her. She then backtracked to another hallway, but she could not find her again. With each empty hallway, she felt her anger continue to grow. She had to find Mariam before anything serious happened. Her desperation grew quickly as she pulled on her hair. Where was she? Where was Mariam? She wanted to scream, shout her name, ask anyone to help her. Though she could do none of that. A sob rose in her throat, one that was full of helplessness, desperation, and anger. She just wanted to go back to sleep, to forget all this was happening.

Just then, a thud happened down the hall that sounded like a body hitting the floor. Verona broke into an all-out sprint as her anger turned to worry. She had to help Mariam. It wasn't until she saw the scene before her that she screeched to a stop. There, at the end of the hall, was Mariam lying on the ground, frozen in fear. Above her, with a wicked grin and sharp claws aimed to kill, was a Telana. The very beast that they had been chasing all this time, the very beast that had almost gutted her. It was standing here in the castle and was ready to do the same thing to her friend. She wanted to scream, to say anything to help Mariam, but she was frozen in fear amongst the shadows of the hall. She didn't know what to do, and she felt helpless at that moment.

The door behind the beast swung open a little farther, lighting up the scene. A dark figure stepped out, its frame silhouetted by the cloak that adjourned its body. Though as the person spoke, it was a woman's voice. Verona tried to see if she could recognize the voice, but with the panic and fear in her mind, she couldn't do anything but stand there in shock as she watched her friend try to crawl away.

The beast turned towards the woman behind it. "What do you want me to do with her?" it hissed.

The woman crossed her arms, letting out a deep sigh of frustration. "She was listening to our conversation. She knows too much. Kill her." The woman then turned around and walked into the room.

That was the moment that everything felt so slow. The beast raised its hand, and then with one big swipe, it aimed toward Mariam's chest. Though it kept on going, it kept on swiping and slicing her body. Blood was spraying everywhere. The fear on Mariam's face turned to pain as she screamed. Then everything snapped back in place as Verona fell to the floor in anguish. She couldn't do this. She couldn't lose another part of her family. She wanted to crawl over there and hold Mariam, to tell her everything was going to be okay like she did to her.

The creature halted its torture, but Mariam didn't stop her screaming as her body convulsed violently in pain. Verona couldn't keep her screams back as she joined in unison. Her own pain of watching was too much to handle. Mariam's head fell to the side as she panted. She looked at Verona and mouthed at her to run. But Verona couldn't run. She couldn't leave Mariam alone like this. She started to crawl towards her, sobs wracked her body as she reached out toward her friend.

"I won't leave you, Mariam. I won't leave you like this," she sobbed loudly. "I can't do this without you. I love you, Mariam, from now until forever."

Mariam shook her head, her throat raw from screaming, she was unable to speak. She mouthed the word run again. Her eyes widened in fear as the beast stepped away from her and moved toward Verona. Though Verona didn't run from her oncoming attacker. Her mind was elsewhere as she was reminded of a woman with a cloth over her eyes who looked so solemn at Mariam. 'Don't be afraid tonight, little one. It will happen fast, but you will feel loved.' The words were echoing through her mind, over and over again. This is what she meant.

The woman once again stepped out of the room, shocked by Verona's presence. She looked at Verona and then at the creature. "Don't kill that one. I have plans for that one."

She silently wished that wasn't her fate as she lay there only inches away from grabbing Mariam's hand, watching her friend take one final breath. The word 'run' was still on her lips as her eyelids slowly became unmoving, gaze forever fixed on Verona.

Part Two

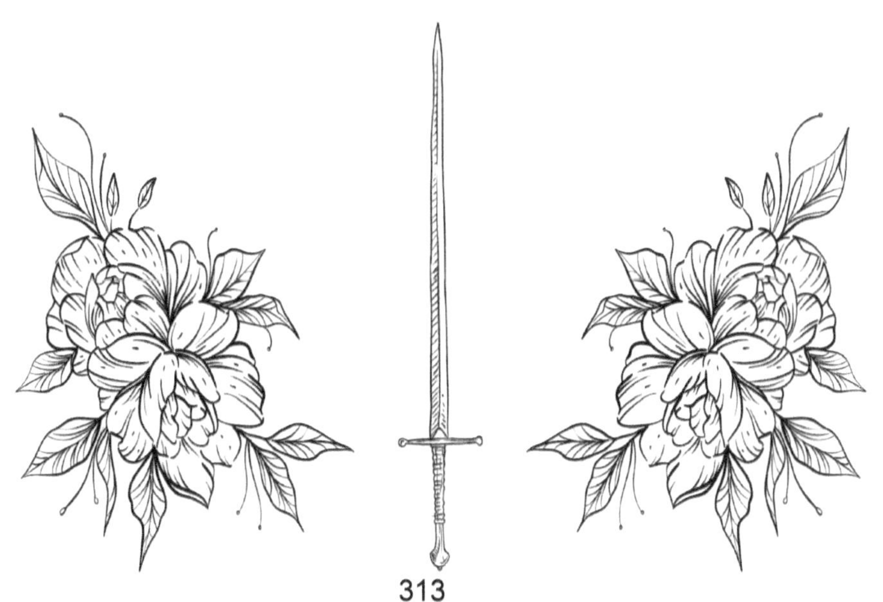

Chapter Nineteen

Verona

There she lay, on the cold dark floor, curled into a ball. Her wrists hurt from the shackles they had instantly put on her wrist. Her body hurt from being dragged down to the dungeon by these beasts. They had gagged her with a rag to stop her from yelling, though she did anyway. Her voice was muffled and raw from the onslaught of her screams. Her eyes were dry because she did not blink. She knew that if she did blink, all she would see in the darkness of her mind was Mariam's dead, unmoving eyes looking back at her. The coldness of the floor bit into her bones; her torn and ragged silk robe was the only thing that covered her body. She didn't care, didn't care at all because she was down here and Mariam was up there all alone. She couldn't do anything to help her, to save her. Verona felt pathetic and weak for just standing there when it happened, for watching it all without even taking a step. She wanted to scream at herself, kick the walls, do something to punish herself; but all she could do was lay there on the cold floor, staring at the stone wall before her, hoping that soon she would wither into the ground and become one with the stones.

Verona didn't know how much time had passed since they threw her in this small dungeon. It could have been minutes, hours, days, or even weeks. She didn't care at all. The only thing she cared about was seeing her friend and getting someone to help Mariam. She needed to get her body to a safe place; Mariam needed to be transported back to Ashfall where she belonged. She needed to get out of this dungeon because she wanted to be the one to bring her back. She needed to carry her back there because it was all her fault. Mariam wouldn't have been bleeding out on the floor above her if Verona hadn't asked her to come on this godsdamn journey with her. Desperation, denial, sadness, and regret were crawling up her throat and flooding her veins. It was all threatening to escape. She couldn't handle it any longer. She pushed herself up and started to bang on the bars of her small, dank cage. She tried to scream, but all that came out was a silent wail of mourning.

The beast that was her guard materialized from the shadows and hissed at her with bared teeth. "Ssstop that noissse and lay down, you mongrel. I don't want to deal with you any more than I have to."

With wide eyes full of rage and panic, Verona kept hitting the cage. "Get me out of here or I swear to the gods, the day you let your guard down is the day my hands will be wrapped around your throat."

The beast snarled in annoyance. "You pathetic little thing, you could never do sssuch a thing. We have torn you apart once. We will do it again."

The sound of clicking heels on the stone grew louder with each step. Verona looked over, hoping for help, hoping it was someone who could let her out. The swish of a skirt was followed by the image of the queen. Her hands were bound behind her back, and a gag was wrapped loosely around her face to stop her from speaking. Telana was holding the chain that bound her hands together, roughly leading her toward Verona.

"My queen," Verona whispered hoarsely. "What have they done to you?"

The queen bowed her head in shame as her eyes flooded with tears. "They have finally captured me along with you. They have sent me down here to give you a message. Your friend can be saved, but you must lie to your friends. Tell them to leave, make up any excuse to get them out of here, and they will save the blonde girl."

Verona's eyes danced around the scene before her wildly as she tried to comprehend the words the queen was saying. "We can't! They are our only hope of getting out of here. If we send them away, we will wither away down here."

The queen furiously shook her head. "If we do not listen to their commands, they will kill us by midday tomorrow. They are having me set up a farewell meeting with them at dawn to get them out of here as soon as possible. You have until then to figure out something to say to them, or else we will both surely be doomed."

Verona looked down at the floor as she wrapped her hands around the metal bars of her cage. "What if we send them away, and they still kill us afterward?" Her voice was nothing but a whisper as anxiety shook through her body.

The queen shook her head. "They will not do that, they have agreed to spare our lives if we meet their demands."

Anger boiled in Verona as her eyes, full of anguish and despair, met the queen's. "How can you know? These are the monsters that have already taken countless lives; many villages and towns have been leveled to the ground by them. Their end goal is to wipe us clean from Esnia, so what is stopping them from killing us now?"

The queen opened her mouth to answer, but the Telana behind her hissed in annoyance and pulled her by the bindings around her wrists. The queen grimaced, baring her teeth at the monster behind her before the gag was placed back on her mouth. The click of her heels once again echoed through the silent chamber as they led her back upstairs, where they were keeping her hostage.

Verona fell back onto the floor of her dungeon cell. These vile creatures were going to use her against her remaining friends to get them out of there. Without her, where would they go? Would they continue with the mission? To Verona, there seemed to be much more going on than she thought. They had the queen captured, and this kingdom was under their control. They could do anything at this point, and that scared Verona. She didn't know what she could do. All she knew was that she needed to get a note to one of her friends to tell them what was going on.

Verona looked to her guard, who was now slumped in a chair, slowly dozing off in the midnight hours. She studied the table next to him, seeing a piece of paper with a feather and a jar of ink nearby. The table was close enough that she could touch it with the tips of her fingers. She knew that was all she needed as she slowly and quietly stepped towards the bars. She pressed her body tightly against them and reached towards the table. Grabbing the piece of paper was easy, though the feather and ink were another struggle. It had proved quite the challenge as she knocked over the ink when her hands landed on the feather. As soon as the jar hit the table, a thunk echoed through the quiet chamber. Verona stood as still as she could, her eyes clenched as she waited. Her guard made a sound of annoyance but didn't wake up as it shifted in its seat, moving to another position before falling back into its deep sleep.

Verona let out a sigh of relief as she pulled both items through the bars. With the limited amount of ink on the quill, she could only write so much; every word she wrote down would need to matter to its fullest potential. She sat there, thinking long and hard about what to write. Minutes passed before she finally set the quill to the paper. When she was done writing, she looked at her words. She closed her eyes, hoping it would help her, help them, and most important of all, make these lands safe again for all those who live here.

Once the words were dried, she folded the paper neatly and placed it in the pocket of her robe. Silence filled the space around her in the cell as she sat on the cold stone floor. It was deafening for her; the silence was too much to bear as her mind was racing, thinking of her friends, of Mariam, of her family, of the queen, of the beasts, and of her dooming fate. She knew she would spend the rest of her fatally short life here if the note didn't work. Her mind was telling her to give up, to accept her fate, but she didn't want to. Her heart was still fighting. It wanted to fight for everything, especially for the life Mav had softly whispered to her. She wanted it more than anything.

Verona slowly fell to the floor of her cell as the weight of the night and lack of sleep rushed over her like a massive tidal wave. She couldn't keep awake any longer, so she closed her eyes to take advantage of the few hours she had left to sleep.

Her dreamless sleep had slowly turned into one filled with nightmares. Wildfires were burning houses before her. She stared at them, dazed as she looked down at her burnt flesh and soot-covered skin. Shock fell over her again as she re-lived all the terrible moments she had endured these last few months. Screams sounded from the houses before her. She ran towards them, even though her body hurt and exhaustion fell over her. She could feel her burnt skin stretch and tear every time she moved. Waves of pain were ebbing and flowing through her, but she kept running towards the houses. However, with every step she took, the houses would disappear farther into the horizon, moving farther away from her. But the screams would get louder with every step until she had to cover her ears to block them out. She squeezed her eyes shut as tears gathered in them.

Verona fell to her knees as she screamed in frustration. She couldn't help everyone, and she was feeling their deaths weighing on her shoulders. As she opened her eyes, she found herself in a room. She stood up, feeling the pain of her skin and body tenfold. Though when she turned around, the pain disappeared as she saw a stack of bodies before her. On the bottom were her parents and siblings, above them was the charred body of the woman who she could not rescue from the town, and above her was Mariam, who lay there with her body in ribbons. All of their heads moved toward her, looking at her. In unison, they all opened their mouths and spoke.

"You did this. Our blood stains your skin. You are the one to blame. We are dead because of you."

Verona backed up, hitting the wall behind her. It was moving. All the walls were moving and they were enclosing her with these bodies before her, getting smaller and smaller. It was all too much for her to bear so she screamed.

Verona bolted awake, seeing only the dungeon before her. She pulled the robe tighter against her sweaty body. Her hands shook violently as her dream wracked her mind; it was all too much at this moment. She felt like that girl at the start of this all again, the one who was weak and afraid of everything. Though she couldn't be that person again, she was more capable, so much more strong-minded, and her body could do so much more than it ever could before. Though she knew she had to be stronger than who she was now to be able to survive this dungeon, to escape from her cage. With a little bit of reassurance from her own mind, she knew she could be that person.

The sound of clicking heels echoed the chamber once more, and the swishing of a silken dress skirt let Verona know the queen was being escorted down once more. Verona stood up, walking to the bar of her cage with worry etched deep into her brows. She wanted to see if the queen was alright, if they had done anything to her yet. Though as soon as the queen turned the corner, Verona could see that she was still unharmed besides the loose restraints covering her wrists and the gag still loosely tied around her mouth. The queen eyed the sleeping Telana, a hint of rage echoing in her eyes before she smothered it and schooled her expression back to fear, so plainly written on her features. The monsters that escorted her down here ripped off the gag, and she hissed at them before turning towards Verona.

"They want to know if you have come up with a plan yet. We will be meeting with them very soon, " the queen whispered to her.

Verona sighed, looking down at her feet before moving her gaze to the queen and the beasts surrounding her. "I have, but I won't do any of it until I have clothes of my own. I will not wear this robe to the meeting unless you want them to be suspicious of what is happening."

The queen turned towards the beasts and hissed out the words she spoke. "You heard the lady, go get her some clothes."

Verona's eyebrows raised in surprise at the order the queen gave the beasts. That was quite some nerve for someone to have who was, in turn, their captive. Though Verona's mind didn't linger on it too long as she watched a set of the beasts wander over to a set of stairs to grab some clothes for her. Verona's eyes then drifted back to the queen, looking her over once more.

"Have they been treating you okay?" Verona said softly.

The queen sighed as she turned towards Verona once more. "They have, I have been kept up in my room to avoid any suspicion, that is the only reason I am not down here with you. After you get dressed, we will walk upstairs and out of the castle to a nearby valley. On the way there, I will tell you everything you need to say. You need to repeat it word for word because that is what they want you to say. They will have a couple of the human guards they have recruited to watch us so we cannot run away."

Before Verona could say anything else, one of the Telanas came out of the shadows with a handful of clothing. Verona stepped back as the creature shoved them through the bars and dropped them on the stone floor. She snatched the clothing before quickly getting dressed in the dark corner of her cell. When she was finished, she nervously wiped her hands over the tunic and pants, making the wrinkles disappear. Verona then stepped towards the bars of her cage, waiting for them to be opened so she could go to this meeting.

Two human guards opened her cell door and stepped in. The first thing they did was snap a pair of shackles to her wrists to stop her from escaping at any point during her time out of her cell. She cursed under her breath for thinking of that. If she wanted to get out today, it would be nearly impossible. These guards were heavily armored, with swords and even crossbows slung over their backs. So, if she even got out of their reach, they could easily put an arrow between her shoulder blades.

Without a second thought, the guard who placed the shackles on her wrists forcefully grabbed her by the arm. His grasp was so tight she gasped in pain, knowing it would bruise. Though he didn't care, he yanked her up towards him without a single thought. She stumbled and yelped as she was thrown up and out of the cage. It took her a few steps to catch herself, though when she did, she lunged at the guard with bared teeth, hoping she could hurt him back. Though the beast that was standing near them grabbed her hair and yanked her back toward its snarling fangs. The beast's other hand reached out, slapping Verona across the face.

"If you try that one more time, I will beat you until you can no longer ussse that mouth of yoursss ssstupid girl, and I will not let it be easy. Do you undersssstand?" The monster before her growled.

Verona bared her teeth and snarled like a wild animal. She wasn't going to agree to any of these monsters' terms, and she would stick by that even if it led to her death. She would never bow to these life-takers, they had done so much to their lands, they had even captured a queen in her very own kingdom.

The beast sighed and threw Verona away from itself. "I wisssh I could be done with you already... but ssshe wantsss you alive, unfortunately."

"Who wants me alive?" Verona growled back.

"The knowledge of who ssshe isss, isss beyond your importance you mongrel," the beast hissed back with an eerie laugh.

Verona wanted to snap back at it with whatever she could think of, any words that would be as vile as the monster before her. Though she kept her mouth closed, knowing it was for the best. She was led out of the dungeon cellar and upwards through many hallways until they were by the back of the castle. There was a set of large glass doors that opened up to a grassy knoll where, in the far distance, she could spot Daelyn, Calder, and Mav standing together. Even from this distance, she could see the tension rising. Worry and nervousness were heavy in the air.

As they walked closer, the queen told her everything she was to say to them. Before the men could see, the human guards behind them quickly got rid of Verona's iron restraints that once donned her wrists. Verona felt as if she wasn't fully in her body, as if she was watching herself walk toward them with slow steps. She wanted to run to them, to tell them that she was a captive, that the beasts were in this castle, and that they killed Mariam. However, as soon as she took a step out of line, she knew she would be dead as soon as she was back in that cold cellar.

Verona watched as Mav turned, finally noticing them coming up. She watched as relief flooded his face, watched as Daelyn stood there with worry still plastered heavily across his face, and watched as Calder looked between her and the queen with confusion in his eyes.

She looked towards them all, tears pricking her eyes. She knew what she had to do now, though she shoved it down, placing a mask smoothly over her features.

"I am glad we all are here, there is much we need to discuss to finally wrap everything up," Verona said flatly.

Daelyn looked towards her, anger boiling in his eyes and lips tight. "Not everyone is here, Verona. Where is Mariam? Why hasn't anyone seen either of you this morning? I haven't seen her since last night."

Verona looked away, the memories of the night prior coming back felt like a slap to the face. The tears threatened to escape once more. She let out a sigh, turning back to them. "We had a break-in last night, and Mariam was unfortunately killed by our intruders. She didn't listen to our commands telling her to stay in her room, so she brought her death upon herself."

Daelyn looked at her with wild eyes. He threw his hands up with a yell of frustration. "That was your friend, Verona, and you act like it's nothing for you. You're not the same person. I know it has to affect you somehow."

Verona looked toward the group and away from Daelyn because all she could see was Mariam in his eyes; all the love and hope for an unending future danced in his vision, and she couldn't stand it. "I also talked to the queen this morning, and we have come to an agreement. There is no threat to us. I thought there was a threat to the lands when it has only been a very dry season for us. It has only been heavy wildfires that are impacting our lands."

Mav looked at her, his eyebrows scrunched, and his jaw hung loose. "A wildfire doesn't almost gut you, Verona. We can fight this together. We can work through this outside of this kingdom. We don't need any royals to back us. Just come with us and help us."

Verona shook her head. "I will be staying here. I have found a home here. I am sorry I have dragged you three away from your lives, please go home and forget about everything I have put you through."

Calder looked at her incredulously but kept silent throughout the conversation.

Mav walked up to her, grabbing the back of her neck and pulling her in closely. "Please, Verona, tell me what's going on. I want you here with me. I want to be by your side for eternity. I need you with me. Please just tell me what is wrong, little flame. You aren't acting like yourself."

With a quick flick of her wrist, before she pushed him away, she placed the note she wrote in the dead of night into the pocket of his pants. "Mav, I don't want you anymore. You were just something to keep my spirits high. I am too broken for you, and you are too broken for me. I don't want you the way I made it seem, you were only something for me to use."

He stumbled back, wincing. "Why would you do this to me again? I thought you truly meant it. I thought we could be together. I thought you wanted me."

She wanted to scream at him, to tell him that she wanted him, that she didn't want him to leave. She wanted him to wrap his arms around her to tell her it was going to be alright, to wipe away all the sorrow and pain she endured in one night alone. But there she stood. As she watched him walk away with hurt written across his face, her heart shattered into piece after piece with each step he took. In silence, the other two walked away. Daelyn shook his head clearly in anger.

When it was just Verona, the queen, and the guards, she let her shoulders slump feeling so helpless, so alone in this battle that was her life. The queen relaxed too, as she knew her life wasn't on the line anymore.

"Now that they are gone, we are safe for now," the queen sighed.

The guards behind them laughed wickedly at their fragile reassurance about their fates. "Now that they are gone, we have all the power, the fates are now in our favor."

"The fates will never be in your favor. As long as I am around I will make sure of that." The queen turned around without even a glance at the wretched humans that were now leading her back to her dungeon cell.

Verona sent a prayer to the gods that Mav would check his pocket and read the note that she slipped in there. Her life depended on it. When he did, she would soon be free of the prison that was this wretched castle. She had to be saved, if not by them then by herself.

Chapter Twenty

Mav

Mav had been in a perpetual state of anger ever since that fateful morning a few days ago, and because of it, he had been constantly drunk. Even though the alcohol helped fade his memories for a brief amount of time, his mood never shifted from being royally pissed. He was setting a personal record for the number of taverns he was getting kicked out of as he slowly stumbled his way down south. The damned man, Calder, in his stupidly shiny armor, was following every step of the way. Everyone tried to keep a wide berth from the angry drunk, though this man kept a short leash on him like a rabid beast that he was trying to keep from attacking anyone. He could see the apologetic looks Calder was giving to the patrons who frequented the taverns as well as the owners behind his own back. He would have snapped at him if he didn't know they sorely needed the apology.

Verona would have thought him a fool at this moment, but it was her who made him a better man. He wanted to help her in the beginning, wanted to see that broken girl who he had caught in the alleyway sobbing be the great woman she was becoming. His help had quickly turned to admiration seeing her bloom. In the end, he knew he couldn't help himself as he tumbled down that hill into full-on love. He was a damned fool for that. All he got was a slap to the face in the end. He should have seen that she didn't want him, that he was just a plaything to her. He was kidding himself if he thought someone like her could ever love someone as broken and damaged as him. He should have known.

He looked down at himself as several barmaids wrinkled their noses in disgust. He was wearing the same clothes that he left M'Ralz in. His tunic was stained with puke, his cloak was torn, and his trousers were stained with dirt from the nights sleeping on the cold dirt. He drunkenly mumbled out a 'sorry' as he turned toward his bag. He got a room this time, thanks to Calder's pleading. Where did he place his room key? He was mentally kicking himself for losing it already. All he wanted to do was change out of these disgusting clothes. After rummaging through his bag, he checked his trouser pockets. In one of them was a note; he was confused by it. He didn't place any notes in his pockets. Mav stood up and felt them again, finding the key in the right pocket. With a lazy smile, he held it up to Calder who in return shook his head. Though most of his attention was on the note.

"What is that paper?" Calder asked.

Mav shrugged without a reply. Though when Calder went to reach for it, Mav snapped out his hand, grabbing it. He wanted to read it first. With an annoyed exhale, Mav shoved the note back into his pocket and started to walk to the stairs. He stumbled upstairs, barely finding his room and expending too much effort to unlock it. He rubbed the heel of his palms into his eyes, hoping that it would clear some of the blurriness in his vision, but to no avail, so he stumbled into the spinning room.

This state he was in became all too uncomfortable in only a matter of moments. His stomach was making its way up his throat; he felt sicker with every step. He was used to being on a boat, feeling the unyielding movement of the ship on the water.

Though being constantly drunk for the first time in forever was now way too much. He reached into his pocket, fingers fumbling for that suspicious piece of paper. He slammed it against the dresser with a little too much force, though he didn't care about it at that moment.

Mav stumbled across the room and towards the bed, where he flopped onto it. He planned to take off his shoes and clothes when he lay down, but as soon as he felt the warm bed under his body, his eyes fluttered closed, and he quickly drifted off into a dreamless sleep.

⁘

The stream of sunlight through the open windows awoke Mav in the late morning hours. With a groan, he picked himself up, eventually moving to sit upright on the bed. He rubbed his eyes with the palms of his hands, trying to wake himself up more. As he looked up towards the ceiling, a throbbing headache echoed through his skull. With a grimace and clenched eyes, he looked around himself. The first thing he noticed was the puke-stained bed, and he sighed once more. He looked down at himself, still wearing the clothes that were weathered from the many days on the road. Mav wished he had been able to remove them last night; he felt disgusting just sitting in them now.

With a grimace of pain, he pushed himself off the bed and towards the door. As he opened it just a crack, he popped his head out and looked around. Right away, he noticed a maid just down the hall. He waved to get her attention.

She quickly walked down the hall towards him. A look of annoyance was visible for just a heartbeat before she smiled at him. "What could I do for you, sir?"

He smiled back, way too sweetly for the amount of pain he was in. "Could I get some warm water for a bath and some opium and vinegar for a headache I have?"

She nodded. "I will fetch those items right away for you, sir."

He gave her a curt 'Thank you' before closing the door. He walked over to his bag and pulled out a new set of clothes. He set those aside on top of the dresser, along with a towel from the drawer and a bar of soap that was also found in his room. Once he was done, he opened the door once more and saw the maid just down the hall with the items he requested. With another 'Thank you,' he quickly grabbed the items and started to set up his bath in the tub that was on the far side of the room. Once he was stripped naked, in the bath, and relaxing, he applied the liquid medicine on his forehead. He sat there in silence and waited for his headache to go away.

Once he felt slightly better and the water was way too cool for him, he stepped out of the bath. He walked towards the dresser and wrapped the towel low on his hips. He went to grab his clothes but noticed the folded paper first. It was the same one that he had placed there last night, the one he didn't remember having at all.

With a confused expression, he slowly opened the paper and read. His confused expression morphed into denial as his eyebrows knitted. Though, another read-through caused his jaw to hang loosely in worry and sadness. He rubbed his eyes, not wanting to believe the written words before him, so he read them once more:

Mav,

Everything I told you was a lie that the beasts made me tell. The very same monsters that are ruining our lands have the queen locked in her room and me down in the dungeons. They hurt Mariam badly; they say she can be saved, but I fear that she has passed.

They have promised to spare my life for lying to you, but I cannot promise that agreement will last forever. I will not force you to come and save me, as it would be a death sentence for the three of you. I will try to get out by myself if I can, but we must still go through our mission; we need to get them out of our lands and save Esnia. We cannot defeat these creatures alone, we need an army.

Forever yours,

Verona

Mav quickly threw on the fresh clothing he had set out along with the shoes that were sitting on the side of the bed. He threw open the door and walked quickly toward the room next to him. He started banging on the door, needing to talk to Calder now.

"Calder!" Mav yelled into the wood door. "Wake up now! I need to talk to you!"

The door swung open, revealing a very unamused and slightly irritated Calder. He sighed and closed his eyes at the sight of a wildly untamed Mav before him.

"What is it this time, Mav?" Calder said, walking back into his room with the door wide open in invitation.

Without a word in response, Mav handed the note over to Calder. As soon as it was in the other man's hands, his mood instantly changed to worry and then to curiosity.

He looked up at Mav with a raised eyebrow. "Is this the paper you found last night?" Calder asked.

With only a nod in response, Calder looked back at the paper and started to read. It had taken him a couple of times over to read it as well. He knew Calder didn't believe the words before him, the ones Mav also saw. He knew Calder felt just as much of a fool as he did reading the words over and over again.

Mav paced the room nervously with a hand running through his hair. He felt frustrated beyond belief. He wished he had pushed her more, wished he had demanded to stay, wished he had said something about the bruised and reddened wrists he had seen on her. He was kicking himself over and over, wishing he had not made such a large mistake. If he had done something differently, maybe talked to her that night, invited her to sneak over to his room, or even told her that very morning that he thought she was lying, maybe something could have been changed. Though he did none of those things, and now she was in a cell locked up with beasts doing gods knew what wicked things to her, and he was the damned idiot getting drunk over hurt feelings.

They had to do something, they had to do anything in their power to get her out of there before they did something terrible to her. The beasts had made her lie to them, made them leave to get them off their land, to disband, and to destroy their rise of power. No lying words would stop them now; they knew the truth and it was time to do something about it.

Calder looked up at him with knitted eyebrows and eyes full of uncertainty. "This is her handwriting?"

Mav nodded. His arms were crossed, though he continued his pacing. "Yes, it is. I've seen her write a time or two, and it looks too similar to be anyone else. We need to do something to get her free. What do we need to do to accomplish that?"

Calder walked away, still looking at the note. He sat down on his bed and rubbed his chin as he thought quietly for a few heartbeats. He then looked over to Mav, who still stood at the doorway of the room. "Close the door," Calder said quietly.

Mav closed the door before walking over and standing by the foot of the bed. "Do you have an idea?"

Calder huffed out a sigh as he set down the note. "You broke ties with the Southern King, The

Queen of M'Ralz is being held captive in her own castle... There is a Northern King. Verona believes the only way to stop these beasts is to gather an army. We could talk to the Northern King to see if he can lend us his. If not, it's up to us to rally the people of the smaller towns. Those who have witnessed the burnings, the ones who have lost everything, the ones who seek justice, just like our friend who lost her family. There are more out there just like her. We just need to bring them to the cause."

Mav nodded, the most determination that he ever felt running through his body. He would crawl through Azarath to get Verona out of the damnation she was in now. He would do anything for her, and now was his chance to do just that. He walked over to the door, opened it, and looked back at Calder with a wicked grin. "So, what are we waiting on, then? Let's do this."

Chapter Twenty-One

Verona

She had spent the past week in the dank cellar in excruciating pain. They had hit her multiple times and flogged her back several more. She had wounds trying to heal from the times the beasts had come in and tore at her flesh. Her days were spent in a living realm of Azarath with the torture they were putting her through, and her nights were filled with endless hours of excruciating pain. She wished they killed her alongside Mariam.

Some days, they would try to get information out of her, asking what she and her friends knew, what they would do next, and what their end goal was. She couldn't give them answers, wouldn't give them what they wanted. She would let them torture her to death before they got anything out of her. When days like that would pass, she knew the next day there would be no food arriving for her in retaliation. Though she couldn't care less.

The food they gave her, on the days they blessed her with it, consisted of stale loaves of uncut bread, almost rotten vegetables, cheese that should have been thrown out many days ago, and meat that was surely beyond edible. Though it was horrid, and she wished she could have gotten anything else, she ate it anyway. She knew she had to eat to be able to see her friends again. She had to eat to regain any strength she had lost, and she had to eat to get out of there. Every moment she was alone, she was coming up with any plan she could to escape, any way she could be free from this torture.

For days, it seemed as if it was impossible. There were guards by her cell bars every minute of the day if they weren't inside beating her. They made sure nothing got inside the cell that she could make into a weapon. So, the plates that the servants would bring her food down on would not make it into her cage. Instead, they threw her food onto the dirty, musty floor of the room that she now lived in. She had to grab it before the starving vermin that skittered amongst the shadows of the dungeon could take a bite. On the days she didn't get any food and she saw them inside her cell; she couldn't say the thought didn't cross her mind to grab one and eat it. Though she felt pity for the starving little animals living amongst her, she was no better than them. They were the same amongst the shadows, two hungry beings doing their best to survive the day.

The only thing that did make it into her cage every day was a bucket of water. There was enough water in there for her to survive, and that very same bucket, after it was empty, was to be used to relieve herself. It would always be taken out of her cage in the morning and replaced with a new one.

It was at the end of the week when things around her small, empty cage started to change. It was the middle of the night when the shouts of guards had awoken Verona from her rare few moments of sleep. The sounds of countless footsteps echoed off the stone walls, casting a loud and sharp sound around her. Verona bolted up, shuffling herself to the back corner of her cage. It was earlier that day that they had started to carve pieces of her flesh from her body. She hadn't thought she could live through another session of that. She was terrified that was their reason for returning a second time that day. However, when they passed her cell, not paying her any mind, and dumped a skinny boy into the cage next to her, that was when she knew they weren't down there for her. It was the first person she had seen besides the guards or those terrible beasts. As soon as the guards locked the cage and left, Verona moved over to the bars that separated their cages.

"What is your name?" Verona asked in a whisper.

The boy whipped his head around, fear still locked in his eyes. He scuttered back as he saw the shape Verona was in, jaw hanging loose in absolute horror. "Who are you? What have they done to you? Are they going to do that to me?"

Verona reached over to comfort him, though when the boy moved back a little more she just grabbed onto the bars. She sighed, looking down at the ground. "I am no one to concern yourself with. I'm sure they won't do the same thing, depending on what you have done."

The man settled down, almost relieved. "I'm glad you're here then. Maybe my punishment will be lighter. I only stole a few pieces of food to try and feed my family. Though in the end, they caught me."

Verona winced at his words, feeling the sting of his relief. He was glad she was here all because he wanted a lighter punishment. After all, they would be dead set on leaving her on Azarath's doorstep, so the fact that they would forget about him and, in the end, let him go with only a slap on the wrist.

She turned back to him with the scorn of fury deep in her eyes. "Well, maybe they will kill me quicker than you'll think, and then they'll be on the lookout for a new thing to play with, just like they played with me," she snapped at him.

The boy floundered for a second, though Verona didn't give him a chance to apologize as she walked back to the tattered furs that were her bed. She placed the better one over top of herself and drifted off back into slumber.

A stream of sunlight filtered in from the staircase on the left, painting the stones around them in a light gray hue and lighting up the dank, musty dungeon just a bit little more. Verona squinted her eyes as she had been used to the darkness that had surrounded her these past few days. She had a far better view now; she could see the rows of empty cells that ran down a large, expansive hallway. At the end, it turned toward another row of cells, which she sure was also empty. Her new companion was still asleep in his cage, curled up atop the threadbare furs of the small bed he had. Verona paced amongst the space she had in her cage, eagerly awaiting the food that was yet to come.

She didn't know how much time had passed when she finally heard footsteps echoing on the stairs before her. Verona paused, staring at the shadow that accompanied the unknown person. Though, as soon as a pair of feet ending in claws came into view, her blood ran cold. Fear and dread hit her harder than being kicked straight in the chest by a Rilasi. All the air escaped her lungs as she struggled to breathe. When she felt like she could move, she crept backward into the familiar corner of her cell. She crouched down, feeling so small, and trying her best to disappear from everyone around her.

Though, when the queen appeared at the bars of her cage, bound with restraints, Verona let out an exhale despite still being terrified of the creatures that led her here. Behind her were two of the beastly Telana's baring their too-white teeth at her. Verona looked around, trying to find anywhere to go, anything that could help her against these monsters before her. Her eyes landed on the boy next to her. She had last seen him sleeping, but he was now wide awake and terrified, backing further into his cell. He looked at her with those wide eyes; even though they were there for her, he was still terrified nonetheless.

The queen unlocked the gate, and the two beasts moved into Verona's cage. They took each step with such lethal grace as they stalked their prey before them. Yellow fangs glinted in the shadows of her cage as they snarled in hunger. Their long claws twitched in anticipation of what was to come. The fur and feathers along the crest of their heads that trailed down their spines ruffled as they crouched before her. The queen stepped into the cage, backing into the far corner and looking somewhat afraid. Verona didn't know why she was in here with them as her eyes bounced between the queen and the monsters before her. The beasts snarled and snapped their jaws, ready to do their leader's bidding and primed to act in their feral ways. The queen held up a hand to them, eyeing the monsters with such suspicion. She then stepped from the corner and towards Verona. She smiled a sad, pained smile, keeping a part of her facing the beasts, not trusting them not to attack her as well. Verona snarled, her teeth bared in defiance to the Telanas that were in there with them. She would never bow down to them. The queen frowned, knowing that such actions would displease the leader who was commanding these monsters.

The queen looked between the Telanas and Verona before speaking. "I am sorry that we are here, though their leader is quite pleased that these Telanas have not quite broken your spirit just yet. They wanted me to come down here to send a message." The queen sighed, walking closer to Verona. "They want you to know that they will eventually win and break you no matter how hard you try to fight against them. So, to show you that, they have sent the Telanas that have recently stepped on Esnia's soil. They are more feral and brutal than the ones you have met so far."

The queen stared at the Telanas as they paced the room; right now, they were starving creatures that were staring at their next meal trapped perfectly in the corner.

Verona looked from the queen to the beasts who stood there so smugly. "You can tell their leader that they will never break me, I will always be stronger than them, I will always be braver than anyone they throw at me. I am the epitome of righteousness, I am the leader of justice, and I am the person that the people will follow when they need hope. I will be the one they fall back on when they see who these things truly are. I am the leader of the broken, of the people these beasts have wronged. They will never outwit me or outrun me. I will be their downfall, their killer. So tell them they can do what they want to me. I will survive until I can see their leader's head on a spike."

The queen bristled slightly, looking down at Verona before a small smile lit her face. "They also told me to tell you that they will miss the girl you were, the one who cried on the ashes of her home, the one that begged for death as she watched her parents die, the one who hid amongst the stares and whispers of the townsfolk, the one who was terrified of fire."

Verona snarled once more, showing her teeth to the queen in fury. She forced herself up to her feet, staring at her eye-to-eye. "You can tell them that they can miss her, but I don't. She was easier to control. She was easier to manipulate. She was easier to kill. This me, the one that stands before you, is their undoing. I will be the one who will watch their leader's life fade before their very eyes. I will remake this world with their death."

The queen stared at her, lips pulled taunt, before nodding. She turned, her heels clicking on the stone as she walked out of the cell, led by a human guard who materialized from the shadows. The beasts tracked her every move as she walked out. When another guard locked the cell doors, he snapped his fingers as a signal to them. They snarled in pleasure as they whipped their heads towards Verona. She stood in defiance, her eyes never leaving the beasts before her. The world seemed to slow down as the beasts lept from

where they were crouched, their jaws wide open and
their yellow fangs on full display. Handfuls of
dagger-sharp claws reached out to her, ready to tear her
flesh apart. The boy next to her screamed in panic as
the scene unfolded before him. Verona slowly lifted her
chin toward them in a show of power as pain erupted
through her. Her world disappeared into a cloud of
feathers as a clash of fangs and claws descended onto
her flesh. She would never give up, no matter how
painful it would get. She made that promise now to
whoever led these monsters, and she would do
everything in her power to see their demise.

Chapter Twenty-Two

Mav

Calder and Mav left the crumbling inn that same day they read those fateful words. Mav's nerves were running higher than ever as he couldn't get her words off his mind, with the feeling of unease running amok in his veins. He couldn't stop kicking himself, either. He blamed himself for not seeing through those lies. They had left her there to endure whatever she was going through, and they blamed everything on her. They were all fools, such damned fools. Despite it all, he was going to right all these wrongs. He was going to do everything in his power to get her out, to apologize to her, and to make her feel safe once more. Even if it meant his death in the end, as long as she was safe and sound, he would be happy.

It only took a few days' travel for them to be on the outskirts of M'Ralz once more. They could see the large, menacing walls on the horizon, the queen's flags fluttering in the wind, a symbol that masked the evil within. It felt as if the sight alone was taunting them, showing them how close Verona was, but also how far she was from their grasp. Mav wanted to run into the kingdom in a fool's mission to rescue her himself. Every ounce of his body was telling him to do so, though her note was the only thing holding him back: the fear of the unknown. There was something that lay in those walls, something that only an army could defeat. So, the only way to get her out was by getting one. And Mav was not an army. His desperation was choking him, consuming every part of his being. It was overwhelming, to say the least. He wanted nothing more than to hold her again, though his hands felt cold and void of her skin, and his body felt the bitterness of the air that surrounded him. So he continued, looking away from the castle and towards the open valley before him.

On the first day of their travels, they went through all their options regarding what to do. It took them a while and a lot of arguments about whether they could trust the Northern King of Fel. Calder had wanted to trust him; he knew that this was the better brother of all the royal siblings and thought they could go to him with anything. Though Mav, on the other hand, was skeptical. He knew Calder had trusted this queen too, and now their group had ended up shattered so easily with Verona trapped in a dungeon by these monsters and Mariam possibly lost to them too. Mav didn't want anything to do with any of these royals anymore, didn't want to even talk to another one ever again. Though he knew gathering townsfolk with only two of them would prove to be a monumental task that would be nearly impossible. So, once again, desperation had won, and now they were two days into a journey to the northern edge of Esnia in search of the King of Fel. The journey there would surely be nothing short of challenging for them. As they would soon pass the flatlands of M'Ralz, they would encounter the dangerous and wild terrain of the mountainous regions of Fel.

The northern folk of Esnia were a different breed of people. Not by looks or by blood, but by strength and resilience. There were no rolling hills, no endless horizons full of farmland, and no banks of soft white sand. Enormous mountains that touched the clouds blocked the horizon of the kingdom of Fel. It was also filled with dangerous pockets of wilderness that only the tough survived in and valleys of dense forests one could easily get lost in. Towns were built along steep mountainsides or IN the deep pockets of valleys between mountain ranges. The people who lived within them were malnourished and often hunted in the wilderness to survive. It was hard to trade outside to other towns of Fel and even harder to trade with other parts of Esnia. They relied on each other within the villages and towns. Mav and Calder would be seen as outsiders, and it would prove to be a challenge to find a place to rest within these small communities if they didn't have anything to give upon entering them. It would be no easy feat for them with this journey ahead, and it would mean they would need to prepare as well as they could for this journey. There was a larger town near the border of the two lands that they would reach by nightfall today. That would be where they would prepare for their journey. There, they would acquire a room for the night, and then the next day would be filled with time to prepare for what was ahead of them. As they walked to their destination, their journey was filled with scattered nerves and heavy silence.

As the sun started to set, they knew they had to be getting close to the town. However, something felt off. A major route to the Kingdom of M'Ralz was empty of any travelers. For the warm evening that it was, it was odd not to see a single soul. Mav could tell it was worrying Calder as well based on his furrowed brows and taunt lips.

Mav coughed, clearing his throat before turning to Calder. "Where do you think everyone is? It's too quiet out here, and I don't like it."

Calder was silent for a few heartbeats as he studied the stone pathway before them. He turned toward Mav; the worried expression hadn't moved from his features. "I do not know where they are, but something's not right here. Prepare yourself. We may be coming into something we do not like."

Both men pulled out their swords as they crept over the hill that blocked the horizon. When they reached the top, they finally understood why no one had passed them. Off on the horizon, a plume of smoke billowed up from the heart of the town before them. Large golden flames danced amongst the houses as they engulfed them one by one.

Mav stared at the scene in horror. "When will they stop this reign of terror?"

Calder's head drooped down to the ground as he squeezed his eyes shut tight. He squatted down, running his hands through his hair. "That's Kingdom Crossing. That's the town we needed to be in."

Mav gritted his teeth and stared at the scene before him. "We need to help them."

He twirled the sword in his hand before sliding it back into the sheath that was strapped onto his back. Once it was sheathed, he took off into a dead sprint towards the horror before them. Calder cursed at his back before pushing up and following him. Together, the two men didn't stop running until they entered the burning town. Many people stood outside, witnessing the carnage before them. Mav looked at all the shocked faces and blank stares as they watched their lives go up in flames. It reminded him of that fateful day, watching from the tavern as soot-covered faces walked into his old town and seeing a girl with red-orange hair walk lifelessly into the center. It felt like he was breaking all over again.

A woman with wide eyes and tears flowing down her cheeks ran up to him; she grasped his arm so tight that he winced in pain. Mav gently peeled her hands away and held her shoulders.

"What's wrong?" he asked the woman, his face painted with worry.

"My daughter. My daughter, she's still in there! We were running out, and I lost her. Please! Please help me! I need to find her! I need to help her! She's probably so worried, she's probably so lost in there!" The woman sobbed into his chest. Her knees buckled underneath her, though Mav held her steady.

Calder walked over to them, placing a hand on her back. "Do not worry, ma'am. We will find her. I promise you that."

The woman sighed in relief at those words. As a man walked up to them and pulled her into a hug, weeping along with her, Mav and Calder looked at each other. Mav nodded and didn't hesitate at all as he sprinted farther into town. Many houses before him were blackened husks of their original selves. Toppled stone cascaded across the streets from the buildings that once stood on the sidelines. Mav jumped over the mounds of stone, trying everything in his might to save whoever he could. Looking up into the sky, he saw the ashes fall like gray-speckled snowflakes. He felt it gather on his skin, speckling across his face and blurring his vision. The smell of burning flesh, wood, and hay assaulted his senses. He wanted to gag at the mix of it all. The screams of the trapped townsfolk were deafening to him, though he followed the sounds. Mav pushed himself faster toward the screams, a laugh bubbling in his throat. In any other situation, he would have been running the opposite way. Though, this time, these screams meant someone was alive.

He ran through streets and alleys, following the young-sounding scream. Mav turned a corner and saw a young blonde-haired girl at the end of the alley. She looked so scared as she huddled in the corner. He went to run to her, but before he could move a muscle, a resounding crack splintered through the silence. Mav backed up as fast as he could as a burnt wooden beam fell and blocked the alley with flames. He cursed out loud; he was so close, if only he had been a few seconds faster. The alley didn't seem like a dead end to him. Mav took off, backtracking. When he came to a crossroads, he took a left to go around to the other side of the alley. He pushed himself harder than he ever had before.

It would have been what Verona would have done. She would have pushed herself to death to save this little girl. He knew the pain she would have been feeling right now, the anguish of a family resigned to their fate. Mav skittered to a stop, seeing an alley to his left where he saw a tiny and afraid girl and sighed in relief.

By the time he carried the girl out of the town, he saw Calder surrounded by more people. Calder was covered by blackened soot and ash from the

destruction of the town. Though he had a wide smile
plastered on his face as many people were thanking him
for his help and crying tears of joy. As Mav walked
closer, silence blanketed over the group of townsfolk.
Only a cry of joy broke the silence as the mother rushed
to grab her daughter.

"Thank you so much. What can I ever do to
repay you?" the woman sobbed in joy.

Mav leaned forward, wrapping the woman in a
one-armed hug. His eyes were closed so tightly to stop
the tears from escaping, his breath still ragged from his
frantic sprint through the town. He leaned back,
looking at the sight before him. "Reuniting you both
was enough for me. It brings me enough joy."

He gave the woman a small smile before
walking over to Calder. He watched as all the
remaining townsfolk looked towards them, waiting for
them to say something.

Mav looked around at all their faces. He saw
the fear, the anger, the helplessness, and the confusion
surrounding everyone. He let out a sigh, bracing
himself, and then began. "We are in the midst of
history that will be told for generations to come.
Today, here and now, we may see destruction. We may
see homes lost, families gone, and a town demolished.
We may look upon this today and think that this is it;

we may feel helpless. Though I assure you, it is not in vain, we must look upon this for what it is. We must not feel helpless and afraid at this very moment. We must take action, fight for our rights, fight for those who have lost their lives, and most importantly, fight for our future. There is an evil plaguing our lands. These monsters are burning our villages, killing helpless families, ruining our livelihoods, and we must do something to stop them! We must stand and fight against this evil! It is time for us, for the farmers, for the townsfolk, for the ones who keep these lands afloat, the ones who keep food on the royals' and nobles' plates. It is time for us to stand against this injustice that is happening to us! It's time for us to make history!"

A war cry erupted amongst the crowd. The very crowd who felt that pain and helplessness now felt empowered, too. He gave them a sense of purpose, an invisible strength, a glimpse of a better future.

Calder looked at him with gratitude, like he was proud of him. Calder turned towards the crowd. "Go, find places to live and rebuild your lives. Many towns still stand strong. Though tell them what we have told you today, spread it far and wide. When it is time, we will send a call to arms, and that day, we will make history. We will make an unstoppable army to combat any force that may come, for we will have the strength of the many, the strength of the opposed. Together, we will prosper in our time of need! We will not bow down to those who try to stomp us out. Most importantly, we will not go down without a fight!"

The crowd before them erupted into a scream of fury. The faces before him were painted with rage, determination, and anguish. Even though they were the oppressed, with their families torn apart and their homes being burned, they still stood tall and proud. These people were ready to fight for what was right, for the justice they deserved. It made Mav feel proud as he watched them leave with what little they had on them. They were such powerful people.

It was that feeling that fueled him to push himself. He and Calder walked through the night as they journeyed further into the mountains. It was a desperate situation they were in and they needed to reach the King of Fel as quickly as they could. They pushed on for days, traversing the wild and rugged landscape of Fel. They traveled up countless mountains, walked in the valleys between rocky giants, visited towns, and traded for what they could. The surrounding air was colder than what they were used to, so they had to trade for fur clothes to keep themselves warm. Their path had already given them quite a scare, as loose stone had collapsed underneath their feet and rocks had tumbled from the tops of mountains. Mav feared that this path, if they stayed on it long enough, would eventually take one of their lives if they weren't careful.

When they were a week into their travels, they decided to stay at the last small village before they reached the Kingdom of Fel. The town was small, with only one inn, a couple of shops, and a handful of houses. The townsfolk had stared at them, as they were not used to outsiders in their village. Not many people would travel this far north, and the Kingdom of Fel rarely had any visitors from any other lands. Even though they were hesitant about Calder and Mav entering the town, once they had traded goods, they offered the two men a room for the night. Though watchful eyes were on them with every move they made. It made Mav's skin crawl, all he wanted to do was leave. Though he was drained from the almost non-stop trek they had made to get them this far, all he wanted to do was sleep in a bed again. It didn't take him long to find his room for the night. As he kicked off his boots and fell into bed, the feeling of sleep quickly dragged him down into slumber.

The excitement of what was to come woke him before dawn. All he wanted was the rest of the trip to come already. Mav wanted to walk into the castle and talk to the king, all in the hopes of finally sending armies out to rescue Verona. Quickly, he slung on a new pair of clothing, his boots, and his furs to keep him warm. As he waited in the bottom part of the inn for Calder to arrive, he watched the sunrise from the windows. Hues of brilliant purple lit up the sky that was once filled with an endless amount of darkness. Soon, the sun peeked over the valleys of the surrounding mountain range, lighting up the town below with its blinding white light as the rays licked the valley below. The town started to awaken with the world as people stepped out into the streets wrapped in thick furs. The sound of howling wind swept through the crack of the door, and Mav could tell that it wouldn't even be close to a warm day today. It didn't take long for Calder to step down from his room, dressed in his furs and ready for the day. After a quick breakfast from the inn, they started on the last leg of their journey to the Kingdom of Fel. They would arrive midday, though it wouldn't be easy. The townsfolk had told them that this last leg would be the most treacherous of the path, and only the strong would be able to make the trip. It was dangerous solely because the Kingdom of Fel sat on the peak of the tallest mountain in Esnia. To reach it as quickly as they wanted to, they would have to leave now. As soon as the sun was fully visible and the sky showed no sign of night, they started their trip to the Kingdom of Fel.

These rumors were proven true as they climbed higher and higher, becoming more tired and out of breath with each step up the rocky slope. The path was man-made, though it sorely needed to be redone as many parts of the path had eroded or disappeared from view entirely. They had made it this far without getting lost due to the wood signs that still stood in place, pointing them in the direction they needed. In some parts, Mav found himself climbing up on his hands and knees from the steep slope they were on; he grabbed onto anything from trees to rocks to pull himself up. All he wanted to do was stop and rest, though the thought of Verona being chained up pushed him on. The thought of the townsfolk who needed their help pushed him on. The thought of the many people who died in this short time alone pushed him on. Every one of them deserved to see this reign of terror come to an end, so he had put one foot in front of the other. He kept going for his cause and was focused on accomplishing it with every fiber of his being.

At that moment, when they were halfway through the day, and all Mav wanted to do was stop, he grabbed onto a stone ledge and pulled himself up. He was tired, his muscles ached, and he was so out of breath. He was curled up into himself, trying to catch his breath. Calder came up behind him, and Mav knew he felt the same way, but he tapped Mav on the shoulder. He looked up, seeing that Calder was pointing at something, and when he looked, he saw the large, magnificent walls that surrounded the Kingdom of Fel. Relief and joy rushed over him like a massive wave swallowing him whole. They had finally made it.

Mav pulled himself up, clapping Calder on the back with a wide smile. "This sight makes it worth it. It's time to finish what we started."

Calder nodded with an equally large smile. "Let's get our girl out and help free these lands."

They both rushed to the guards, who stood by the outer gate of the kingdom. The men in armor nodded, motioning to the open doors. "Come in, you are welcome in the Kingdom of Fel. We have food for sale, rooms for rent, and anything else you might need. Please abide by our rules and cause no trouble."

Mav nodded as he chewed on his bottom lip. "We need to speak to the king. There is an urgent matter at hand."

The guards looked at each other, though they said nothing. After a few heartbeats, one of them looked towards the two men. "I don't believe our king is taking any visitors today."

Mav closed his eyes tightly, sighing in frustration. He clenched his fists tight. "It's an urgent matter. People are dying. The queen, his sister, has been captured. We need to talk to him now."

They looked toward Mav in disbelief at what they heard. Though, as Mav stood before them, not cracking one bit, they knew what he said was true. The second guard stepped forward toward them. "Stay inside our kingdom. I will send word to the king of this urgent matter, then I will find you."

Calder nodded his thanks as one of the guards rushed off toward the castle. Calder and Mav stepped into the Kingdom to wander around, waiting for word. Mav felt useless and impatient as he stood around, trying to kill time. All he wanted to do was talk to the King already. He couldn't imagine what would take so long to set up a meeting. Mav walked around, looking at all the shops and stands in the market not once, not twice, but three times. He wanted to just rush into the castle himself. Mav damned the guard who was wasting his time now. His anger was boiling with each heartbeat that was passing without any word. Just as he was about to throw all caution to the wind and storm in, a familiar guard rushed into the market towards the two men.

"The king will see you now. Come, follow me. We have no time to waste," the guard said, his words now filled with fear and worry.

Calder and Mav rushed after the fleeing guard as he ran through alleys and streets toward the large and looming white castle. This castle was more presentable than the castle of Lo'Kil, though not as fancy and beautiful as the castle of M'Ralz. It was built with white stone and gray banners with green accents hung underneath large glass windows. Pillars loomed large at every corner, touching the clouds above them. They quickly entered the large wooden doors and into the castle. These doors opened up straight into a small hallway and in front of them was an open doorway to a great hall. A small handful of noble men and women chatted amongst themselves, some sat at the long tables that took up most of the space and some stood by the outer walls of the room. Large windows were scattered on the walls, letting in streams of sunlight. Several paintings of the royal family and picturesque mountainscapes were hung in between these large windows.

Sitting on a throne at the very back of the room was the King of Fel. He looked almost bored, but content sitting there with his chin resting on his propped-up hand. Pale skin lay across his features from the lands he lived in, and dark circles rested underneath his pale blue eyes. A crooked nose sat in the middle of his face. His lips were plump with a curved cupid's bow. His face was framed by a set of sharp cheekbones that jutted out and an even sharper jawline. The sides of his white-blonde hair were cut short, though the top was long and pulled back into a small ponytail. He was beautiful in an almost artistic way as if he was carved from stone. His attention was pulled towards them as he saw the guard walk into the room, and his expression perked seeing Calder and Mav. The king stood up and walked towards them, holding out his hand he shook both of theirs, one after the other.

"It is nice to see you both, well and one piece from this treacherous journey you have made to reach me. I hear you come with some very fateful news," the king said as he leaned against a table.

Mav nodded, "I was traveling from the lands of Lo'Kil with several companions. One of them, Verona, had lost her family to a fire. It was her goal to find out why their house burned down and why so many more homes were burning down along with them. We learned that these beasts, called the Telanas, traveled across the sea from Ro'l in search of revenge. What we did not know is that they had a larger end goal in mind and have now captured your sister. Verona has been captured, and her friend, Mariam, was possibly killed in the midst of it all. We are here to ask for your hand in helping us to defeat this evil." Mav spoke to him, the rage and desperation thick in his voice.

Calder stepped forward, pain written clearly on his face. "Your people need your help, and the people of Esnia need your help. If someone does not step in, more people will suffer by their hands, and these beasts will continue to wreak havoc in Esnia. They will find their way here if we do not act soon enough. We will have no more farmers, no more villages, and no more kingdoms."

The king paced around before them, obviously distraught by what he had heard. After a few heartbeats, he looked back towards them. "I cannot say this news does not affect me. It hurts to hear that they have my sister captured. We live by a set of rules and a promise to serve our people and protect them. These beasts need to be punished for their wrongdoings. I will help you in any way I can. So what is it that you need?"

Mav looked towards Calder. He swallowed quite audibly from the nerves running high in him. He turned towards the king. "We need your army. Verona is being held hostage with the queen as we speak. She is inside and sees what we cannot. If she thinks we need an army, then there is a good reason for us to gather one. These beasts are impossible for us to stop alone. We need men. We need trained fighters."

The king paced around them as he thought over his words for a few heartbeats. He looked deep in thought before turning back to them. "I cannot give you my army, for they do not know how to operate under anyone else's command except my own. So I will join your cause, and together we will defeat this evil."

Mav let out a breath of relief. "Thank you, my King. I appreciate your help greatly. There is much we need to do before we are ready. We need to send out notes of warning to all the remaining towns of Esnia and, with it, a call to arms to anyone who can fight. We will spend that time training until the beasts hear our endeavor to stop their plans."

The king nodded in agreement. "I will send out my best riders to deliver these papers. Until then, we will prepare for this war."

Together, these two men who were fighting for a cause and the King of Fel were in arms for what was right. In a matter of weeks, papers filled with warnings and a call to arms were sent out to towns far and wide in the continent of Esnia. Mutters started to rise amongst the lands filled with talk of murderous beasts and war.

Chapter Twenty-Three
Verona

It had been a couple of weeks since that fateful attack. She remembered it all so vividly. The pain still echoed through her body and bones where they were trying to heal. Every noise she heard made her wince and cower; she didn't like being like this. She was stronger than this, though here in this moment; she felt so weak.

The boy next to her tried to comfort her the best he could in his short time there. He had become more sympathetic since that attack and often gave her half of his food when they gave nothing to her. It had been a week since they released him, and his last words to her were a promise to help her get out. The guards had laughed at him for that. They called him a mongrel, that he would never be strong enough to achieve such a promise, that she wasn't even worth the effort. She wanted to strangle these guards for their laughter and abuse. She sent a silent promise up to the gods that they would get what they deserved in the end.

It had also been a couple of weeks since she heard the click of heels against the stone stairs, telling her the queen and her beastly captors were coming down. She thanked her lucky stars that it had been that way. Every time she had seen the queen or the beasts, it meant the worst was about to come, so these last two weeks without them were a godssend.

Verona had spent that time healing, building up her strength, and thinking about ways to get out of the hellhole she was in. She thought about Mav the most; every time she closed her eyes, she saw the look of pain and distrust that had flashed across his face when she lied to him. She hoped he had found her letter. She tried to make it so easy to find. Though a part of her mind told her he didn't. *If he had, wouldn't he have been here by now? Wouldn't he have rescued her? Or worse, what if he had read the letter and didn't find it worth it to even rescue her, and she was stuck here in this cage till her death?* If something didn't happen soon, she feared her death would happen sooner rather than later with the abuse and torture they had put her through. She wanted to be strong, wanted to survive, but it was becoming too much. It was getting harder and harder to hold on.

One morning, when Verona was wrapping cloth around her wounds, a servant walked down the stairs. She whipped her head up towards the sound to see who it was, though she grew even more confused when she saw the large plate of food. It was filled with steaming hot chicken, potatoes, vegetables, soup, and non-molded bread. Verona was wary of the sight before her because she knew something was going to happen. There would be no way they would come with this plate of food for her with no strings attached. She scrambled towards the corner of her cell and wrapped the blanket of furs around her. Something had to be happening, right? Just then, the sound of heels clicking against stone stairs confirmed her suspicion. The queen came walking gracefully down the stairs, her long, dark red dress trailing after her. The dark corset was pulled tight against her body, and the sleeves were draped over her shoulders, leaving her chest an open expanse of perfect skin. Her blonde hair was braided and pulled up into a bun. A mask of apprehension showed clearly on her face, though Verona could see the deep sadness she tried to hide. Verona was nothing short of afraid. The queen was more worried than Verona had ever seen before, and she knew nothing good would happen here.

The queen stopped before her cage with tears pricking her eyes. "I believe you have noticed the gift I have brought down for you." She waved over to the food that sat on the table. "Their leaders have been feeling quite guilty about the way they have treated you these past few weeks, and they wanted to give you something as a little gift."

Lies. Lies. Lies and more lies were all Verona heard. She pushed herself deeper into the corner. "What is the catch here? I don't believe your words one bit."

The queen's eyes shifted toward the shadows in the hall before wearily moving towards Verona. "They just want me to ask some questions. That is all."

Verona snarled. She was getting tired of their games. "I told you, I don't know anything. How would I? I've been stuck in this cage since they made you throw me in here. My friends are probably back to living their lives like they did before they met me."

The queen stepped closer to the cage and grabbed the bars. Her eyes wildly moved to the shadow once more before her voice dropped to a whisper.

"That is where you are wrong, child. They are not living their normal lives. Somehow, they found out about me being captured, my kingdom being overtaken, and the Telanas. Somehow, two of the men from your party have traveled to Fel and talked to my brother. My brother believed them and has now rallied his army against these beasts to take back this castle once more. Papers are being sent through Esnia, calling for arms. Their leader wants to know how they found out about the castle being overtaken. They are displeased and want to know right now, or more harm will come not only to you but to me as well." Her eyes were growing more wild with each passing word she spoke.

She was shocked at first. Mav got her note. He had read it, and he had done something about it. They were coming to get her. They were going to rescue her. Tears threatened to escape as she found the answers to the questions she had been pondering for weeks. She was relieved that these beasts would never get their way. Not this time, nor in this lifetime. Verona couldn't help but laugh at the onslaught of questions they shot at her. She was overjoyed to know she had the advantage over these monsters. She was stuck here in this cage, and she still had the upper hand, she still was the one calling the shots.

The queen's expression cracked as anger shone before a blanket of sadness once more covered her face. "Why do you laugh at my words? They will harm me if you do not give the answers now!"

Verona stood up, walking to the set of bars. Her body was stiff, worn, and in a tremendous amount of pain, but there she stood with defiance in her eyes. "I am sorry, but I cannot give you such answers as they are the cards up my sleeve. You can tell them that I will be better and smarter than them, and I will always have the upper hand in this game, even from this cell. I am Verona of Felkeirn, I am the leader of the people, the savior of the broken, and I will be the death of their leader."

The queen bared her teeth at Verona. "You will be the death of me, child. I hope your pride is worth it all. I hope you can live with yourself knowing you have the blood of a queen on your hands."

Verona sat down, wrapping the furs around herself once more. "I am sorry that not telling you will lead to the first amount of harm done to you, but these answers only belong to me. I have a promise to keep to people like me."

The queen threw the platter of food onto Verona's cell floor in a rage. She stormed out and walked up the stairs without a single look back. The guards stood by Verona's cage once more, though she didn't care to pay them any attention as she grabbed the food on the ground because she hadn't eaten in days.

Chapter Twenty-Four

Mav

Mav and Calder had spent the last couple of days in the Kingdom of Fel. They filled all their waking moments training with their soldiers, learning their ways of fighting and the style of their fine movements on that battlefield. It was harder for Mav to learn the sleek moves and precise steps of a soldier's way of fighting as the style he learned on Death's Skull was ingrained into his very being. The pirates' way of fighting was blunt, forceful, and rash movements. Mav had learned that was not the best way when he used them on the battlefield and had ended up on his ass more often than not. It frustrated him to no end, though he eventually learned a mix of both fighting styles and became of force to be reckoned with on the training grounds.

When they weren't practicing on the snowy fields, they were in the king's war room, going through every choice that could be made in these next few days. They went through every way they could fail from this moment on, every success they could have, and every move that could advance them further. But the only thing that was on Mav's mind was Verona. He wanted to get her out as soon as possible, and because of that, he was there for every meeting. He advocated the best he could for her release, though every time he spoke, they had shot him down. It would be too risky, they said, especially during battle. Though they would do everything possible to get her in the end. Mav was growing weary at the thought of her staying any longer than she needed to; he just wished it was that moment already. So, instead of lingering on the pain of it all, he pushed himself into training at all hours of the day. He needed himself stronger for that moment, the one where he would get her out. He would fight for her until he couldn't any longer.

At nights, when they sat in the hall amongst the nobles and other guests of the King, rumors would float amongst the small conversations during supper.

Rumors of uproar in towns and villages following the news of the queen's capture, of people foolishly risking their lives to save her themselves, of people leaving their homes for safer grounds, and of those who were anxiously waiting for the call to arms. Some said the leader of the Telanas knew of their plans and that they were furious. Though they had yet to hear any formal declaration of war. It unnerved him that the queen had to sit there without a word as she watched her kingdom crumble beneath her. They were waiting in tense anticipation for that moment when the leader of this catastrophe would finally break. When they would finally raise their sword in declaration. Mav knew it would only be a short time until that moment finally came.

One morning, he woke up feeling off; he wanted to go to the war meeting once dawn arrived, but they wouldn't let him in. He tried everything possible to get himself in there, though when he looked through the cracks, all he could see in that room was the King, his general, a few figures he did not recognize, and Calder. He was confused and hurt, but he was pissed off most of all. *Why was Calder allowed in there and not him? Were they getting tired of him telling them to free Verona? Did they not want him there anymore?* He couldn't figure out why he wasn't allowed in that room, but that godsdamn man in his shiny Daekari armor was. Why was he so important? It frustrated him to no end. And so, without a single thought, he rushed down the stairs and to the courtyard. Several other men were training outside; they all nodded at him, though Mav rushed straight to the man he had been training with this whole time.

Markaal was an older man, and he reminded Mav a lot of his father with his short brown hair, stubbled jaw, wrinkles slowly forming on his face, and stern expression. He stood tall and fought like a beast who had seen many wars. He was a no-nonsense man and told Mav his faults straight to his face after he knocked him on his ass over and over again. Though with each blunt reply of his faults, Mav would get up. Markaal hated Mav at first and thought he was a kid who was in way over his head, though when Mav had shown him how determined he was, the man started to take on all of Mav's training. He taught Mav the secrets he knew and showed him their way of fighting.

He had even given him a sword of his own after they had bonded one night. Mav had told him about being an outcast to his family, watching them die, growing up on a pirate ship, being forced off the ship, drowning in his sorrows, and then finally finding Verona and losing her. Markaal had known his pain as he had lost his child and wife to the fires in a small town bordering the mountain ranges. He had made his journey here and pledged his allegiance to the King. Markaal had guessed this was from something other than human before Mav and Calder had shown up. They both wanted revenge, and that had fueled them both to keep training and fighting until that moment came.

There, in the middle of the courtyard, Mav saw Markaal training a recruit who had come from a small village just south of here. He was younger but full of spirit, though that wouldn't get him anywhere when they would be on that bloody battlefield. Mav prayed to the gods that this kid would be stationed in the back. As Mav walked up, the kid grew skittish and asked Markaal for a break. He had left, skittering off into the armory without a single reply.

Markall sighed at him. "What is it this time, child? Could you frown any deeper? You're scaring my trainees."

Mav rolled his eyes at him, uncrossing his arms and letting out a large sigh. "There was a meeting this morning. I wasn't told about it. I tried going in, and they wouldn't let me in."

Markaal shrugged at him. "I wouldn't take it personally, boy. Sometimes, the king needs meetings without outsiders in there with him."

Mav threw his hands in the air. "Then why was Calder in there but not me?"

Markaal raised an eyebrow in confusion. "Is that so? It's because your friend has a notably famous family. I'm surprised you don't know who you travel with; I was sure a smart boy like you would at least know that."

Mav looked at him with a wary glance. "What do you mean? He's just an adventurer. I don't know how you can get famous for that."

Markaal looked at him with a blank stare. "They're not allowed to fully reveal themselves, but they wear the crest on their armor. He has houses amongst the inner walls of the kingdoms. He can get any meeting with any of the royals whenever he pleases. It's not my place to tell, but maybe it's time to ask who your friend really is."

Mav shook his head in annoyance. This man had to have been playing with him, but he would save whatever Markaal was telling him for later. Mav pulled out his sword. "Whatever. I didn't come for information, I came to train. Pull out your sword, old man, and fight me."

In a matter of seconds, steel met steel, and the sound of metal clanging together reverberated through the silent courtyard.

They fought hard for hours, and as soon as Mav could no longer raise his sword, he knew it was time to stop. He collapsed onto a wooden bench, panting for air. Markaal sat next to him, as calm as ever, as if they hadn't just trained the hardest they had ever trained before.

Mav looked over to him wearily. "How does this not affect you?"

Markaal looked over to him, giving him a sad smile. "It doesn't affect me because I have trained for war. When the time comes, and we are on that battlefield, there will be no stopping, no breaks, and no time to breathe. You will be amongst the throng of our people and the enemies, jam-packed amongst bodies, not knowing who your enemy is and who your ally is. Your body will scream at you to stop, to give up, but your life will depend on you continuing to fight. When you stop, you become the easiest target on that field."

Mav's face pinched with an emotion he didn't know how to describe. Was it pity, sorrow, anguish? He didn't know. He opened his mouth to ask something, to find out how Markaal knew, but just as he was about to speak, the wooden doors of the castle slammed open. Mav snapped his neck at the sound to see Calder walking towards them with a serious look. Mav sighed, closing his eyes for a heartbeat to control his emotions. Just as Calder said a curt hello to Markaal, Mav opened his eyes and plastered a smile on his face.

"What brings you here, Calder? Is the meeting done already?" Mav asked, bitterness dripping from his tone like poison.

Calder sighed as he rubbed his head in annoyance. "I know you're understandably upset, Mav. It was a meeting for only a select few people, but during that meeting, we got a letter that you must see. Follow me."

Without another word, Calder walked back toward the castle, not even waiting to see if Mav followed him. Mav threw his hands in the air in disbelief and annoyance. He snarled at the back of Calder but followed him anyway. His curiosity always got the better of him.

"Will you slow down a bit? It's not like I've been standing in a room all day!" Mav huffed out, trying his best to catch up to Calder.

They were finally inside the castle, though Calder did not slow his pace. He looked back for only the briefest heartbeat. "There's no time to slow down."

"I just have a few questions, that's all! Why were you there but I wasn't allowed? What status do you have that I don't? Who are you, and what are you not telling me? Does Verona know these answers?" Mav yelled to the man in front of him.

Calder abruptly stopped, turning around to face Mav. A few heartbeats of deafening silence passed before he spoke. "She doesn't know, she never asked. There are many things I wish I could tell you, but I run under a strict set of oaths that binds me to secrecy unless times of great unrest run rampant through our world. Those who know me will ask for my service, and that is what the king has done. In a time of unrest like today. So just be patient, Mav, soon all will be revealed."

Mav sighed, shaking his head. Those were far from answers; they only made him more confused. Was Calder some cult leader? Was he bound to a dead person to help some cause? Was he some kind of person from the future? He didn't know how to wrap his head around it all. Though if he said he would learn soon, then he guessed he would learn soon.

The two men walked to the doorway of the war room. Shouting was heard from inside, and Mav could tell one of the voices was that of the king. The two guards that stood by the door nodded to them and then opened the double doors. As the doors opened, they saw the scene before them. Papers were strewn across the floor and table with a large map sitting in the middle of it all with a single note atop it. The king radiated anger as the general was leaning against the table. Other notable figures were also disheveled from whatever had happened. Calder walked to the center of the room, grabbed the note from the table, and handed it to Mav.

With a single look toward Calder, hoping to get any word of what was going on and receiving nothing back, Mav grabbed the note and began to read.

Hello brother,

I have received word that you are raising an army against my captors, and I regret to inform you that every word you have heard is true. However, do not take this letter as an act of standing down. These monsters plan to take Esnia back once more as their blood rite demands. If you do not stand down and let them claim what is rightfully theirs, my life will be taken as a consequence of your actions. Your people will not survive their army. They are bigger than you, stronger than you, and they will destroy you. You must stand down, brother. Bow to them; you will not win against their mighty army. This is your last warning. Please do not kill me, brother.

From,

Vandalia

Queen of M'Ralz.

Mav placed the note back on the table before walking over to where Calder now talked to the King. "How are we going to respond to this?"

The King pulled out a chair and sat down as he stared at the table before him. Heartbeats of silence passed as he sat there staring. He turned to Mav, his face clouded. "There is only one way: war."

The captain of the army walked over to the King. "Did you not read the letter, sire? We do not stand a chance against them!"

The king looked at him flatly. "We will rally anyone to our cause. I will not stand by as innocent people die, as my *sister* dies, if we do not act sooner!"

Calder walked over to the king and kneeled before him. He slammed his fist against the symbol etched on his chest plate and bowed his head. "I, Calder Brannon, Clan Master to the Shields of the Just and protector of the realm, aid your cause. My brothers and sisters, come out of the shadows and join you in war to defeat what plagues this kingdom."

The king stood up and faced Calder, placing a hand on his shoulder. "I accept your aid, Clan Master.

Send what letters you must to awaken your members. We will need all the help we can get."

Calder nodded and walked out of the room at a quickened pace. He was the leader of the Shields of the Just. A clan that Mav had believed was just a tale told to dreamers and children. Though no one knew for sure because of the strong oaths that forbade them from ever saying anything unless it was a time like now. It surprised him, though everything added up: the meetings, the houses, the status. Everything finally added up.

The King stood up, walked over to the map, and studied it with his general. They pointed at a few places before Mav walked over and joined them. He could hear that they were arguing about where to place their army and where this war would eventually happen. Mav took one look at the map and knew where it would be.

"It should be at the northern tip of Fel, on the border of the two kingdoms," Mav blurted out.

The king studied him for a second before standing up with his arms crossed. "Why there?"

Mav swallowed hard as nervousness crept up his skin. "Well, we have the sea to our back, so they won't be able to circle behind and ambush us. That way, we could have the pirates aid us as well. We will still be in our kingdom, so it will be unfamiliar turf for them, but we will know the terrain by heart. Finally, we have the two mountain ranges boarding our army, so if they want to attack us from the side, they will need to climb through treacherous terrain to do so. It is also closer to us, so we can be there before they know it, and when they finally get word of our army, we will already be there in full force."

The king looked towards him warily with his eyes full of distrust. "The pirates? Would they fight with us? I thought they trusted no one but themselves."

Mav sighed as he paced around the table, staring at the map. He chewed at his lip, thinking about it all. "They rely on us more than you think. If Esnia was ruled by these monsters, they would never be able to get anything to keep them alive. They would be stupid to not help us in this war. You also have me, someone who is close to them."

The King nodded absentmindedly, though wariness still clouded his eyes as he continued to stare at the map. "The coast is not a bad idea at all. We will go there. I'd rather not bring it any further into our land than that point." He turned to the general. "Get our army ready. Also, send word to my steward to send out the couriers. It is time for the call to arms."

It did not take long for the castle to turn into a madhouse. Many people scrambled about the halls, women ran around with fear plastered on their faces, and men packed bags for the move to the battlefield. It wouldn't take Mav and Calder long to pack the small bags they had brought on their journey, and in a matter of moments, they were ready to leave this castle.

Days passed in such a whirlwind that Mav felt that the days had blended into one. They walked through the mountains nonstop with the largest group of people he had ever seen. Because of that, it had taken them longer to get through the mountains and unfortunately, they had come out of them with fewer people. Nerves and fear were thick in the air as they found the valley they would set up camp in. The sound of weeping filled the air at all times of the day. Many men and women had left their families behind to spare them, not knowing if that would be the last time they would see their families, not knowing if they would lay here in this forsaken valley for the rest of eternity.

The days that followed were a rush of setting up tents for everybody to sleep in. They welcomed the flow of newcomers who took up the call to arms. Many of them were from smaller villages and towns and had never wielded a sword. It would be tough for the army to train them in time, and Mav feared that they would lose many of them in a matter of moments when the battle truly started. Though he did the best he could and helped the soldiers with training at all hours of the day. It was all he could do because now, at this moment, at this place, it was all just a waiting game. They would sit here and wait for more people to answer their call and wait for the monsters to find out that their army was ready for them to come.

Chapter Twenty-Five

Verona

The word of war spread like wildfire throughout the castle; even her guards were talking about the rising army. People throughout Esnia were traveling to fight for what was right and join this ever-growing mass of people. Even the King of Fel had traveled to join the cause, which was most surprising to her. His townsfolk followed him as they were inspired by their king to join the war effort. She even heard that the Shields of the Just had risen from the shadows and sworn their lives to the cause, led by her friend. That shocked her the most, as she thought he was only an adventurer and not a myth made flesh. Their numbers were growing by the day and Verona couldn't be happier as her cause had sparked a life of its own. She felt proud of her friends who were there helping to defeat this evil. Verona only hoped she would live long enough to see them succeed.

However, that wasn't the only thing Verona had heard. The guards whispered in the shadows, talking about the beasts readying for war themselves. Their leader knew and was gathering an army of beasts, slaves, guards, and townsfolk they had forced to join them. Dozens more ships were being sent out to Ro'L to gather more Telanas for the fight ahead. It wouldn't be long before the beasts themselves were fully ready for war.

Verona had yet to see the queen since that fateful day, and because of that, her fate was still unknown. Would she be stuck here, alone in this cell, waiting for her captors to come back? Would she be rescued? Would she be killed before then to prove a point? Would she be brought along as a message or as a warning? She didn't know, but none of those options were anything she wanted. She wanted to be free. She wanted to be on that battlefield with her friends. She wanted to be fighting alongside them. Though here she was, sitting in this cage as she was starved, beaten, and slowly losing hope of everything around her.

Commotion was constantly happening around her in this castle. Swords were being readied for war, tents were being packed, and armor was being fitted to each soldier. It wouldn't be long before they left, and after that, it was only a few days' journey to arrive on that battlefield. After a few days of this constant hecticness throughout the castle, the queen had made her way down to Verona. This time, she was alone, wearing a beautiful set of silver armor etched with filigree.

Verona stood up shakily, walking over to the bars of her cell with confusion written on her face. "I see they finally found out about the army. Though why are you here alone? Why are you in armor?"

The queen shook her head and looked away from Verona. Her anger boiled up inside of her, and she was ready to burst free. She bawled her fists tightly. In a matter of heartbeats, she took a deep breath and turned to Verona with a smile on her face. "It's a good thing that I am preparing for it now." The queen sighed, looking down at her hands. "Oh, Verona. I'm tired of all these lies between us. So, I want to make amends. I am the one who gathered the army of Telanas, the one who started this war. I was the one who told them to start causing chaos in the two other kingdoms, though it was their idea to burn down villages. So I am sorry that it got, well... a little out of hand. Though it is all in good faith because soon everything will come together."

Verona's eyes widened in anger and confusion. "What do you mean you did all this? I thought you were captured with me all this time. I thought you were their prisoner, too."

The queen laughed so viciously that venom dripped slowly from her words. "Oh, you foolish girl. If you thought that, then you aren't as smart as I thought you were. It was all a game. I pretended to be captured to get information from you. To make you think that we were on the same side, but no. You somehow slipped information to those godsdamn boys, and now an army has risen against me!"

Verona barred her teeth as she pressed against the bars of her cell. "If this is all true, then you deserve to have an army rise up against you. You are nothing but a delusional wench. They will defeat you in the end, and this fool's errand will bring you nothing but death in the end."

The queen looked at her with wild eyes. "That is where you are wrong, stupid girl. They don't stand a chance against me. It will be a shame when they are all gone. It will be a pain to watch my brother go. I tried to kill my other brother once, but the assassin was stupid enough to get killed. Though in the end, it will only help my plan, so I think I owe you thanks for that. Soon, when they are all gone, I will be the Queen of Esnia, the *only* ruler of this continent. All of these people will bow down to me."

Verona laughed loudly at her words. "The only thing you will be queen of is a broken land. You will be a queen of people who don't trust you, and, most of all, a queen of a kingdom of lies. You will be nothing to no one."

The queen looked down at Verona, her nostrils flaring and lips tight with anger. "When it comes time for us to leave, I am going to take you with me so I can keep an eye on you. I do not trust you here. We will be leaving tomorrow. So be prepared."

Verona walked back to her furs, sitting down and wrapping them around her body. There was so much to process in only a few moments. So many pieces fit together that finally created a full picture. From the creatures in the woods talking about a 'she' to the woman in the shadows the day that Mariam was attacked, to the loose restraints, to the way the queen looked at the monsters. It was all too much to process, and she didn't have time for it because there was more she needed to worry about. Like how she was being moved to the battlefield. She didn't know how to feel about the news, but she felt a little happy at the thought of being closer to Mav than she had been in a very long time.

Verona whipped her head up, staring at the queen once more. "Bring me more clothes tomorrow if you don't want me to die from the cold."

The queen turned around without a word and walked back up the stairs, disappearing from Verona's sight. They were leaving tomorrow. Verona couldn't comprehend the idea of them leaving already. Only a few more days and she would be close to her friends, she would see Mav once more. That thought alone was the only thing that had kept her going this long and had kept her fighting.

It was a sleepless night for Verona, as this war was all she could think about. When the guards walked down in the morning, she knew they could see the bags underneath her eyes, though they didn't say anything about it as they threw a pile of clothes into her cell. Another guard had given her a plate of food. The guard who gave her food stuck around. "Get dressed and eat quickly. We're leaving now."

Verona quickly ate the food and threw on the warmer clothes. The food was better than anything she had received during her time here, and the clothes weren't great, but they were by all means better than the rags she wore before. Once she was done, she was led out of the cell and the front gates of the castle, and toward the fields where the army of people and beasts waited for her. She felt the warmth of the sun touch her skin as she closed her eyes and sighed with relief. It felt so good to feel the sun once more. With a sharp jolt, her eyes snapped open, and she was shoved to the front. There, sitting on a bright white rilasi, was the Queen of M'Ralz, and in her hands were a set of chains and cuffs. She sat there in her set of silver armor that was carved with trim of golden filigree. She lacked a helmet, but her golden hair was elegantly braided into a crown, and her golden crown sat gently amidst the braids.

The queen looked down at her with a wicked smile. "You will be locked up and walking with me. You better keep up, or you will be dragging behind me."

Verona grimaced at her, never taking her eyes off of the queen as they locked the cuffs on Verona's hands and feet. The queen pulled on the chain sharply, making Verona fall to her knees. In her mind, she was killing this woman in a million different ways. All she wished would come true.

Those next few days of travel were a living nightmare for her. She was being pulled behind the queen during the days, and she was chained to a tree at night. It was hard for her to sleep like that, and when she did get any, it was rough with only a few hours of peace. During those hours, when she was awake, she would stare up to the sky, wondering if Mav was looking at the same stars and wisps of green light streaking across the sky. Verona didn't know what day it was, and when they saw the coast at a far distance, she felt surprised. She felt relief, even. She was so close to him.

There was a large hill that had blocked most of their view that led down into a large valley, and when they reached the top, the sight Verona saw had taken her breath away. There, in the water, were a dozen pirate ships, their cannons prepped and slid out of the ships. She recognized Death's Skull, but there were many she had not seen before. On the sandy coast, thousands upon thousands of tents were set up, with countless people bustling amongst them. Hundreds were training in front of the tents, preparing for this war. A small delegation of people walked towards them, and as soon as they drew closer, Verona could tell who they were.

The group consisted of the King of Fel and the King of Lo'Kil, both of their generals, and trailing behind them were Mav, Calder, and Malakai. Verona wanted to sink to her knees in relief at seeing them. She wanted to scream, to cry, to ask them to help her. Though all she could do was stand there and watch them walk towards her ever so slowly. Mav spotted her as soon as they drew closer, and he winced in pain as he saw how frail and skinny she had become. She gave him a reassuring smile in return, hoping to give him some peace. Calder had looked at her for a heartbeat and saw all the scars and fresh wounds that littered her body. He squeezed his eyes closed, trying to mask the pain that was so clearly written on his face. Malakai, on the other hand, knew not to show his emotions and only looked at her briefly before looking at the queen.

She smiled at the delegation before her. "Hello, brothers. This revelation may be a surprise to you. I assure you that your fight to save the queen from her awful captors is not in vain. As you can see, I am not captured. I am simply raising an army against you to take Esnia for myself once and for all. I'm sure you are here to give me a grand speech and all, but I do not have time for that, so I will give you an ultimatum for this war. I will give you the girl, you will stand down as rulers in your lands, and I will sit on a throne as the one and only Queen of Esnia."

The King of Fel stepped forward. "Have you gone mad, sister? We did this all for you, and you are the leader behind all this chaos? You are foolish. What if we do not accept your terms? What then?"

The queen's smile grew wider and more wicked. "Then I will kill Verona, and war will ensue."

The king looked at her for several heartbeats, then spoke those final damning words. "We do not accept your terms."

The scream that came out of Mav was deafening. She wanted to cry with him, wanted to force her way over to him. But she couldn't do any of that because, with a snap of the Queen's fingers, Verona's chain was passed to a guard who pulled her toward the back of their party. She didn't know she was screaming; she couldn't feel the tears rolling down her cheeks; all she could feel was the all-consuming despair that ran through her.

The revelation ran through her body like a tidal wave. This war was starting, and she wouldn't be alive to see it end.

Part Three

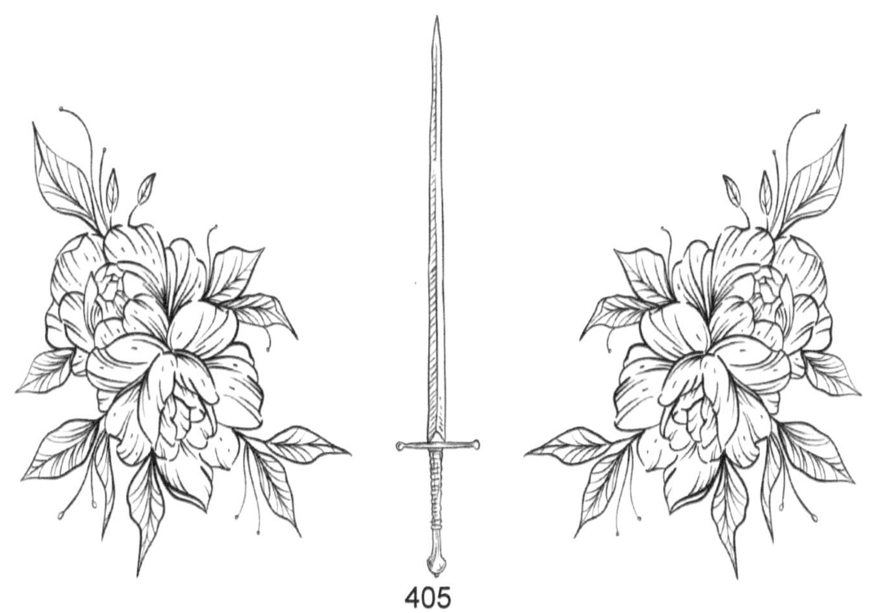

Chapter Twenty-Six

Verona was led to a large tent in the back of the valley. She could tell it was the first to be set up and knew, with the luxuries inside, that it had to be the Queen's. There, inside the tent, a large wooden pole was struck into the ground and had metal rings on it for her chains to be attached to. She would sit here until the Queen deemed it time for her promise to be fulfilled. Verona wished it wouldn't have been this way, she had fought so hard for so long, and now she would die behind the battlefield. Though she couldn't blame them for their decision. As a matter of fact, she applauded their decision to keep up with the war. She was only one person, and they had the entirety of the kingdom to think about. She was glad her sacrifice would save Esnia.

As she sat there chained to a wooden pole in silence, her mind kept replaying how Mav fell to his knees and screamed when they didn't want to save her. She was hearing it over and over again. The tears gathered in her eyes as she could feel his pain through that very scream. She could feel his desperation, his rage, and his fear through it all. Verona tried to push it out of her mind, tried to forget it, but she couldn't do anything; she didn't want to die like this, in such a pit of despair. She wanted to be strong, happy, and feeling accomplished when that time came.

The sound of commotion broke her from her thoughts. She was confused. They had to have all been on the battlefield by now, so why would there be a guard or someone else here in the Queen's tent? She tensed on the ground as the flaps of the tent moved. Though instead of a guard coming in, it was a boy with a mass of brown curly hair that appeared. Verona's breath caught in her throat as she recognized him. It was the same boy that had been in the dungeon with her.

A cry of relief escaped her, and tears rolled down her cheeks. "It's you! I didn't think I'd ever see you again."

The boy smiled as he walked towards her and squatted down right in front of her. "I promised I would free you, and when I make a promise, I stand by it. So, here I am to fulfill that promise."

Sobs wracked her body as she finally relaxed for the first time in forever. "I am so glad you are here. I didn't think I would make it out of this one, but look where we are at now. I don't know how I will ever repay you for this."

The boy looked at her with those green eyes full of determination. "You can repay me by coming to the other side and fighting alongside me in this battle."

Verona watched as the boy pulled out a set of keys and began unlocking her cuffs. She looked back at his face, which was pinched in concentration. "Where did you get the keys?"

The boy looked up at Verona. He was silent for a few heartbeats before he continued unlocking the cuffs. His voice was soft when he did speak. "I did what I had to do to get these keys."

Verona absentmindedly nodded. As soon as all of her cuffs were off, she gently rubbed the raw skin where they used to be. "Thank you. I never got your name down in the dungeon."

The boy smiled widely at Verona. "The name is Elis, Ma'am."

Verona stood up. "I thank you, Elis. You have saved my life. Now, let's go fight this war."

Verona and Elis climbed out of the tent and into the world. Laying next to the tent was a guard whose neck was sliced open. Verona turned away, knowing exactly what Elis had done to free her. The two of them quickly snuck out of the enemy's line of tents and up toward the hill they arrived on. They would need the cover of the hill to circle around to the side they needed to be on. The fight had already started; the clang of metal on metal was deafening as it filled the air. Men screamed as some charged their way through the mass of bodies while others screeched in pain as they died on this forsaken land. Cannonballs were shot from the pirate ships. As they hit, the ground groaned and shuddered from the force. Another one was shot and wooshed through the air. Verona watched as it came closer and closer to them. With a single yell, she threw her arm around Elis and pulled him down to the ground. The land shuddered and exploded from the force of the cannonball as it hit the other side of the hill. Chunks of dirt and grass rained down on them from the sky; when it was safe to do so, they both got up and ran. Verona pushed herself as fast as she could, she pushed herself to her breaking point as she saw the side her friends were on come closer with each step.

It didn't take them long to stumble into the
tents, and Verona knew exactly where she needed to go.
She found the biggest tent of them all, knowing it was
the tent for the Kings. Without any hesitation, she
threw open the flaps and found a handful of people
leaning over the table. The two kings were the ones
facing toward her, and when she forced open the tent,
their heads snapped up to meet her gaze.

She straightened her body, lifted her chin, and
stared at them with determination. "My name is
Verona of Felkeirn. I have escaped the queen to fight
alongside you."

The back of one of the men facing away from
her stiffened. As he whipped around, she knew she
would recognize that face anywhere as Mav stared at
her with astonishment. She smiled at him and that's all
he needed to run to her. Without hesitation, he
scooped her up in his arms. She knew he could feel how
frail she was, he could feel everything she went
through.

He looked at her with rage and pain in his eyes.
"We need to get you checked out." He looked over to
the kings. "Get her a healer now. She needs to be
looked over."

A man she did not recognize ran out of the tent
in a quickened pace. She let out a sigh of relief,

knowing everything was finally okay, but that did not mean it was done yet. "I want to fight with you. I know you will say no, but I will not listen. This is as much my fight as it is yours."

The King of Fel wandered over to her with his arms tucked behind his back. His eyebrows were furrowed in an inquisitive look. "And how might you do that with the state you are in now?" The King walked even closer as he studied every inch of her. "I've heard a lot about you, Verona of Felkeirn. You are a tough girl indeed, but you are barely standing right now, so what will you do when you get on that battlefield? Could you even lift a sword?."

Verona looked at him with such determination in her eyes. "You belittle me, my king. I can do so much more in this state than you think."

The king walked back over to his place on the other side of the table. He looked back down at the paper on top of it. With such nonchalance in his voice, he started to speak. "If she wishes to fight, then she will be allowed to. If she dies, then her blood will be on her hands only."

Mav moved to set her in a nearby chair as a healer came into the tent. He crouched down next to her and held her hands in his. "You don't need to do this, Verona. You don't need to get involved, just stay here and rest. You deserve it with everything you've been through. Please, do it for me."

She looked at him with her eyebrows knitted, eyes hooded, and lips turned downwards in sadness. "That's the problem, Mav. I have been through too much. I have started this all, and I have found the answer I have been looking for since the start. I'm too far in to stop now. I am the voice of all this, the ember that started the fire, and the heart of the cause. I cannot let all of these people down by resting when they are fighting for what I have started."

Another man moved from the shadows, facing Verona. Calder smiled at her widely. "You are all of that and more, Verona. I think we should let her go. It is what she wants, so who are we to stop her? I will protect you with my sword and shield, Verona of Felkeirn."

Verona smiled widely at Calder. With a teasing tone, she quipped back. "I will do the same for you, Calder, leader to the Shields of the Just."

Mav sighed as he leaned his head down towards the ground. He was silent for several heartbeats. "If you must be out there, then I will not leave your side."

Verona nodded. "Then it has been decided."

They waited in silence as the healer took her time checking every wound Verona had received during this adventure. The healer wrapped several bandages around various parts of her body before she was satisfied. When the healer was done, she stood up and walked out of the tent. Without hesitation, Verona stood as well; she was tired of sitting down and waiting.

The King of Fel looked back at her. "We did not know what state you would be in, though these two men before you knew you would not stand down." The king waved to a set of armor hanging from a dummy. "That is yours if you would like to use it."

Verona stood up, walking to the armor that sat on the stand. Covering every inch of the dummy was a baselayer of black chainmail that shimmered against the sunlight streaming in. The armor itself was made of a strong silver metal and broken down into several pieces. The calves and boots were connected into one piece. An intricately patterned circlet sat mid-thigh on the left, and attached to it was a leather sheath for a dagger. Instead of a full set of armored pants, they had given her an armored skirt. Its design made it look layered with the metal overlapping itself in several areas; it was etched with a filigree design along the edges. The top of her armor was a small piece that circled her neck and armpits for easy maneuverability. The bottom of the top ended around the edge of her hips. The chest piece had designs of filigree etched into

the metal along her hips and in the small space
following along her collarbones. Finally, several small
pieces of metal protected her shoulders, biceps, and
forceps, all decorated with the same etched filigree.

Sitting beside the armor stand was a smaller
stand that held a shield and sword. Verona walked over
to the sword, recognizing it in a matter of moments.
There was Fury, the very same sword she had left in the
care of Calder's house. She was astonished because she
had been fully set on the sword being lost within the
kingdom of M'Ralz, but here it sat. Verona knew full
well that the sword had survived its own journey,
wherever Calder and Mav had gone.

Verona turned to the king with a small smile on
her lips. "I love it. Thank you for bringing it with you."
She then turned to Mav. "Will you help me put it on?"

Mav nodded and walked over to Verona and
the armor. He took his time, carefully unstrapping
each leather strip that held the armor together and
slowly placing it on Verona with hesitant hands as he
tried not to touch her wounds. When she was all
strapped in and held her sword, she looked down and
admired herself. She felt powerful with a set of armor
on her body and a sword in her hand. She looked at the
war party, who all stared at her with awe on their faces.

She smiled back in return. It was time for her entrance onto that battlefield.

With a quick flick of her wrist, she twisted her sword, feeling its familiarity in her hands once more and making it a part of herself once again. With a look towards the war table, she knew it was time. "Let's get out there and fight for what is right."

Without a word, Verona walked out of the tent. The outside world was something entirely different from the calm demeanor inside the tent. Cannonballs were flying over the tents, soaring far into the air. Her head throbbed from the sound of clashing metal. She could hear the screams of men dying. The smell of blood, sweat, and tears was so thick in the air. She could see the fear written on all the faces of the men she passed who would step onto the battlefield with her. She laid a hand on the shoulder of each person who looked lost, afraid, and broken. She held them close and told them that it would be okay and that they would make it out just fine.

Mav, Calder, and the two kings slowly followed her through the line of tents. When they finally approached the line of the battlefield, she looked back at them and smiled. Behind them, many other soldiers gathered in a mass. They whispered her name, they spoke in awe about what she had done, and they looked at her as if she was a god who was walking among them. She knew what she needed to do. These men were fighting for her. They were fighting for a cause she inspired and now it was time to show them that it was all worth it in the end.

"We have all lost friends, parents, siblings, and children. We have lost so much to these monsters that plague our homelands. Today, we say enough. Today, we stand up to those beasts. Today, we will make history. We will right what has been made wrong. We will avenge the fallen, and the innocents who have died because of the darkness plaguing us. Today. We. Will. Fight!" she screamed.

Men screamed with her, raising their swords in a rallying war cry. She joined them, raising her sword high. With a single glance at her friends, Verona charged into battle, leading the soldiers with her. She waded into the throng of bodies that swarmed into a mass of metal and death. Men were shoving others to the ground, shoving their swords into their bodies. Those who had lost their weapons were using their arms and fists to fight until they couldn't fight anymore.

The first line of the queen's defense was normal human men, and it made it difficult to fight those who had no choice, who had been enslaved and forced to fight for her. Behind those mortal men, in the far distance, were her beasts. Hundreds of Telanas waited, claws drawn and teeth bared. They were dressed with leaves. They had human skulls dangling from their necks and war paint smeared across various parts of their bodies. They all had primitive weapons ranging from spears to handmade bows. Many of them were on beasts that Verona had never seen before. They were sleek, black felines that were covered in scales. Three sets of large slits flared underneath their jaws as they breathed. Two sets of ears were pinned back as they snarled. Large fangs were bared as they paced, staring at the enemies before them. They were crouched and ready to pounce. Verona could tell these beasts were far more deadly than the Telanas, and if given the chance, they would rip through their army in seconds.

Men and women had surrounded Verona as she pushed further into battle; they all had familiar armor on, and she knew they were the Shields of the Just. They pierced any enemy that came near, creating a protective ring around her. She didn't quite care for it. Verona didn't want to stand in a safe spot when people around her were dying as they fought for her cause. She would break free of this bubble as soon as she could. She needed to fight, needed to show these men hope for the greater good. She needed this for herself as well, needed this revenge for what she had been through. Most important of all, she needed these monsters to suffer the way she suffered.

As soon as she saw a break in the circle, she rushed out of it. She could hear the men screaming her name behind her, but she did not stop as she went deeper and deeper into the mass of bodies. She kept moving until she was on the front lines with the seasoned soldiers and war generals. As Verona got closer to that front line, everything was assaulting her in every way.

The rancid smell of sweat and the tangy smell of blood was thick in the air. The sounds of screaming and metal were assaulting her ears as she felt her head thrum from it all. Her ears felt like they were going to explode. She was stepping over men who died on top of each other, stacked in piles of bodies. This wasn't like Verona expected it to be. It was more gruesome, more devastating, and more traumatizing. These men below her died for what she started, and she couldn't handle it. The world was shifting in and out as her breath became uncontrollable and her vision blurred. She couldn't handle this. It was too much, too fast. She wanted to be strong for these men, wanted to inspire them. But here she was, panicking in the face of war. The world snapped out of focus for Verona as she closed her eyes, trying to control herself. She took several deep breaths and then opened her eyes once more. When she did, everything felt as if it was going in slow motion, as if she was seeing everything from outside of her body.

A man behind her elbowed her trying to get to the front, Verona fell from the sudden push. She had not braced herself, had not felt any warning, and so there she was, lying on top of the mass of bodies. She wanted to scream, though nothing came out of her open mouth. Her eyes were wide and full of fear. She felt another man pull her up. He grabbed her sword and shoved it into her hand. She didn't know what to do, so she did all she could do: she went forward as the mass of her men behind her kept moving toward the enemy.

A man with the queen's sigil on his armor ran towards her, screaming, with his sword raised and pointed at her abdomen. On instinct, Verona raised her sword and shoved it forward. She clenched her eyes closed as it met with resistance, sliding slowly into the man. She opened her eyes to see him mere inches away from her. His body was slack, his jaw hung loose, and his eyes widened in pain. His sword dropped to the ground with a thud as he slowly died before her.

Verona looked at the man in horror and whispered to him. "I'm so sorry, I didn't mean to. I promise."

Verona and the man stood there in silence as she watched life fade from his eyes. Slowly, she pulled her sword from his body and shivered as she saw the blood-coated sword. She knew she'd have to do it. If she didn't protect herself, the roles would have been reversed. Verona looked around the battlefield, trying to find some sense of familiarity, someone who could help and ground her. She looked around for several heartbeats before she saw Calder. He was surrounded by enemies; he was all alone, though he fought like a thousand men as he cut each one of them down. Verona shoved her way towards him. She screamed his name, feeling relieved to see him. As he heard her voice, he whipped around towards her, his eyebrows furrowed, and his lips stretched in a thin line. He knew she broke that protective ring he made for her and she was about to hear it all.

A blur of movement made her head snap as she watched a Telana warrior leap through the throng of men and straight towards Calder. Fear washed over Verona like a wave of freezing water. Her eyes were wide, and her mouth was open wide as she tried to scream, though nothing came out. Everything was moving too slowly. It felt like she was wading through a thick patch of mud; she was doing everything possible to push forward and get to him, but her body was moving so slowly. She fell to her knees and screamed as she watched the beast fall on Calder. They both landed on the ground with a thud. Teeth and claws shredded his armor with ease. Metal flew through the air, and following right after was so much blood. The world snapped back into place, and all Verona could hear was her own scream as she watched her friend get hurt right in front of her.

Chapter Twenty-Seven

All Verona could hear was her screaming, it drowned out everything around her and rang in her ears. She screamed and screamed until she couldn't anymore. Shock ran through her veins like bolts of lightning that had hit her body. She couldn't move, she couldn't feel. Nothing registered for Verona as she sat there and played the moment over and over again.

Her eyes never left his body as she watched the beast jump off of him onto another soldier, its feathery body still covered in Calder's blood. Her eyes finally moved as she watched the beast rip through their line of defense, many more following in its wake.

She slowly got to her feet and started to move to her friend, though it felt like she was wading in deep mud. She wanted to run over there; she tried everything in her power to get to Calder. She wanted to be over there to comfort him in his last moments, she wanted to place his head in her lap and tell him everything would be just fine. Though as she slowly moved over to him, more soldiers ran in between them. She was getting elbowed, knocked down, and stepped on by the charging men. Each time she fell, she got right back up, determined to be over there holding him.

She started to grow frustrated at everyone around her. There were too many people between them and she was moving much too slowly. He would pass by the time she got to him. She hated everything about this moment, she didn't want this to happen like this. She didn't want to keep losing people like this. She wanted the war to be over and to have everyone by her side, though now she only had Mav. Verona wanted to scream again, both in despair and rage. With every step she took toward her dying friend, more rage filled her body. There was a part of her that wanted to go after that beast. She wanted to make it suffer like her friend did. Like she did. She wanted them all to suffer. Verona wanted the gods to feel her anger and throw their wrath down on every living Telana that roamed this world. If she had to do it herself, then so be it. By the time she was done walking this world, she promised that every one of them who served under the queen would feel her pain, anger, and vengeance.

As she started to get closer to Calder, a hand gripped her arm and pulled her back. She looked back, ready to snap at whoever stopped her. Though as soon as she saw it was Mav, everything in her body broke down. Every part of her crashed like a wave breaking against a jagged wall.

"He's hurt, Mav. That monster attacked him," she whispered, tears starting to run down her cheek as she slowly spaced out. She wanted all this pain to end, she was done with it all.

Mav pulled her into his embrace as he tucked her head into his chin and wrapped his arms around her frail body. "I know. I saw it all, too. It's going to be just fine, Verona. I will find someone to get him, we need to get a healer for him right away."

Verona looked up at him with rage filling her eyes and the empty void inside her. "I want to make them suffer, Mav. I want them all to be dead by the time we are done here."

He looked down at her with worry written on his face. "You don't mean that, Verona. They are as much of pawns as we are in the queen's plan. You can't blame them for what is happening here."

Verona bared her teeth. "I blame them all for what has happened. Just because they are her pawns does not mean they are not responsible for their actions of killing these innocent people and burning their homes to the ground. If you don't think the same, then you're a fool, Mav."

Mav opened his mouth to talk to her once more, though she shoved him away. She knew what he was about to say. She would not calm down, she would not back down. They killed her family, they killed Mariam, and now they may have killed Calder. She was a force to be reckoned with. She was a phoenix rising from the ashes of pain. A terror in the dark. She was the epitome of wrath, and they were about to suffer from the burning inferno she was going to create. They would all suffer in the end because She. Was. Death.

She ran through the crowd of people, getting as far away from Mav as possible as he ran to get a healer for Calder. Any enemy she saw, she pierced her sword right through their abdomen. She had separated her mind from her body, forced it deep inside herself, and let instinct take over. Verona knew some part of herself would slowly die, knowing how many lives she would take on this battlefield. She would lose that innocence she had carried around inside herself during her younger years. That feeling of hope for a world full of good. The lack of knowledge she carried about anything close to evil and death. Though a new part of her would be born today, one that consumed vengeance and walked closely beside death. A new part of her that craved war and violence. She would walk between these two worlds, torn between good and evil. She would forever be changed by the events today.

Slowly, Verona moved closer to the center of the battle. With every step she took, more bodies fell in her wake. Her sword was becoming increasingly tinted with the blood of the humans and beasts she slashed down. Her armor was spotted in thick, red dots. She would keep doing this until every single one of them was lying beneath her feet.

There was a break in the fighting not far from her, and Verona made her move to get to that break. She had paid so much attention to her enemies that she didn't notice the smoke that was billowing above her and around her. It was thick, black smoke that suffocated everyone in its wake and it did not care who was in its path. Verona elbowed her way into the fold and when she saw what caused the break in the fight, all she could do was stop and stare.

There, in front of them all, the Telanas had lit the world on fire. Branches, leaves, piles of grass, and even dead bodies laid in a mass of fuel for these flames they created and it was making its way towards them. This fire was slowly growing more out of control as it consumed everything in its path, if they did not stop it now, there would be no end in sight for it.

Though Verona did not care as a flake of ash landed on her skin and everything snapped out of place. She was transported back in time to a place where she had begged the gods to never be back again. A place where she had lost everything, and a time where she had to watch her mother die.

She was reliving it all at this moment as the smell of burnt skin made her stomach roil: the feeling of the heated flames once more, the way her eyes watered as the smoke finally made its way to her, and the ash that fell like snow against her skin. It was all too much for her. She couldn't handle this again, she couldn't watch her family die once more.

She clenched her eyes, hoping that when she opened them again, she would be back on that battlefield. The hairs on her body rose and her stomach dropped as she felt like she was falling. A scream was stuck in her throat as she felt an impact against her chest. Her eyes flew open in horror and her mouth fell agape. She was looking down a large open hole in a fallen, charred home. Down in the opening, staring back at her, was her mother's charred body. Her mother's mouth cracked open and screamed so loud it pierced Verona's ears. Pain reverberated through Verona's body as she squeezed her eyes shut and clenched her jaw with bared teeth. She slapped a pair of hands over her ears, though all she could feel was wetness. She pulled her hands back towards her face and all she saw was blood before everything went black.

Verona didn't know how long she was out before she was awoken by the jostling of people who were kicking her, stepping on her, and moving around her. She slowly pushed herself up, though she did not have any strength left in her. Her arms collapsed underneath her and she fell back on top of the others who perished in this fight. She tried again and again, though each time ended similarly with her landing back where she started. As she lay there, feeling lifeless, all she could do was let out a weak chuckle. This is where she would die, she had promised this queen that she would end her life, though it was ironic that Verona would die before even getting that chance. She accomplished all this for nothing and pushed this far just to not be able to see the ending. Though a part of her had felt at peace, if this was the end of the line for her, at least she would see her family again.

Her eyes slowly drew closed as she heard her mother speak to her. "Verona. Verona. Verona." Her mother's voice spoke. It started as a whisper and slowly grew to a shout. "Verona. Verona! VERONA!"

Verona's eyes flew open as she watched the ghost of her mother materialize from the smoke around her. Tears pricked her eyes and threatened to escape as she watched her mother walk towards her broken body. "Mama." She whispered.

"Verona, my love." Her mother said as she kneeled in front of her. "You need to get up. You need to live for me, you promised you would."

Verona closed her eyes, knowing it all was an illusion, a trick her mind was playing on her as she lay there dying. She welcomed it with open arms as she talked to her mother one last time. "I can't, mama. I think I'm dying. But it's okay, I'll be with all of you again soon."

Her mother brushed a curl away from her face as she gave Verona a sad smile. "I will welcome you with open arms when that time comes. But that is not this time. You need to get up, love. You need to fight. You only have to hold on a little bit longer. The world needs you, my love. So I need you to get up. You need to get up, Verona. Get. Up!"

As her mother shouted, a jolt ran through Verona's body and her eyes flew open. She gasped for a breath as if she had held her breath underwater for a second too long. She twisted her body, getting her hands underneath herself, and pushed. She slid one foot underneath her body. Then a second. In a matter of moments, Verona was standing once more. A jolt of energy ran through her and a thrum of energy, almost like another soul was dancing with hers, gave Verona what she needed to fight until the end.

Verona ran into the smoke, not feeling anything from it. She was not going to let it break her anymore. She was stronger than that. She funneled every ounce of that strength inside of her. The smoke clouded her vision, making it so hard to see where anyone was or where these flames were slowly inching towards her. She coughed and waved her hands in front of her face, clearing the air for only a few heartbeats. In the thick of it, surrounded by an innumerable amount of beasts, was a female Telana. She was on top of a sleek black cat who watched the battle alongside its master.

Verona could tell the female beast was a strong one. Her face was littered with scars amongst the tiny feathers that dawned on her skin. Her plumage was full of midnight blues, vibrant reds, bright yellows, and deep purples. Her crest was bigger and fuller than any of the others that Verona had seen. Wrapped around her chest was black fabric and a black skirt that covered her hips. Jewelry made of bones, beads, and large leaves was draped around her neck. White warpaint was splattered across her body. On top of her head was a bronze crown with several gems inlaid in its metal.

Her eyes were set on this queen of Beasts, she knew she was the one to go down next. Verona looked behind her, seeing a group of men in her wake. She screamed as loud as she could to rally these men to her, and when their eyes met, she pointed her sword at the beastly queen. With a battle cry emerging from her chest, she pushed her body forward towards this monster. She pushed herself further and further, to the tip of her breaking point. If she could only do one more thing, this would be it.

The men around her attacked the beasts around the queen while Verona took a running jump toward the sleek cat with her sword pointed at its heart. Her body slammed against the butt of her sword as it slowly edged into flesh. The large cat screamed as it swatted at Verona. The queen hopped off her large, scaled feline as it lunged towards Verona, swiping its paw once more. In a single heartbeat, her body was knocked to the ground by a large paw; she was grateful that none of its claws had collided with her skin. Verona unsheathed her dagger as she pulled herself up. She remained crouched as the telana's steed started to run towards her. As she clenched the dagger tightly, her knuckles turned a pale white. With her lips thin and her eyes focused on the cat before her, everything else faded around them both. As the beast jumped, Verona ran towards it. In a single heartbeat, Verona jumped up in the air and dug her dagger into the cat's neck. It screamed in pain as it wrapped its front legs around Verona, digging its claws into her back. The two of them fell to the ground with an audible thud. Pain skittered through her body as she gritted her teeth. The cat hissed in pain as it tried to stand up, but fell as it began losing consciousness.

Verona rolled the beast off of her body and pushed herself up. As stood up, she came face to face with the snarling beast queen.

"You hurt my friend." She hissed, fury thick in her voice. She looked over to the cat that was taking deep labored breaths at their feet. "For that, you ssshall pay."

The queen bared her sharp teeth as she crouched with her hands outstretched as her claws were ready to slice into Verona's flesh. Verona reached around, trying to grab her sword in defense. Her eyes glanced back to the cat as she realized Fury was still embedded in its body and she was now defenseless. With a single irrational thought, she cocked back her clenched fist and hit the Telana square in the jaw. The beast hissed as her head snapped back, her eyes grew wide in astonishment as she placed a hand on her jaw. Verona took that heartbeat to yank her sword out of the cat, using her foot on its body as leverage. The queen let out a mournful and guttural scream as the cat took its last breath, its eyes looking endlessly towards its last moments.

She launched herself toward Verona, claws slashing with fury until they finally met flesh. Verona screamed in pain as she felt claws shred her skin. With her free hand, she pushed the queen farther away from her, and in a single heartbeat, swung her sword around and used the butt to slam against the queen's ribs. The beast before her yowled in pain, though she did not let that stop her as she barreled towards Verona once more. Verona dodged the slashing claws that came closer with the armor on her forearms. With every step the queen took towards her, Verona took another step back. She tried her hardest to keep the distance between them. Verona knew that this fight was in the favor of the beast. She was pushing her away, and she knew there would be a limited amount of stepping back until there were no more chances. She was so focused on the claws and trying her hardest to deflect them that she didn't expect the queen to bow down and use her long, sharp teeth to dig into Verona's ribs.

She screamed in pain as every inch of her body wanted to recoil. She wanted to escape from that pain, though the sharp object that assaulted her was still attached to her body as the queen's teeth ripped apart her skin. Verona did the only thing she could do as she brought the pommel of her sword crashing against the Telana's temple. With a single soundless gasp, the Telana queen crumpled at Verona's feet in a heap of lifeless feathers.

She placed a hand over her shredded flesh, as she knelt before the queen. After a quick check, she knew the beast was still alive, as deep, slow breaths came from her opened mouth. As soon as Verona saw the flutter of eyelids, she knew that the queen was regaining consciousness, so she placed the blade of her sword against the queen's neck.

Once the queen became aware of the situation she was in, she seemed almost at peace where she was, and that confused Verona. She was fully prepared for the queen to fight back, to do *something* at least, but all she did was close her eyes once more and whisper words in their beastly language.

The telana opened her eyes once more, looking up at Verona. She bared her teeth as she spoke. "What are you waiting for? Kill me already. You have won thisss battle, ssso do what you people have done time and time again. Killing my kind will be nothing new for you humansss. Ssso if I die, then I will die fighting for a caussse that I ssstand by. I will die on the sssoil my ancessstorsss lived on."

Anger boiled in Verona's blood as she stared down at the beast that lay underneath her. "Do not act so innocent when you have bodies lying in your wake. The towns you have burnt, children you have killed, families you have severed for your cause. You killed my family, my friends, my land. This war is because of your actions, and you shall die because of it."

The beast hissed, though she closed her eyes and raised her head, baring her neck to Verona's blade. She moved to press her blade into the queen's throat when a cloud of smoke drifted behind them. A single hand made of smoke landed on Verona's shoulder as she looked behind her. A familiar scent of bread and jasmine filled the air as sorrow consumed every ounce of Verona's being. Her mother was here, she was seeing who Verona was becoming, seeing this monster who wielded a sword. Anger, violence, and revenge had driven her this far; she had let it consume her and shape her until it was all she felt. She was lost in it and let it become something so rage-filled, something so disgusting, that Verona did not know if she could live with herself.

A voice echoed through her mind, one that soothed her all these years. "This is not who you are, my love. Do not let your anger break you. Do not let it lead you down a path that you cannot escape."

Tears were gathering in Verona's eyes as she took a deep breath. She looked back at the queen below her who still had her eyes closed. "I have let my anger fuel me this far. I thought my revenge was acceptable. I thought I wouldn't let it consume me. But I have done everything I didn't want to do, became everything I didn't want to become. I let the loss I experienced turn me into my own nightmare. I will not go further down that path. I will not become the person the queen of M'Ralz wants me to be. So I will not kill you, you are free to go, queen of the Telanas."

The queen's eyes snapped open in surprise, and when Verona offered a hand to pull her up, the beast was even more confused. "Why would you ssspare me? That isss not what your people do."

Verona stood proud, with her chin high. I am not one of them, I am not my ancestor. I am the wave that grows, changing the course of time. I am the voice amongst the many who yell for change. I will be the one who demands justice in the face of injustice. I know the queen brought you over in exchange for our land, something that is unattainable. She was not going to give you any of it. Our people are far too embedded in this land to change that. Her mission was to conquer the land herself and to use your blood to do so. She was sending you to your death for her own cause."

The telana thought in silence for a few heartbeats before looking back at Verona. "I have alssso let revenge draw me into a place that I did not want to be in. I wasss consssumed by it and let that queen ussse my people asss her pawnsss. I thank you for sssparing my life. We have generationsss of prejudice that run between usss, it will be hard to change, but together we can become that wave."

Verona gripped the queen's forearm in a handshake and a sign of a promise. "Together, we will change history."

A war cry was sent out by the queen, and the Telanas ceased their fighting. Verona had let the men beside her know the beasts were not their enemies, and word spread through the army like wildfire. Together,

her army and the Telanas fought together, tracking down the rest of the men from the M'Ralz army. They kept some as prisoners, as they were given word that the queen of M'Ralz was missing from the battlefield. No one knew where she had fled, but once the war was over and everything was settled, Verona would be tracking her down. As the frenzy slowly faded, Verona made her way back to the line of tents with the Telana queen behind her. The only thing she wanted right now was to see Mav's face once more, to know that he was okay. She used it as motivation and kept taking one step after another, slowly getting closer to the line of tents.

Chapter Twenty-Eight

Mav was alive, and she was there, wrapped in his arms. Verona felt herself relax for the first time in a very long time as she closed her eyes and took a deep breath of his cinnamon and pine scent. They stayed in that embrace for several heartbeats as people entered the tent. Verona didn't care, though. She could stay there the rest of her life and be happy. Though they had let go when the king of Fel let out a soft cough as everyone gathered around the table.

Verona grabbed Mav's hand, giving him a shy smile. She went to take a step toward the table, but looked behind her to see the Telana queen still standing by the tent flaps, looking very uncomfortable. Verona let go of Mav's hand and walked over to the queen. After grabbing her hand, she led them over to the table.

"I would like to introduce the Telana queen, Caro," Verona said softly.

The queen gave a nod to the rest of the group before moving forward. "The queen of M'Ralz had not given me much information on her plansss but what I do know wasss that ssshe wanted to wipe out every town and kingdom on the map besides M'Ralz. Ssshe had told usss ssshe wanted the world to be remade for usss and for it to be like it wasss before their people had taken over our homelandsss." The queen nervously shifted on her feet before continuing. "We foolissshly believed her asss we were blinded by our own prejudice and desire for revenge. Despite what we have gone through here, we plan to ssstrive to be better and to have a better relationsssship with Esssnia. We do not have any need to take over your land, ssso we will return home."

People on the council questioned Caro; many people were skeptical of her, though most of the interactions she was getting were positive and trusting. Verona knew she needed to be there, that there would be questions for her. There would be plans to go over, villages to rebuild, and a kingdom to settle. They would need to gather the bodies, heal those who needed medical attention, and help whoever they could. Though today would not be that day. There will be tomorrow and many more days for those questions. So, with a single rash thought, she grabbed Mav's hand and walked out of the tent.

She took a deep breath as she closed her eyes. She felt the wind tickle her skin and sweep through her hair. Along with that wind, a lone hand brushed against her shoulder, and a whisper of proud words danced amongst the gusts. A smile graced her lips and she sent a prayer up to the gods for them to take care of her mother. Once she opened her eyes again, she looked over to see Mav staring down at her in amazement. She looked at him incredulously and wrinkled her nose at him.

He smiled at her childishly. "So, what did you bring me out here for?"

She gave him a wicked look. "So I could finally do this again." She cupped his cheek and wrapped another hand around the back of his neck, pulling him in so their lips finally met.

They stood there for several heartbeats, taking their time and enjoying the moment. Once they had separated, Verona placed her forehead against his as she stared into his eyes. What shone in his eyes was something she had only seen shared between her parents. A love so deep that it was unbreakable by any measure.

His voice was gruff when he finally spoke. "I do not know what the future holds, Verona of Felkiern. I cannot see what will happen tomorrow, but what I do know is that I will follow you anywhere you go for the rest of my life. I love you, Verona. I will love you until I take my last breath."

She smiled widely hearing those words, tears pricked her eyes and threatened to spill over. "And I love you, Mav. I hope to always have you with me, and until that day comes when we take our last breath, we will conquer this wild and crazy life together."

Mav went to lean in for another kiss and she met him only for a few heartbeats. There was something that thrummed against the back of her mind, something that would bother her until her mission was complete. She knew what she had to do, and so that would be her next mission.

She sighed softly as their embrace melted away. "There is something that I must do first, something that will change the tide of our world."

Mav sighed as he watched her walk away from him, and after a few heartbeats, he started to follow her. "And what is that, my love?"

Verona looked back behind her, looking at Mav dead in the eyes with a wicked smile on her lips. She stabbed her sword into the ground. "I'm going to kill the queen."